JO BRAND

The More You Ignore Me

R
headline
review

First published in 2009 by HEADLINE REVIEW

An imprint of HEADLINE PUBLISHING GROUP

Cataloguing in Publication Data is available from the British Library

ISBN 978 0 7553 2231 2 (Hardback)
ISBN 978 0 7553 4886 2 (Trade paperback)

Typeset in Caslon540 BT by Palimpsest Book Production Limited,
Grangemouth, Stirlingshire

Printed in the UK by CPI Mackays, Chatham ME5 8TD

Headline's policy is to use papers that are natural, renewable and
recyclable products and made from wood grown in sustainable forests.
The logging and manufacturing processes are expected to conform to the
environmental regulations of the country of origin.

HEADLINE PUBLISHING GROUP
An Hachette UK Company
338 Euston Road
London NW1 3BH

www.headline.co.uk
www.hachette.co.uk

To Grandma Maisie

Acknowledgements

I would like to thank everyone who's been a help in the production of this book, which has taken an enormously long time. Thanks to Martin Fletcher for not shouting at me and showing patience that was above and beyond the call of duty. Thanks too to Vivienne Clore, my agent, for reading every chapter as it came out and being so enthusiastic. Also thanks to Jo Stansall and everyone at Headline. It's been the hardest to do but is my favourite so far. Finally thanks to my family who managed not to be too annoying or absent when I was writing it.

Chapter 1

1966–9

As a child growing up in a tiny Herefordshire village, Alice had five personalities. These personalities were not buried in her subconscious, appearing randomly during explosions of emotional stress, they were fashioned and refined by her as a response to the circumstances in which she found herself. They functioned as an aid to her emotional survival in a family landscape which was harsh, absurd, histrionic, druggy and unpredictable.

That's not to say that Alice was growing up in an environment devoid of love and care. Love and care were the intention. They just weren't the result most of the time. This may have been because the eye of the frequent emotional storms, her mother Gina, was an unconventional parent whose child-rearing methods were controlled not so much by her experience and instinct as by her mental state.

So she might praise Alice for the sodden mess of paint-soaked tissue with which she had attempted to decorate the kitchen, or she might emit a fearful howling noise and cower in the corner as if she had been stabbed. Either of these was preferable to her wild temper which, when lost, was not found for what seemed like hours. China would be smashed, animals kicked, doors acquired gaping wounds and Alice and her father Keith had either to leave the area or barricade themselves in the bathroom.

When Alice was very small, her dad always tried to downplay the situation by turning it into a fantasy of sorts. Alice wasn't fooled by these games, though. For her, the big bad monster wasn't green and hiding under the bed, it wore tasteless floral prints, bright scarlet lipstick and sat in the kitchen smoking and saying 'bollocks' a lot.

Instinct encouraged Alice to attempt to fade into the surrounding domestic background on these occasions of temper or out-and-out madness and it was because of this that to her family she appeared secretive, apathetic and surly, even though, underneath, she was happy, loved fairies and kittens and wanted to be a vet when she grew up.

Had her mother realised quite what a normal little girl was flourishing underneath the miserable alabaster façade, she would have been extremely disappointed. Gina had always assumed that any child of hers would receive her idiosyncratic genes and translate them into something unearthly and unique. Alice's constitution seemed to have dealt with her mother's genes by suppressing and then ejecting them in favour of her father Keith's. So, despite the madness in which she existed, underneath lay a fairly well-balanced, unremarkable little girl who rarely showed her true colours at home for fear of Gina noticing and washing them away.

Gina was one of those anomalies occasionally thrown up by the gene pool. She came from a family of country labourers named, very appropriately, Wildgoose – they were as aggressive and uncontrolled as geese – and turned out to be extremely bright. By the age of eleven she began to suffer enormous embarrassment as she realised she was leaving her family behind on every conceivable level of social and intellectual achievement. Her father turning up to meet her from school in corduroys stained with cow's piss, her mother taking her shopping with the straps of her enormous bra flapping on her forearms, her two brothers fighting everyone they came into contact with under the age of fifteen who was not in a wheelchair – all of this heightened and basted Gina's feelings of embarrassment into an angry shame. University was not an option for Gina, not because she wasn't bright enough but because, to her family, it was as alien a place as the moon. Eventually Gina came to the conclusion that the only way she would lift herself out of her gloomy future would be to find someone to marry who didn't have hands the size of shoeboxes and the social graces of a rutting boar. Gina's unconventional looks dictated that she could not pin down a potential husband simply by fluttering her stubby eyelashes or laughing as genuinely as she could at a wealthy man's jokes, so she began to stalk the farmyards and towns of Herefordshire. By her mid-teens this had become a full-time occupation, much to the disdain of her parents and her feral brothers nicknamed Wobbly and Bighead, but it was a pursuit made much easier by the advance of what came to be known as the swinging sixties.

Eventually Gina came across Keith, a rare bird in the Welsh Marches because he read books and loved nature. Anyone who has grown up in the country soon comes to realise that those who make their living from the land tend not to romanticise their brutal lives and so Keith, basking in the sun on a verge reading Wordsworth and appreciating the call of the curlew, was unlikely to be from around those parts. Gina liked the look of Keith's long hair, his humorous face and his long fingers capped with nails which were clean and trimmed, not cracked and gnarled like the talons of a troll. Keith liked Gina's breasts, the mad look in her eyes and her forwardness, which seemed to promise him disturbing sex in a hedge.

Their first encounter, noted by Gina in her diary, lasted thirteen minutes, during which time she found out that he came from a suburban estate in Wolverhampton, he was an only child and he had gone to agricultural college, much to the despair of his parents, Jennifer and Norman, who had wanted him to be a surveyor.

Gina knew her power lay in the rationing of her body for the pleasure of men, coupled with her sharp wit, and she had decided her strategy for capturing a partner would consist of these two weapons. It didn't occur to her that just because Keith was the only man she had met who seemed sensitive and educated, there weren't thousands more like him out there with bigger wallets she could have. No, he felt like her one opportunity to escape and therefore she knew she must cling on as tightly as she could, whilst appearing as nonchalant as an heiress, in order to buy her ticket out of purgatory. She was seized with a mixture of love, lust and pragmatic planning and her intelligence was put to work compiling a graded list of encounters which would drive Keith to distraction and assure his commitment to her.

Meeting her family lay at the end of this project because she realised, quite correctly, that however much someone loved her, her cartoon family would inevitably weaken that love, possibly to the point of extinction. So, as the months of their relationship passed, she held herself aloof sexually, meting out just enough physical contact to keep Keith going, fuelling the flames of his fantasies, and denying access to the rest of the Wildgoose family, despite repeated requests.

Keith had no such qualms about introducing Gina to his parents, although he should have had, and within a year of their relationship beginning, an invitation to tea was reluctantly extended by Jennifer, whose reaction to her son's description of his new love was a lot of shuddering and shaking of her head.

Keith and Gina's relationship had become one of snatched meetings in strange places to ensure her family did not get to know about him. She never took him home and they could not go into the local pubs because she would have been recognised and either thrown out or asked to elucidate on her relationship with this stick-thin, pleasant-looking hippy. So instead, Keith in his battered Ford van with the customary sacking in the back and Gina on her bicycle would make their separate ways to the high points of Shropshire and Herefordshire. At Bury Ditches they would sit holding hands, windblown and cold as they surveyed the countryside from the Black Mountains to the Long Mynd; or they would race round the battlements of Clun Castle, laughing and falling over in the long grass; or stand by Hopton Castle, oppressed by the atmosphere, both temporarily transported back to the Civil War and the shocking history of the slaughter that took place there. Keith rather uncharacteristically hoped Gina would get so upset he could have sex with her. In fact, each time they met, Keith thought they were going to have sex and each time they didn't, it had the required effect: a growing desperation which was not eased by beer or masturbation. Gina had him exactly where she wanted him.

Then they went to tea with Jennifer and Norman.

For Jennifer, a big week was one in which she bought a Mr Kipling's Battenberg cake and served it on a silvered cake plate with a cake slice. She constantly attempted to refine her husband's utterances and behaviour on these occasions as Norman was prone to farting loudly and saying things like, 'Better out than in,' oblivious of the presence of guests.

But when Gina Wildgoose turned up for tea, Jennifer

realised that Norman was a veritable aristocrat in comparison to this country bumpkin, however bright she may have been.

Jennifer's raison d'être immediately became the prevention of her son's marriage into the Wildgoose clan, which only served to increase Gina, Keith and Norman's determination that it should happen.

The teatime debacle that took place in Jennifer's pristine home with its beige Dralon furniture and the routinely twitched net curtains was something akin to a badly performed West End farce in which people forgot their lines, began to laugh or fell over.

When Keith and Gina arrived, Jennifer was sitting in the front room toying with her freshly laid and polished hostess trolley, hoping against hope that the front door would open to reveal, attached to Keith's arm, a smartly dressed fresh-faced graduate with a talent for modesty and deference, and child-bearing hips.

The child-bearing hips arrived satisfactorily, but above them sat a wild-haired temptress who appeared slightly grubby and out of the pages of one of those dreadful magazines Jennifer occasionally found in Keith's toolbox or bedside cabinet, which revealed a series of catalogue model types dressed in very little, breasts primed and pointing straight at the camera, and on the odd, truly shocking occasion – for Jennifer at least – legs wide open and what she called their 'foo-foos' on show to all. To Jennifer, Gina looked like a porn queen.

Norman, who had been instructed to turn off *Grandstand*, his favourite sports programme and sanctuary from Jennifer's constant monologue on his shortcomings, felt an unmistakable stirring in his loins and a wave of pure jealousy at his son's good fortune.

The hostess trolley groaned with a traditional suburban tea of egg and cress sandwiches, a salad consisting of the truly banal trio of lettuce, cucumber and tomato, and of course the Battenberg cake.

Despite Gina's appearance, she had made what she considered to be a gargantuan effort for Keith, who had begged her to bury her cleavage and watch her language. She was clad in a green nylon cardigan, tweed skirt and some shoes she had bought at the local jumble sale for a pound, which were too high for her and caused her gait to become a totter, resulting in her moving into the lounge like a cutprice geisha with Parkinson's disease. As she swayed forward to shake Norman and Jennifer by the hand, a fixed, determined gurn on her face, the heel of one of her shoes gave way, propelling her forward at quite some speed and depositing her on top of the hostess trolley which collapsed under her weight and sent her sprawling to the ground on top of it, her skirt flying up to reveal stocking tops and no knickers, a state which she had planned to employ in the van later to make Keith implode. The final nail in the coffin of Jennifer's support for Keith's union was Gina's response to this accident. She turned and said, 'Oh fuck, oh shit, sorry, Keith, oh bollocks, sorry Mr and Mrs Wilson.'

'They think it's all over . . . it is now,' said Norman to himself quietly.

As most adults of a certain class and age would in this situation, Jennifer and Norman tried to pretend nothing had happened, but it had destroyed their suburban idyll and the visit was curtailed almost immediately.

Keith sat, mortified, in the van, running the incident over and over again in his head. The closing scene of the horrified face of his mother and the slightly horrified (combined with more than slightly aroused) face of his father refused to subside, and he wondered to himself why a serially unremarkable person such as himself should have fallen in love with an uncontrolled, mobile wrecking machine such as Gina.

But Keith was remarkable. He was intelligent, humorous, kind, altruistic, warm and very funny and these qualities together, unsullied by any negative accompaniments, were rare in most men as they often came with the initially hidden price of moodiness, drunkenness and laziness to puncture the woman's joy at having found the man of her dreams.

Within a few days, however, Keith found that the image of Gina's disgrace in his parents' front room, which had initially gnawed at his entrails ceaselessly, had faded completely and he and Gina continued their courtship, with Gina safe in the knowledge that the blip that had occurred in Wolverhampton had not ruined her chances of snaring Keith. Paradoxically, it had the opposite effect and it gave

Keith more impetus in his journey away from his parents towards independence and Gina.

Gina realised a proposal was close. If it was possible, Keith was more attentive, more dreamy-eyed and more sexually charged than ever. And so it happened that one day, as they lay squinting at the late-afternoon sun in a field very close to the Welsh border, looking up at a hill where King Caractacus was rumoured to have fought his final battle, the much-awaited moment arrived. Despite appearances, Keith was uncomfortable. Gina's head lay on his arm, which had gone to sleep; she looked so peaceful, he couldn't bear to disturb her but he had to do something to shift his paralysed arm from under her big, heavy head.

'Do you want to get married?' he said almost inaudibly, so that Gina, with her eyes closed, listening to the breeze, thought it was an auditory hallucination.

'What did you say?' she said.

'Nothing,' said Keith.

Gina quickly became agitated. She was sure she had heard a proposal but didn't know if it was bad form to ask him to repeat it. Would he be offended that she'd missed the proposal? Even worse, what if he hadn't proposed and she started to badger him, insisting he had? She heard a low chuckling and looked across at Keith who seemed highly entertained by her pain.

'You fucking bastard,' she said. 'You did propose.'

'I'm afraid you're too late,' said Keith. 'You should have answered straight away.'

'So what does that mean?' said Gina.

'Well, you'll have to wait and see if I ask again,' said Keith, 'and pay attention next time.'

Gina felt tears pricking at her eyes.

'Keith . . .' she said falteringly.

Keith was smiling broadly. 'You silly bag,' he said. 'What's your answer?'

And that was probably the last time Keith had the upper hand in their relationship.

Their wedding took place in a small chapel in a neighbouring village, although the minister took some persuading before he let the Wildgoose family across the threshold of his territory; long hours spent asking God if it was all right to hate an entire family produced little encouragement.

There had been a serious threat to Keith and Gina's relationship arising from Keith's introduction to the Wildgoose family. But this mountain had been climbed and everyone had safely coasted down the other side. An uneasy camaraderie existed between Keith and Gina's brothers Wobbly and Bighead but Jennifer and Norman kept their distance during and after the wedding for fear of some breach in social etiquette that would force them to cut the lines of communication completely. Keith was terrified of his mother-in-law-to-be and found himself taking seriously the idea that one's wife's mother is what one's wife will become eventually. This horrifying reverie overtook him during the ceremony and when the kindly elderly minister asked Keith if he took 'this woman', his mouth formed the word, 'No.'

Something akin to snarling emanated from the back of the chapel and Keith, waking from his strange depersonalised state, realised what he had said and quickly converted the 'no' into a 'yes'.

The reception in the village hall was a rather subdued affair because the legendary stag night the previous evening in Hereford had left the major players in the drama virtually blinded by hangovers. Keith, knowing that vast amounts of alcohol would be poured down his throat before some kind of rustic humiliation was visited upon him, had attempted to water down or spit out his drinks during the evening, thus ensuring that when he was finally dragged into a fight and then tied naked and protesting to the back of a milk float, the suffering was doubled by his relative sobriety.

Still, he and Gina were happy at last and, with what many of the older relatives considered to be slightly bad-mannered haste, headed off for their honeymoon in Aberystwyth. The elderly relatives had little idea just how unseemly the haste was; had they processed behind the couple in Keith's old van, decorated with a few old cans and some badly spelled obscenities, they would have seen the van swerve into the first field it encountered and within a very short time begin to rock to the accompanying sounds of Gina's shrieks and Keith's low, mournful whoops.

'And that was 'ow you came to be, littl'un,' Nan Wildgoose

would often say to Alice as she sat her on her bony knee and talked her through the post-nuptial encounter.

'Mum, for Chrissakes,' Gina would say, even she baulking at the idea of a three-year-old being regaled with her parents' first sexual encounter in place of a bedtime story.

'Shall I tell 'er 'bout the stag night instead then?' asked Nan Wildgoose.

'Jesus,' said Gina, her eyes swivelling towards the ceiling.

Chapter 2

1974, aged 5

As Alice began to grow into a little girl, she realised she would have to go out into a world populated with even more people like her grandma, grandpap and disturbed uncles, and for this, at the unsophisticated age of five, she would need to develop a persona which would charm yet protect her from the unwanted approaches of the county's over-bearing people. She was a sweet-looking child whose dirty blonde curls immediately put one in mind of a sad little orphan; consequently people, especially middle-aged women, wanted to pick her up and hug her to their cushiony ample bosoms, a berth she did not particularly want to occupy. So she developed an outward ambivalence towards the rest of the human race, which made it hard for them to judge whether she was in desperate need of their care or too disturbed to warrant it.

She learned from her uncles Wobbly and Bighead how to effect socially unacceptable behaviour and on occasions would dribble whilst clasped to a fervent do-gooder. This resulted in an immediate loosening of the hug and on one or two occasions a swift plummet to the ground, accompanied by an exclamation of disgust. Word quickly went round that 'the Wilson child's a bit simple', and this meant that people were wary of her, which, to Alice, was a good thing.

When Alice started at the local primary school, she quickly became known as the problem child by the teaching staff. This was not because she was a problem but because her mother Gina was. Teachers would hold their breath most mornings until they saw Keith amble into view, because on the rare days when Gina appeared with Alice in tow, it would be like negotiating with a hostage-taker. Some mornings Gina was all right but her unpredictability only served to increase the frisson of fear amongst the small group of teachers.

This stemmed from an incident when Gina had thrown a tantrum following a slight disagreement between herself and the headmaster, John Jarvis, who found it absolutely inconceivable that anyone would challenge his authority. On a frosty February morning, as he stood at the gates redefining the meaning of welcoming children to school, given that his face disagreed so violently with his relaxed posture, he threw out a remark to Gina as she passed, on the inappropriateness of her daughter wearing short socks in such cold weather. Gina, who had spent some twenty minutes trying to find any socks at all that remotely resembled each other in colour, let alone a pair of long ones, was in no mood for this rebuke and turned, still holding Alice's hand, to face Mr Jarvis.

'Pardon,' she said, with a homicidal glint in her eye.

John Jarvis, who was incapable of either predicting impending human storms or indeed preventing them, blithely repeated his statement.

He could not quite believe he had heard the words, 'Mind your own fucking business, fat arse,' and launched into a speech concerning the use of bad language in front of children. This was curtailed by a sharp pain in his stomach and he realised that the child's mother had hit him.

The altercation began to catch the notice of the other parents and John Jarvis escalated it tenfold by attempting to restrain Gina with what he would describe as 'a firm hand' and she 'a pervert's clamp'. Had not one of the teachers, a little bird-like creature called Miss Mount, intervened at this point, serious injury might have occurred. Miss Mount knew Gina Wilson of old and her instinct to steer John Jarvis away from her proved to be the saving of his reputation, as his anger at being challenged was rising so ferociously that he was about to slap her.

Gina's temper always subsided quickly but never down to the point of shame. She rearranged herself and harrumphed off home where Keith got the abuse intended for Mr Jarvis, delivered with both barrels.

Alice gained a huge amount of kudos as a result of her mother punching the headmaster, although the calibre of those who were impressed left something to be desired.

They included three eleven-year-olds who had pretty much already signed themselves up for a few short spells in prison, and Mrs Jarvis, who would have liked to take the occasional swing at Mr Jarvis herself but trod the path of least resistance. The mothers, however, shied away from Gina, even though they had known her since they were children. They had been slightly unsettled by her behaviour as a six-year-old but were far less judgemental then than they were now. As adults, having taken on board the ignorance and prejudice commonly displayed to the outsider, they kept their distance. And when they noticed a subtle change in Gina's manner which grew into increasingly frequent episodes of really strange behaviour, they became even more wary.

Although Alice couldn't really understand the lack of invitations to tea and was perplexed by children being gently moved away from her when the clutter of mothers who hung around the school gates came to pick up their brood, she didn't really mind; her inner life was becoming much more exciting than the superficial life she lived in public.

Inside herself she was like a good witch who controlled the world and made it the way she wanted it. So when her mother raged through the house, Alice retired to a rotting shed in the garden where she kept a shoebox full of spells (a dead dragonfly, some string, two dead beetles and a handful of tadpoles she had plucked from a pond, not realising that the lack of water would soon finish them off). She only came out when she heard her dad's gentle voice calling her in for tea.

Life improved immensely when her mother was absent or 'lying down', as her father put it, which meant, in Gran Wildgoose's language, she was 'pissed out 'er 'ead'.

When Alice was about five, television and especially the weather reports began to take on a huge significance in Gina's life. Alice would notice her, transfixed, in front of the screen, smiling, and she would turn to Alice and say things like, 'He's a bit tired today,' or 'Look at him, the little devil, he's flirting with me again.' Alice didn't really understand what Gina was talking about and didn't care because at least, her mother seemed calmer and happier.

One day, a Saturday, Gina announced to Keith that she was going shopping in Hereford for some curtain material, and Alice noticed that he looked at her mother as if she had said, 'I'm going to learn how to ride an elephant today.' This was understandable. Curtains were as far down Gina's list of important things to do as keeping the house looking nice.

'And I'll take Alice with me,' added Gina.

Keith stiffened and a look of concern flitted across his benign features. He, too, had noticed the hitherto subtle changes in Gina's behaviour.

'It's all right, I'll have her,' he said. 'I'll take her up Coxall Knoll and show her where the owl lives.'

This was something he'd been promising to do for ages and Alice immediately rose to go and find her wellingtons and slightly too big denim jacket bought at the village jumble sale.

'Sit down, Alice,' said Gina. 'You're coming with me.'

Alice knew better than to try and argue. Last time she had tried to change her mother's mind, Gina had thrown a cup at her which had shattered on the fridge and knocked off her picture of Miss Mount.

'What's the big deal?' said Keith. 'Have a day out on your own and enjoy yourself.'

'Alice, go in the garden,' said Gina.

The words 'Alice, go in the garden' usually prefaced a row and Alice, not wanting to see her sweet dad once again at the receiving end of her mother's temper, obediently headed out to the shed and chanted a 'Don't Make Me Go To Hereford With Mum' spell over the dead tadpoles.

It didn't work. After some pretty concentrated shouting, Gina appeared, handbag on arm, and beckoned to Alice.

They got the bus from the village and as it moved slug-like through the Herefordshire countryside, Alice felt an inexplicable sense of dread wash over her as if something really bad was going to happen. Gina, however, seemed cheerful, as if she was anticipating something wonderful, like a day at the seaside. Some time later they alighted, not as Alice had expected in the town centre but on the outskirts, and began to walk down a suburban street of thirties houses that looked well kept if not a little dull. This passed for the posh bit of Hereford.

Gina stopped outside a house where a pristine silver sports car was parked in the drive.

'Wait here,' said Gina, and Alice sat down on the pavement

while her mum walked up the short lavender-lined path to the front door and rang the bell.

A man in his thirties answered and the rictus grin that obviously sat very easily on his attractive yet rather doughy features turned to a frown. Although Alice could not hear what was said, it was clear to her that the man was not very pleased to see her mum. There was a short exchange before her mother reacted almost as if she had been slapped and turned sharply back down the path, muttering angrily and looking like Grandpap did when the cider ran out.

'Don't say a word,' said Gina to Alice. 'I'm not in the mood. Wait a minute.'

She ran to the sports car and kicked it, shouting a very loud 'Bastard!' at the top of her voice. Then she shot off down the road and Alice raced to keep up with her.

The word 'bastard' was not a stranger in the Wilson and Wildgoose households and Alice knew it meant a bad thing.

'Are you cross with bastard?' she said to Gina.

'Yes I am,' said Gina, 'and if you tell Dad about this, I'll be even crosser with you.'

Alice didn't like having secrets with her mum. It felt dangerous and out of control but she knew it would be even more dangerous if she disobeyed Gina.

They spent a couple of hours looking round the shops but Gina was in such a bad mood it wasn't a pleasure and every time Alice asked for something, Gina tutted loudly, looked straight ahead and carried on walking, so in the end Alice gave up.

They arrived home in time for the news. Keith always made an attempt to shield Alice from the more tragic and violent stories but he wasn't in, so Alice sat through a couple of horrible murders and a war story and was just about to try for a sandwich and a drink when the weather came on and Gina shushed her loudly and urgently.

Alice was aware of her mother once again staring transfixed at the screen and realised that the man talking and pointing to a map with clouds and sun on it was 'bastard' from the house in Hereford. Gina became agitated and took her shoe off and threw it at the television. It missed the screen and bounced off the controls at the bottom, somehow managing to turn the television off. Gina began to sob uncontrollably, managing to say through her tears, 'Bastard weatherman. Look what he's done, he's turned me off from his life, I hate him, I hate him.' Her tragic snot-covered face put Alice in mind of Susan Winston, a girl in her class who often burst into tears if even slightly reprimanded by a teacher. Alice wanted to give her mum a hug but knew there was a good chance of this escalating the proceedings to hurricane level so she sat motionless, wondering what to do, when like a mud-spattered knight in shining armour her dad stepped into the room to rescue her.

'What's up, sweetheart?' he said to Gina. 'Nothing much in the shops?'

'Don't take the piss,' said Gina. 'Can't you see the state I'm in?'

'Come on, Alice,' said Keith perkily. 'Shall we go and see how Smelly is?'

Smelly was Alice's guinea pig who lived in the porch; the overpowering aroma from the emissions he was responsible for had been deemed too unpleasant to allow him access to Alice's bedroom.

While they checked Smelly's progress, Alice said to Keith, 'Mum's gone a bit funny, Dad.'

Keith tried to retain a normal expression but his heart jumped. It hadn't occurred to him that Alice had picked up the nuances of Gina's deteriorating mental health.

'Don't worry, sweetheart,' he said. 'I'll sort it out. Did you and Mum have a nice time at the shops today?'

'Not really,' said Alice. 'Mum kicked bastard Weatherman's car.'

Oh Jesus, Keith thought. It's happening again.

Just after Alice was born, Gina had had what psychiatrists might call a psychotic episode, which is to say she lost touch with reality for a few weeks. She was eventually deemed to be a danger to others and sectioned under the Mental Health Act and admitted to a local psychiatric hospital. This episode had involved Gina becoming obsessed with a mechanic at the garage where Keith took his van for servicing. The unfortunate mechanic in question had been terrified, being a small, mousy and spotty little thing who still lived with his mother. Eventually Gina had to be forcibly removed from under a Morris traveller by the police and was taken to hospital. Alice had been only a few weeks old at the time and Keith had had to take on a tiny baby, visit his wife in hospital and somehow manage to keep the offers of help from the Wildgoose family at bay. One day, desperate to find someone to have Alice for the afternoon while he went to see Gina whom he still loved fiercely with a blind loyalty, he foolishly allowed Wobbly and Bighead to take Alice out for a walk. The walk, of course, was to the pub and they took great delight in letting her pushchair run down the hill and then racing to see who could catch up with it first. The pair then decided to take her fishing and accidentally dropped her in a pond while they were trying to show her a big carp that kept rising to the surface. Keith only found this out some years later when Grandpap had had too much cider and related it fondly as one of the few stories that showed Wobbly and Bighead in a good light.

In the porch with Smelly, Keith attempted to get some more information from Alice but she realised that she shouldn't have said anything and her mouth set into a determined line, out of which came no more details of the day's proceedings. She looked a bit frightened, thought Keith, and he left her alone. Together they tucked Smelly into bed, even though Smelly didn't want to be tucked into bed, and then Keith took Alice up to her scruffy little room and read her a particularly silly story to try and take both their minds off the lurking explosion downstairs.

When Gina had gone to bed that night, exhausted by her racing thoughts and rejection by Hereford's weather forecaster, Keith phoned Marie Henty the local GP, whom he had got to know well during Gina's last psychotic episode. He felt he could tell her anything and he even thought that if he asked her to come round and give him a cuddle, she wouldn't refuse, such was her capacity to fling herself wholeheartedly and empathetically into her work. Keith had no idea that it was he himself who provoked these feelings because of his sweetness, his humour and his grinding, thankless job of looking after Gina at her most mad.

'Marie, sorry about the time of night, it's Keith,' he said, causing her stomach to give a slight lurch.

'Is it Gina?' she said.

'I think she's on the road to Bonkersville again,' said Keith, trying to sound relaxed about the fact that his wife was metamorphosing once more into a scary, stigmatised member of society. 'She's been chasing that weather forecaster off the local news, according to Alice. She took her to his house today and there was some sort of incident that Alice won't talk about.'

Marie wanted to laugh.

'What do you want to do?' she said with her fingers crossed.

'Could you talk to her?' said Keith.

The crossed fingers having failed to secure the right result, Marie asked a question she already knew the answer to.

'Can you get her to the surgery?' she said.

Keith did a horsey sort of snort down the phone.

'You're joking, aren't you?' he said.

'Yes, I suppose so,' said Marie. 'Shall I try my usual very

normal stroll past the cottage, bearing in mind that last time she threw a cabbage at me?'

'Would you?' said Keith. 'Be ever so grateful.'

'All right,' said Marie. 'Tomorrow afternoon after surgery.'

'Thanks,' said Keith. 'Tomorrow it is then.'

'Was that bastard?' said a voice and Keith turned to see Alice sitting on the stairs in her teddy pyjamas.

'No, silly,' he said. 'Now back into bed before Mum catches you.' And given the circumstances, that was all he needed to say.

The following afternoon, Gina saw Marie Henty's head going along the top of the hedge, back again and then past again, until, curious to know why their GP seemed to be out for a very boring walk, she went outside.

'Marie,' she said. 'What the hell do you want?'

'Well,' said Marie, 'I haven't seen you at the surgery for a bit and I just thought I'd pop down and see how you're doing.'

'Bullshit,' said Gina. 'Someone's been talking about me. It's not that creep John Jarvis, is it?'

'I'm not allowed to say,' said Marie, thereby getting Keith off the hook and implicating John Jarvis, a good result.

'I'm fine,' said Gina. 'In fact, couldn't be better.'

Her appearance belied this statement. She looked unwashed and out of control and Marie wondered how Keith could have let it go this far without trying to do something. But she knew the answer really. Keith's head was buried in the comforting mire of denial, because Gina's threats to kill him last time and her screeching accusations of betrayal as she disappeared into the back of a police car were something to be avoided at all costs even if it meant allowing her to deteriorate further.

Marie wished she could just lay it on the line. In an ideal world she would say to Gina, 'Look, Gina, it's obvious to everyone, even your five-year-old daughter, that you're as mad as a snake and you need some treatment. Let's not let it go any further or we'll all be up shit creek and the emotional debris will cause even more damage than last time.'

Instead, she smiled a benign smile, which irritated Gina enormously, causing her to look for a missile. Marie encouraged her to call if she needed to and quickly walked away. A handful of chicken droppings landed a few feet behind her, accompanied by Gina's personal parting shot.

'There's more of that in your face if you come back, you nosy cow!'

Marie knew it wouldn't be long before the woman would be sectioned again.

And it wasn't. The following day, a Monday, Keith took Alice to school before work up at the farm. Gina seemed to be completely absorbed in a book about the weather in space that she had managed to pick up in a second-hand bookshop in Ludlow on one of her shopping trips. The more disturbed Gina became, the less likely she was to come back from a shopping trip with what she had originally intended to buy. On the Ludlow trip she had gone on market day to get some fresh vegetables and meat but had come back with a book and a barometer she'd found at the back of an antique shop. Inner Keith said, 'What the fuck are we going to do with a barometer, you silly mare?' Outer Keith said, 'Hmm, a barometer. Well, I suppose that'll come in useful.'

Gina caught the humorous edge in his voice and said, 'It'll come in useful for knocking you out.' And that statement had no humour in it.

Keith wished the Wildgoose family could be a bit more help but the last time he'd called upon them to try and persuade Gina to go into hospital voluntarily, Gina's mum had screamed down the phone, 'Over my dead body, you useless lump,' and hung up. Not a bad exchange, Keith had thought and took refuge in some mother-in-law jokes he'd heard on telly.

Keith's parents were equally unhelpful. Their dislike of Gina had moved up the scale from 'Give her the benefit, Norman' to 'Can't abide the woman'.

It was hard to even get them to come to the house and look after Alice. They didn't like the countryside because it had a funny smell and all the people they met looked like sex offenders. Added to that, Jennifer didn't have any suitable shoes and refused to wear her beige suede K-Skips anywhere near mud, of which there was copious gloopy amounts down Keith and Gina's lane.

So Keith was a lone sailor in this sea of madness, apart from a few lifebelts thrown at him by Marie Henty and Doug in the shop. Doug was an ex-psychiatric nurse from Chester who had realised that he was so inured to people's pain after ten years on a general psychiatric ward that he was surplus to requirements in the field of solace. Ironically, though, he was the last person who should have left nursing because he possessed a cheery disposition, true empathy and an endless supply of fags.

Chapter 3

It was Saturday morning and Keith, exhausted from grafting all week and lying awake all night smoking some very big joints, trying to work out a way to talk Gina into some treatment, lay in bed snoring gently, protected from the day ahead by a thin sliver of sleep. Alice had woken and, as she normally did at the weekend, ran downstairs in her pyjamas to see how Smelly was and give him some food.

Her heart somersaulted in her little chest when she saw that Smelly's cage was open and her beloved guinea pig was nowhere to be seen. She hoped that her mum or dad was up and had put Smelly's garden run out for him to sniff and nibble at some fresh grass. She went out on to the dewy lawn in her bare feet and looked, panicked, around the small garden.

A strange moaning noise from the top of the house distracted her and she turned to see her mother sitting naked on top of the roof, holding aloft the aforementioned Smelly and crooning a song with which Alice was unfamiliar.

'Mum,' she called. 'Why are you on the roof with no clothes on?'

This perfectly reasonable question was greeted with a string of random words which Alice didn't understand and she thought she'd better call her father. Sucking her thumb, as she did when the world presented an insurmountable problem, she climbed the stairs to her parents' bedroom and gently shook her dad. He opened his eyes.

'Hello, sweetheart,' he said, his voice thick with sleep. 'Everything OK?'

'I think so,' said Alice, because at this point no one had fallen or died. 'But Smelly and Mum are on the roof and Mum's got no clothes on.'

Keith, still half in his dreaming state, laughed.

'Alice,' he said, 'what a daft thing to say. Come on, let's get you and Mum some breakfast.'

'But how are we going to get Mum and Smelly down for breakfast?'

Keith sat up in bed. 'Jesus Christ,' he said.

'I think he's too busy to get Mum and Smelly down,' said Alice.

Keith threw the bedcovers back and ran downstairs and out into the garden, the last few blissful seconds of half sleep tearing away from his brain and catapulting him into the familiar waking nightmare of his wife's deteriorating mental state.

Sure enough, there was Gina, on the roof holding the guinea pig – minus her clothes.

'Go away,' she screamed at him. 'I don't want you, I want little Teddy Fairfax.'

The possibility of luring the local news programme's best-loved weather forecaster down to their scruffy cottage seemed unlikely and Keith found himself shifting into the most banal of communications to try and resolve this farcical scenario.

'Come down for breakfast and we'll talk about it, love.' He tried to say this as if his wife wasn't sitting naked on the roof clutching the family pet.

'Mum, I want Smelly!' shouted Alice and began to cry, realising that even for her unpredictable mother this was most unusual.

'Smelly's my present for Teddy,' she called back, 'to show him I truly love him.'

By this point Smelly had set up a fearful squeaking and was wriggling dangerously in Gina's hands.

'Come on, love,' said Keith. 'Poor old Smelly's scared. Let him come down and we'll clean him up a bit and feed him. We couldn't give him as a present to anyone in that state.' Keith realised with some surprise that he was as concerned for Smelly's safety as Gina's.

Gina turned Smelly to examine him as if he was a piece of old rag.

'All right,' she said. 'Here you go,' and she rolled Smelly from the top of the roof down towards Keith.

Alice squealed with delight. Not realising the consequences of Smelly hitting the ground at some considerable
speed, this was the funniest thing she'd seen for ages, her
rotating pet heading earthwards, a bit like when she rolled
down the top meadow in summer, gathering speed until,
hysterical with laughter, she landed in a heap at the bottom.

'Fuck!' Keith braced himself for the most important catch
of his life.

Smelly dropped off the bottom of the roof and landed in
Keith's large and capable hands. Alice clapped with joy and
gently relieved Keith of the luckiest guinea pig in
Herefordshire.

'Take Smelly inside,' said Keith, 'and I'll talk to Mum.'

Alice, only too happy not to be caught up in the naked-
mum-on-the-roof-drama any more, disappeared inside the
cottage while Keith came at the problem from another
direction.

'Gina, come down and I'll drive you to Hereford to see
Teddy,' he called.

'I don't believe you,' she shouted back, clinging to some
vestige of sanity. 'You're just saying that to make me come
down.'

Never had Keith felt such a strong desire to walk away
from a crisis. I could take Alice, he thought, and we could
spend a lovely day at the seaside, have fish and chips and just
walk along the waves until she gets bored. We could drive
to Aberystwyth, find a little B and B and then come back
the next day and see if she's still up there.

But poor Keith wasn't made of that kind of stuff. Irritating, demanding, out of control as she was, the lovely, wild Gina was still under there somewhere and he just wanted her to be better and to be the weird and wonderful woman he had married. He knew at this point that there was no getting away from treating her against her will. She must go into hospital and suffer the indignity of forced injections and twenty-four-hour surveillance by the motley crew of people who staffed what the locals called 'the bin'. But how best to do it? He knew the police would take one look, laugh inwardly and drag her screaming from her perch with all the empathy of a group of teenage boys given sole responsibility for a younger brother. Would Marie Henty be a better bet? Or what about Doug from the shop? He might help and at least he had some experience of this sort of thing. Keith ran into the house and dialled the number. Doug picked up after one ring.

'Doug, I'm sorry,' these days Keith seemed to preface every conversation with these words, 'but I've got a problem at the cottage. Gina's on the roof, starkers, and won't come down.'

'Righto,' said Doug, as matter-of-fact as if Keith had asked for his newspapers to be cancelled for the weekend. 'Give us five minutes.'

The ability of time to stretch itself never ceased to amaze Keith. He heard the chug of Doug's ancient Escort in the lane after what seemed to be forty minutes and yet when he glanced at his watch, Keith saw that it had only taken six minutes. Doug parked his car in the lane and walked up to the cottage. His red, quizzical face appeared round the hedge first – he seemed to be checking this wasn't some sort of joke before he dragged the rest of his body after it.

'Blimey, Keith,' said Doug, 'see what you mean. We'll need to get her down and take her to hospital, get her sectioned and then everything will be fine. Just give me a brief picture of how long this has all been going on and what it involves.'

'Well, she's been deteriorating for weeks,' said Keith, 'but this very mad behaviour's only been going on for a few days. She's obsessed with this weather forecaster on telly and has been to his house, not really sleeping very well, talking a bit of rubbish, you know.'

'Oh yes,' said Doug, for he did. 'What we gonna do then? Shall I get a ladder up and talk her down?'

'Do you think you can?' said Keith, more grateful than he could say to this big, bumbling giant of a man for taking the responsibility off his shoulders.

'Dunno,' said Doug, 'but I'll give it a try.'

Keith produced a rusty ladder from the shed and Doug laid it up against the house.

'What's going on?' said Gina, suspicion evident in her voice.

Keith shouted up, 'Doug's coming up to talk to you.'

'Oh, not that ginger fat arse,' said Gina loudly.

'Sorry,' said Keith.

'That's all right,' said Doug. 'I've heard far worse than that, you know, mate,' but a little arrow of pain still flew directly towards his heart, a minor injury in the lexicon of the tragedy of the fat bloke, re-lived time and time again at the hands of drunks, teenagers and mad people.

Doug struggled up the ladder, with Keith at the bottom trying to control every seismic wobble as the ample frame above him neared its destination.

'Hello, Gina.'

'Fuck off, Doug.'

'Aw, Gina, come on, you know you need help.'

Sounds like the title of a country and western song, thought Keith.

'Come on down, Gina, you look freezing up there,' Doug persisted.

'Well, actually, if you'd listened to little Teddy Fairfax, you'd know the temperature this morning was going to be sixty degrees Fahrenheit so that's hardly freezing.'

'You're doing a Valerie Singleton, though,' said Doug.

'Pardon?' said Gina.

'Erect nipples,' said Doug. 'Don't you remember her coming out of the water on *Blue Peter* with that swimming cossie on? Ooh, I was shocked.'

Steady on, thought Keith.

Gina began to laugh and an expression crossed her face for a split second that gave the merest of hints that some insight into her situation was still possible.

'Come on, Gina, for Gawd's sake,' said Doug, 'or this

ladder's gonna break, I'll get killed and you'll be responsible.'

Gina hesitated. 'You promise you won't do anything.'

'Like what?' said Doug.

'Like drag me into that Godforsaken hospital again. I couldn't stand it.'

Doug's honest, open face belied his duplicitous intent.

'Gina, do I look like someone who would bullshit you?'

Gina began to edge down towards him, looking magnificent in the morning sun, Doug thought, whereas Keith was thinking, Christ, I hope she doesn't roll like Smelly.

She didn't and between them they managed to get her intact to the ground. Rather shortsightedly they had not agreed what to do next, but they both instinctively moved towards her to contain her so they could begin the long journey to hospital and some treatment.

Gina, realising they were bearing down on her, began to scream as loud as she could, which brought Alice out into the garden from the safety of a cartoon on TV.

'What's the matter with Mum, Dad?' she cried above the noise.

'She's not well, tiddler,' said Keith, 'and me and Doug are going to take her to hospital.'

Gina screamed louder.

'Hold her, Doug,' shouted Keith. 'I'll get some clothes.' He ran into the house and reappeared with her dressing gown which seemed to be the only article of clothing they had a chance of getting her into.

'Get in the car, love,' Keith said to Alice. 'In the front.' He turned to Doug. 'I'll take Gina in the back with me, you drive, and we'll swap if it all gets too bad.'

'It fucking will get bad, you bastard,' screamed Gina. 'How dare you, I have my rights, let go of me, scum.' She tried to bite Keith who managed a body swerve away from her jaws.

'Can I help?' said a voice. It was Marie Henty who, having dropped into the village shop and heard that Doug had gone up to the Wilsons' cottage, had walked up to help.

'Oh Jesus, so you're in on it as well,' said Gina through clenched teeth. 'You fucking witch, keep your hands off my husband.'

Marie Henty blushed and hoped Keith hadn't noticed. He hadn't.

'Just help me get her in the back of the van, will you?' said Keith. 'We're going to the hospital.'

Keith opened the back doors of the van and he, Gina and Marie all tumbled in together. Doug banged them shut, put a seatbelt round Alice and the van began its epic journey through the lanes, accompanied by much screeched abuse from Gina and some familiar squeaking.

'What's that?' Doug asked Alice.

'It's Smelly,' said Alice. 'I didn't want to leave him on his own.'

All went reasonably well until they reached the outskirts of Hereford. Doug and Alice sang along to some hits on the car radio and Keith and Marie Henty lay in the back of Keith's old van on some oily blankets, listening to the disordered thought processes of Gina as she oscillated between pathetically begging them to let her go and railing against them as if they were handmaidens of the devil. Keith's warm breath occasionally drifted towards Marie and she found herself inappropriately wishing he would lean across and kiss her. She took in the pained expression on his face and loved him all the more for it, not realising he was desperate for a pee. Gina quietened down and as they approached the first set of traffic lights, a strange moment of calm descended on the little group. It was short-lived, though, as Gina, sensing a loosening of their hold on her, gave the doors one almighty kick and made a bid for freedom, leaving Keith and Marie clutching one arm each of her dressing gown.

Doug saw Gina's naked figure fly past the van and with an oath he skidded into the side of the road and leapt out to find Marie and Keith looking nonplussed in the back.

'For fuck's sake, you two, let's get after her,' he roared.

For a big bloke, Doug was really nippy on his toes. As Marie plunged towards the pavement, the heel on her new court shoes having snapped off, he and Keith sprinted chest to chest after the escaping Gina. Pedestrians stood transfixed as the latterday horseless Lady Godiva flew past them, wondering if this was indigestion or something more sinister that had been added to their drinks at the local.

Gina made the mistake of running into a newsagents where

the proprietor, one Reg Meston, was having a cup of tea and perusing the sports page.

As the door was flung open he murmured, 'What can I get you?' without even looking up.

'Get me little Teddy Fairfax or I'll die,' shrieked a woman's voice and he looked up to see a wild-eyed, naked woman flailing about near the children's comics.

'Bloody hell, love, are you all right?' said Reg but never got an answer as a fat ginger bloke and a small wiry hippy came skidding through the door.

'Sorry, mate,' said Doug, 'we're taking her to hospital.'

'Be my guest,' said Reg, who didn't fancy his chances against the desperate Gina.

Keith and Doug grabbed an arm each and led Gina from the shop. Marie had followed them in the van and she and Alice were parked outside.

Reg went into the back room to call his wife and switched on the telly just as a strange little man with bleached blond highlights, standing in front of a weather map, said, 'Good afternoon, I'm Ted Fairfax.'

'Well I never,' said Reg. 'Come 'ere, Pat, you'll never guess what I've just seen.'

The van finally pulled up at Hereford's one and only psychiatric hospital. Marie left Gina pinioned by Doug and Keith in the back and Alice sucking her thumb in the front and went to find the duty doctor. Five minutes later she appeared with a couple of scary-looking male nurses and Gina was euphemistically 'escorted' inside and taken to a side room of a ward decorated in the sort of colours that immediately bring on a deep depression.

They were told to wait.

Eventually what was effectively a boy dressed up as a doctor appeared and perched on the edge of a chair.

Having been filled in by Marie Henty, medic to medic, he turned to Gina and said, 'Hello, I'm Dr Desmond. And what is your name, my dear?'

'Oh, I'm the fucking Queen of Sheba,' said Gina with a snarl.

Excitedly, he scribbled 'delusional ideas' down on his pad.

'And how are you?' he said.

'How do you think I am, you prick?' said Gina.

Dr Desmond reddened. He turned to Keith, Doug and Marie Henty. 'Perhaps it's best if I spend some time alone with Mrs Wilson,' he said. 'If you'd like to wait outside, I'll catch up with you soon.'

They all left the room and Doug and Marie sat uncomfortably on some institutional chairs while Keith went out to check on Alice. She had fallen asleep on the front seat, thumb in her mouth, and Smelly had produced an incongruously large bowel movement on the driver's side.

The decision was made to admit Gina to a ward under a section of the Mental Health Act which meant she could be detained for up to twenty-eight days. Keith was so relieved when Dr Desmond informed him of the decision he almost began to cry. Doug put a huge arm round him.

'At least she's in the right place,' he said. 'Let's see what some treatment can do.'

'Let's get back,' said Marie, slightly puzzled by Keith's emotional state. 'You can get some clothes and stuff for Gina, Keith, and maybe pop in and see her tomorrow with Alice.'

A cloud crossed Keith's face.

'What is it?' asked Marie.

'I've got to tell the Wildgoose family,' said Keith, 'and they weren't best pleased last time this happened.' The Wildgoose family being 'not best pleased' was like any other family having a homicidal rampage.

In normal circumstances Marie would have leapt in and offered to go with Keith to inform the Wildgoose family of the situation, but having experienced their particular brand of shoot-'em-up social graces, she kept quiet.

They all drove off together through glorious sunshine, the outlines of old oaks sprouting from ancient hill forts enclosing them as they traversed the valley. Keith dropped Marie off in the village. She wanted to go home with Keith and cook him a meal but the prospect of possibly bumping into the Wildgoose family ensured that she didn't suggest this option and she exited the van with a cheery wave and an aching heart. Doug picked up his car from the lane. 'See you, mate,' he said as if he and Keith had been fishing, and drove off to the local to fend off questions about what he considered to be a private matter. Keith, noticing that both Alice and Smelly had dropped off to sleep, luxuriated in the very rare condition of silence. He almost felt at peace for once. As the van rounded the corner and took a run at the steep drive to the cottage, three figures sitting on the doorstep caused Keith to cross himself – only half in jest. For there sat his mother-in-law, Wobbly and Bighead who was cradling a shotgun.

Chapter 4

'I've got Alice asleep in the van,' Keith shouted out of the window as if this might prevent Bighead shooting him on sight.

The Wildgoose family rose as one and by the time Keith had turned off the engine and got out of the van, they were standing right by him.

'Where is Gina?' growled her mother.

'Put the gun down, Bighead,' said Keith. 'I can't talk to all of you with that thing about to take off my head.'

'Arse more like,' said Bighead and he and Wobbly managed a throaty laugh.

'Put it down,' said Ma Wildgoose and the gun was laid alongside a toy car and a headless Barbie.

'So where is she?' Ma Wildgoose repeated.

Keith desperately wanted to say, 'Oh, she's having a pedicure at that new salon in Hereford,' but instead he forced out the words, 'We've taken her to hospital.'

The 'H' word caused a dark cloud to pass across their faces and Wobbly, with his customary head wobble, was the first to speak.

'You've never put our sister in that fucking place again, have you?'

'Well.' Keith hesitated, trying to form a sentence in his head that would absolve him of all responsibility for this heinous act and enable them all to go in for a nice cup of tea and a biscuit.

'You bloody 'ave then,' said Ma Wildgoose. 'What did we tell you last time that happened?'

The exact phrase they had used was permanently seared into Keith's grey matter so it was not a problem to call it to mind and repeat it back to them.

'You said you'd have my balls off with the secateurs and hang them up in the porch for the magpies,' he said.

'Exactly,' said Ma Wildgoose. 'Now what's made you ignore that and put our precious Gina in the bin?'

The truth was the only option, so Keith detailed the events of the morning and crossed his fingers behind his back as their expressions went through several emotions, including disbelief and horror, and ended up being a sort of quizzical amusement.

'Fucking starkers on the roof?' said Bighead. 'You having me on, Keithy boy?'

'No, I swear,' said Keith. 'And shouting to the four winds the name of this weather forecaster she thinks is in love with her.'

'Bastard.' Alice was standing there cradling Smelly in her arms.

'Alice,' said Keith, 'that's not a nice way for little girls to speak.'

'Sorry, Dad,' said Alice, 'but that's what Mum called him when she saw him when we was shopping.'

'Were shopping,' Keith corrected her. Even in the midst of this potential shooting by his in-laws, he couldn't stop himself steering her towards correct usage.

'We've got to get her out,' said Bighead. 'We can look after her at home, can't we, Mum, seeing as this useless lump ain't up to it?'

'I reckon,' said Ma Wildgoose, although to Keith the prospect of the three of them attempting to manage a serious psychotic illness within the confines of their gothic cottage seemed a non-starter.

'Look,' said Keith. 'Gina really isn't well at all. Please just give them a chance to make her better, a few days even, and if things aren't getting better I'll come and help you get her out.' He couldn't quite believe he had allied himself with the Wildgoose family in a potential attempt to spring his wife from a locked psychiatric ward but, well, he thought, there's got to be some give and take with this lot. He continued, 'And if it doesn't work out after three days you can shoot me then,' he indicated the shotgun.

Wobbly and Bighead laughed out loud.

'Thought we was coming to shoot yer, Keithy, did yer?'

said Bighead. 'No, we're going after some pheasants up in the woods.'

Keith wanted to say, I think you'll find those pheasants belong to the estate and they're being reared for a lot of posh blokes in Land Rovers to knock off more easily than a clump of skittles, but he knew better than to intervene in the minor criminal activities of the Wildgoose family.

'All right then,' said Ma Wildgoose, 'but three days is all you're getting and then we're taking over.'

The terrifying trio then turned on their heels and walked down the drive to where their ancient Cortina was parked half in the ditch. With a splutter of exhaust and a dangerous-sounding roar, they were gone down the country lanes.

The rest of the weekend was spent calmly. To Keith, Alice seemed fairly unaffected by the traumatic events of Saturday. She spent time playing in the garden with Smelly and drawing some pictures of the hospital that Mum had gone into, and on Sunday they went fishing down on the River Clun together, spending hours with their lines bobbing jauntily in the water although they didn't catch a thing.

But a cloud had hovered over them all day, because Keith knew that in the evening he and Alice would have to go and visit Gina and brave the confined space of the acute admission ward which would throw into their path a selection of the Herefordshire mentally ill, an ordeal he didn't want to put Alice through. He had the option of leaving Alice with his nearest neighbours, a kindly old couple called the Wellingtons, and he put this to Alice, but she had spent one too many afternoons in their fusty front room with some horrible biscuits and revolting-tasting milk, and she opted for the visit.

'I've got to pack some things for Mum,' said Keith before they left. 'Do you want to help?'

'Yes,' said Alice excitedly and while Keith laid out a selection of Gina's least sexually provocative clothes on the bed and some toiletries and towels, Alice assembled a couple of Noddy books, some of her dolls and a packet of Gina's favourite biscuits from the back of the kitchen cupboard.

Keith didn't have it in him to veto Alice's little collection which she had stuffed into a carrier bag, so they set off for Hereford, Keith in sombre mood, wondering exactly how Gina would be when they arrived, and Alice cheerfully singing a selection of nursery rhymes.

Keith marvelled at the ability of his five-year-old daughter to seemingly accept without question the admission of her mother to a local psychiatric hospital following weeks of increasingly strange behaviour, but realised he was imposing his own adult values on to Alice; he did not quite grasp the fact that a child who knows no different just accepts what is happening at face value.

I suppose it's the intervention of adults and their values who ruin children's lives, he thought sadly to himself and wished he could suspend Alice in time to prevent the inevitable encroachment of the shame and distress she would feel when she eventually came to the realisation that her mother wasn't like everyone else's.

'You look grumpy, Dad,' said Alice, breaking off from singing her favourite line about a blackbird pecking off someone's nose which she thought was enormously funny and wished it was Mr Jarvis the headmaster's nose.

The interference of the outside world and its harsh judgements on those suffering with mental illness became apparent even sooner than Keith would have imagined. Alice, back at school the following day, after the visit to Gina, encountered Stephen Matthews in the playground at break time. Stephen, the son of a local cowman, had picked up from his parents' gossip in front of the television that Alice's mum had been 'taken away' and locked up somewhere. Stephen was two years older than Alice and about twice her size and he threw his considerable weight around whenever he got the chance. The objects of his disdain were always the children of those adults whom his parents felt most threatened by, and mental illness terrified them because it had been identified in successive generations on both sides of the family. So Alice found herself surrounded by Stephen and his cowardly mates in a corner of the playground less well policed by the teaching staff.

'Your mum's in prison, she's a bloody nutcase!' Stephen led the chorus and the others joined in as best they could.

'She's not in prison,' said Alice, cowering under the eclipse caused by Stephen's huge frame. 'She's in a big castle with lots of circus people. She got on the roof on her own with no clothes on.' Alice was rather proud of this and communicated it as if her mother had achieved something spectacular.

The boys simultaneously uttered a honk of disgust.

'Your mum showed her bosoms and she showed her—'

'Stephen Matthews!' Miss Mount strode across the playground, having spotted Alice surrounded by the little group. 'What are you doing?'

'Nothing, miss,' said Stephen, who had learned at a young age it was best to deny all knowledge.

'Well, off you go then,' said Miss Mount, who defused many a potential drama this way.

She had heard some talk in the staffroom about Gina and felt very sorry for the naive husband and his sturdy little daughter.

'Are you all right, Alice dear?' she said.

'Yes,' said Alice. 'My mum has gone to a castle and is with people from a circus.'

Miss Mount hesitated. Is this what the father has allowed her to believe? she wondered. She resolved to speak to Keith when he came to pick Alice up that afternoon.

Alice fled back to the safety of the two friends she had managed to cultivate in spite of the whispering campaign against her mum and her strangeness. Mark, whose blond, wild hair seemed to have been stolen from a girl's head, was sweet-tempered and effeminate and eschewed the 'hitting things' games that the other boys seemed to prefer in the playground. His attempts at home to shy away from the more manly pastimes of football and shooting had been met with some despair by his father, a red-cheeked arable farmer, but secretly with huge fondness by his mother whose revulsion towards the 'huntin', shootin' and fishin'' ethos of the locals was barely contained. Her unconscious encouragement of Mark's feminine side from an early age was subtle and all but hidden but the constant questioning by his father of why he wouldn't pick up a toy gun or why he wanted to indulge in baking with his mother when wading through mud was on offer was frequent and oppressive.

Karen, on the other hand, Alice's other friend, was tougher than most of the boys in the playground. Her long black hair, secured in two plaits with rubber bands, had been pulled only once in the playground. It had resulted in such a rage that Stephen Matthews, his little bulbous nose bloodied from Karen's flailing punch, retired howling to report the incident to Miss Mount. Her pleasure at this nascent bully receiving his comeuppance from a mere girl was well disguised under the mild ticking-off she felt obliged to give Karen in front of Stephen.

Stephen and Karen accepted the castle and circus performers story without question and both thought this sounded very exciting. Mark wondered if perhaps they could go to the circus, while Karen wisely cautioned a decent waiting time so the performers could get their acts together and find a suitable venue. What she actually said was, 'Let's wait till they're in their tent,' and Mark and Alice nodded sagely.

Keith, having managed to get his employer to agree to his having some time off while his wife was in hospital, found Miss Mount waiting at the school gate for him. Keith felt relieved that John his boss had serendipitously mistaken his reluctance to elucidate on his wife's condition as a sign that her admission was necessitated because of 'women's problems' and he'd escaped without having to explain any further. Now here was Miss Mount telling him that Alice had been saying her mum was in a castle with some circus performers.

'Have you told her the truth?' said Miss Mount, pushing her hand through her thinning grey hair.

'Um . . .' Keith hadn't and thought this made him seem like a bad parent.

'It's just that if she goes round saying these things in the playground, other children may tease her,' she said.

'It's hard,' said Keith. 'She definitely knows it's a hospital but it's so hard to explain to her what mental illness is, so when she said they looked like people in a circus, I just let it pass.'

Miss Mount desperately wanted to ask Keith how it had really been but felt it too intrusive a question. Keith, on the other hand, desperately wanted to tell her but didn't know if it was appropriate because although she was kindly and sympathetic, she was after all one of Alice's teachers and he couldn't be absolutely sure that she wouldn't gossip.

The visit to the hospital had been a pretty dreadful experience. Gina had seemed like a different person, drowsy and floppy like a big, smoking puppet, all her personality carried away by the power of the anti-psychotic drugs she had had pumped into her against her will. Her fellow sufferers were in varying stages of madness and recovery. One had stood singing 'Oh What A Beautiful Morning' on a table, attempting to conduct the rabble in front of him with manic charm, while ghosts moved around him, seemingly barely in touch with the real world. A man had sidled up to Keith and Alice and conspiratorially whispered, 'Watch the nurse with the ponytail, she's working for the government, we're all being experimented on.' Keith could only nod helplessly, having not the faintest idea how to handle this half-dressed blank-eyed giant and shielding Alice in case he lashed out. At the other end of the ward, several patients sat on threadbare chairs watching *Songs of Praise* and singing along barely audibly to Keith's favourite hymn, 'For Those In Peril On The Sea'.

The charge nurse, a middle-aged time-server called Steve, wearily informed Keith that Gina would probably be 'zonked out' for a week or so and that once the drugs wore off, a period of assessment would take place. Keith felt it imperative to explain to the nurse that the Wildgoose clan might pay a visit and not be best pleased, but Steve reacted to this with barely a flicker of anxiety, so Keith decided to hand over responsibility and let the Wildgoose family be an unpleasant surprise at visiting time.

Chapter 5

1979, aged 10

Nan Wildgoose threw back her head and roared with laughter.

'That head nurse's face when we pushed him into the office, tied him up and took the keys,' she said. 'Looked like 'e thought we was going to kill 'im. What was 'e called now? Some bloody dull name like Andy or Dave, wasn't it?'

'Steve,' said Alice, who had rather liked the flat, emotionless Steve and his ability to react to everything with the same passive expression. 'But what did Mum think?' she asked. Alice got most of her information from Nan Wildgoose and although she had heard this story many times, the retelling of it by her nan was always entertaining and heroic.

'Oh, your mother was completely out of it,' said Nan Wildgoose. 'They'd filled her up with drugs, she didn't know where she was. Wobbly just threw her over his shoulders like a sack of spuds and we opened the doors and ran for it.'

'Did everyone else get out too?' said Alice.

'Oh Jesus, no,' said Nan. 'We didn't want them running around raping and pillaging.'

'There was one,' said Grandpap, waking briefly from an elongated snore by the fire.

'You're right, Bert,' said Nan. 'Now I think about it, there was that woman who told Big'ead she was a member of staff and she was so convincing 'e let her wander through. Why 'e didn't cotton on that a real member of staff might 'ave been a bit upset we was stealing a patient, I don't know. It was all so quick, I s'pose.'

'You had to take Mum back, though, didn't you?' said Alice as if she was describing some shoddy goods from a supermarket.

'Yes, we fucking did,' said Nan, getting cross as she recalled the defeat suffered by the Wildgoose family at the hands of society. 'Not without a bloody brilliant fight first, though, was it, Bert?'

Bert grinned. 'No, love,' he said and dropped back to sleep.

Locally, it had been dubbed the Siege of Dodds Cottage, the name of the mean little cottage occupied by the Wildgoose family. The residents of the village still talked about it now and again when the weather wasn't interesting enough. The local police, with reinforcements from Hereford, once they had familiarised themselves with Wobbly and Bighead's criminal records, had approached the cottage mob-handed with ten policemen. The senior policeman, who had managed to find a loudhailer in a fusty old cupboard at the station, had taken up a position some twenty yards away from the cottage.

Inside, the Wildgoose family, if they were perfectly honest, had already begun to regret their decision to kidnap Gina from the hospital. It had only been one night, yet as the drugs had started to wear off, they could see quite plainly that Gina was not her normal feisty and free-spirited self.

Added to this, as Wobbly so succinctly put it, 'We are not watching the fucking weather report again. We've seen it six times today.'

'Still,' said Nan Wildgoose, 'we couldn't let them think we were giving in easily so your Uncle Bighead stuck his shotgun out of the bedroom window and shouted – what did he shout, Bert?'

'Get back or I'll blow your f . . .' he thought better of swearing in front of a ten-year-old. 'Get back or I'll blow your blooming head off!'

'He didn't, though, did he, Nan?' said Alice, although she knew the answer.

'Course not, you silly old sausage,' said Nan Wildgoose. 'It was only to frighten the buggers.'

'That social worker dived like a good'un, though, Violet, do you remember?' said Grandpap. 'Got a face full of cow shit, as I remember.'

'Yes, and a couple of big spuds on the 'ead,' said Nan, 'from Wobbly. He always was a good shot.'

'Tell me the end again,' said Alice.

'Well, there was a bit of a stand-off,' said Nan Wildgoose,

who spent her time reading a lot of *True Crime* magazines, 'and then eventually they surrounded us and we had to give up your mum to them. She wanted to go really. We knew she wasn't right, she knew she wasn't right, and although we'd thought your dad was being a right scumbag having her locked up, when we saw how she was and what she was saying, we thought it best she had more treatment and went to hospital.'

'What was she like? What was she saying?' said Alice, who had never quite managed to elicit this information on previous occasions.

A rare guilty queasiness swept through Nan Wildgoose, who was well aware that Keith had attempted to protect Alice from the worst excesses of the Wildgooses' behaviour and Gina's illness.

'That's for your dad to tell you, sweetpea,' she said. 'But your mum went out waving a white pillowcase of surrender and they carried her off back to St Mary's where she stayed for the next two months and then came back to us.'

'But it wasn't her, was it, Violet?' said Bert.

'Was it someone else?' said Alice, wide-eyed, conjuring up images of gothic plotting in the hospital and Frankensteinian experimentation.

'No, what he means, love, is your mum was different – quieter, no spark to her any more, all the Wildgoose wildness gone.'

'All for the best,' said Bert and the conversation turned to more prosaic topics like what was for tea and how Alice was doing at school.

What they had said was true, though. Gina had become a watered-down version of her previous self. Controlled by long-term medication which she received once a month at the hospital, she seemed to have had the sharp edges shaved off. She no longer mentioned Ted Fairfax or watched the weather forecast in her previously agitated way, but sat demurely in the corner of the room, the muttering television a constant backdrop as she smoked, or twisted a piece of string in and out of her fingers, the only part of her body that seemed restless and free now.

Keith could see that some flames had been extinguished on the blazing bonfire but for the most part he was relieved. Gina had not been an easy person to live with and the delightful flashes of anger and excitement he had once loved had become coarse and wearing as her illness had progressed. Now, at least, the family home was peaceful and their lives ticked over, thankfully, with little incident apart from contact with his wife's family which was always fraught with weirdness and occasional threat.

Keith's parents had tried to persuade him to leave Gina. They wanted him back near them in a little semi, furnished with a dull and obedient wife and a child who didn't stand in the corner of the room wordlessly observing them and honouring them with the odd monosyllable.

'That child is a bit odd,' Keith's mum, Jennifer, had tactlessly said to him on a number of occasions. 'She needs taking in hand. Why can't she chat nicely and dress prettily like your cousin Lesley's two?'

Keith thought that cousin Lesley's pale-skinned, gawky offspring were as dull as they come and that rather than dressing prettily, they both looked like anorexic toilet roll covers. He waved his mother's comments away with a humorous remark, but her words stayed in his head until eventually he booked an appointment with Marie Henty to talk about Alice.

Keith's name in the appointments book of the gargantuan receptionist at the surgery where Marie worked lifted her spirits as her eye ran through the usual gamut of varicose veins, chronic coughs and the collected complaints of the over-seventies. She wanted to think that perhaps Keith had just missed her and wanted a chat. Gina's equilibrium had been fairly well maintained with monthly anti-psychotic injections, with few side effects, apart from a general slowness, some weight gain and a bum like a pin cushion, so Marie had rarely seen Keith over the past five years. Yet she had rejected approaches from a number of unsuitable suitors in the hope that one day, like Mr Rochester in *Jane Eyre*, he would rid himself of his mad wife and fall into her arms. But it seemed Keith wanted to talk about Alice. Marie rarely saw Alice but she had noted sadly that her mother's illness seemed to have turned her in on herself; the once sparky little girl was now a somewhat sullen and unrewarding miniature adult.

'Should I see someone about her, do you think?' Keith asked worriedly. 'I mean, how likely is it she'll get what Gina's got?'

'Oh, Keith,' said Marie, her stomach doing uncontrolled fluttering, 'it's so hard to say at this point. Shall I talk to her and let you know what I think?'

'Would you, please?' said Keith. 'I'd be so grateful and perhaps it would put my mind at rest. Just informal like, if you can. I don't want to bring her here – she wouldn't want to come anyway.'

'All right then,' said Marie. 'I'll try and catch her around and about and see what I can do.'

'Thanks.' Keith squeezed Marie's hand and the fluttering dropped lower.

Alice, Mark and Karen were all draped over the broad oak tree at the end of the school lane one evening some days later. They had been talking about building a den which none of the adults could find, to which they could escape whenever high emotion boiled over in any of their households. Alice was at her most happy and verbose with Mark and Karen, both refugees from the seemingly traditional happy nuclear family that populated the Bisto adverts and for which both of them yearned with an intensity that would have shocked their parents.

'I could ask my uncles to help,' said Alice, who had very little understanding of the pure unadulterated terror even the mention of their names had on most of the village.

'Nah, we should do it, then it's ours.' Mark tried to say it as nonchalantly as possible to disguise the squeak in his voice that always appeared when he was scared.

'Yes,' agreed Karen. 'It's got to be only ours and if anyone comes near it we'll kill them.'

'Yes,' said Alice, 'and we'll cut off their heads and put them on big sticks to scare everyone.'

'Brilliant,' said Mark, thinking of Matthew Stephens, who had called him a homo in the playground that day because he wouldn't play hitting girls' legs with a stick.

'Oh look, here comes the doctor,' said Karen.

Marie Henty was trying to look as if she was strolling up the lane for no other reason than pure enjoyment. She was thirty years old and not bad looking, but little did she know that Mark had put her age at about fifty recently and the others had concurred.

'Hello, you three,' she said.

'Hello,' they said.

'Alice,' said Marie, 'I was wondering if we could have a chat.'

Alice began to batten down the social hatches.

'Why?' she said suspiciously.

'Oh, just wanted to see if things are OK,' said Marie as airily as she could.

'I'm playing with my friends,' said Alice stubbornly.

'Just ten minutes,' said Marie.

'All right,' said Alice. She climbed down from the tree.

'Let's walk for a bit,' said Marie.

They headed up the hill towards the crop of oaks that stood at the top, flushed with mistletoe.

'How's your mum?' said Marie.

'All right,' said Alice.

'And your dad?'

'He's all right too,' said Alice.

'And what about you?'

'I'm all right,' said Alice.

'School OK?'

'Yes.'

This monosyllabic torture continued for ten minutes until Marie, exhausted by Alice's responses, said brightly, 'Well, I'm glad to hear it. Shall we go back and find your friends?'

Alice looked enormously relieved. 'Yes please,' she said, and they headed back down the hill to where Mark and Karen were still hanging in the branches of the big tree.

Whoops and cheers greeted them and Marie said her good-byes, thinking to herself that she had no more ability to talk to ten-year-olds than she had to the pigeons that flocked to her bird table and stole the food intended for the smaller birds.

That night, heart slightly aflutter, she phoned Keith.

'I couldn't really get anything out of her, I'm sorry,' she said.

'Don't worry,' said Keith, slightly disappointed. 'She's like that with all of us and I suppose I could hardly have expected her to suddenly open up and tell you her deepest darkest thoughts.'

'We'll keep an eye,' said Marie. 'She seems fine but there may be stuff going on underneath.'

Chapter 6

It was Thursday. Fifteen-year-old Alice, languid, miserable, bored, pessimistic and prickly, always felt slightly better on a Thursday because *Top Of The Pops* was on. She loved her dad very much but his repertoire of Dylan and other American folk singers didn't say anything to her about the dark thoughts and feelings she carried inside. Most of these she attempted to suppress in the family home because having a mother who was little more than a ghostly figure in the house these days meant that the balance of good-naturedness and optimism was a step away from disintegrating. It only took one of Alice's fearsome, teenage moods to lay a big black cloud over the place, something Keith with his studied nonchalance and desperate cheeriness could not cope with as well as Gina.

These days Keith smoked a bit more dope than he used

to, carefully avoiding discovery by Alice, as he somehow felt he owed it to her to normalise her life as much as possible, given that her mother set a skewed example of what a child's upbringing should be. But Alice always knew when Keith had smoked a joint because his natural befuddledness would become more marked and he would exhibit a fatuousness not normally present. He laughed much more easily at stupid things and wasn't very good at getting the conundrum at the end of *Countdown*, a word game that had recently started on the new Channel 4.

Gina didn't do much apart from smoke cigarettes and drift aimlessly round the house. Every month she continued to have her long-acting injection which dampened down her spirit to the point of her having no spirit at all. Alice watched her helplessly, hoping that one day Gina would throw off the yoke of her medication and go completely bloody mad for a few days. Alice knew this was unreasonable, though. Gina's psychiatrist had told Keith and Alice that he thought Gina was suffering from de Clerambault's syndrome, a psychotic condition – 'A bit like schizophrenia, when someone is out of touch with reality,' he'd said to them, doing his best to couch his explanation in layman's terms. He'd also explained that the illness involved Gina being convinced that the weatherman was in love with her and interpreting completely innocent actions on his part as a sign that this was the case.

'Like what?' Keith had asked.

'Well,' Dr Desmond said, 'he might make a movement

with his hands or look in a particular way and Gina will impose an interpretation all of her own. We call this ideas of reference.'

He'd also told them about some of the other symptoms. He said Gina might hear voices, may become paranoid or might be confused in her thinking.

'But the drugs will help, won't they?' Keith had said hopefully.

'To an extent,' he had answered, 'but really the drugs are just damping down the worst of Gina's symptoms rather than taking them away, and of course the drugs themselves have side effects that aren't too pleasant. Gina may slow up, become withdrawn and may get a slight tremor.'

'And how do we deal with that?' said Keith.

'By prescribing another drug, I'm afraid,' he'd said, aware that the barely hidden look of disdain on Keith's face was an appropriate response to how little psychiatry had achieved in terms of treating the myriad subleties that made up the damaged human mind.

So Keith and Alice had had to become resigned over the years to the ravaging of Gina and her personality and to gradually accept that through a combination of the illness and the drugs, the butterfly had turned back into a cocoon.

Keith had tried to explain this as simply as he could to Alice and the oversimplification rested in Alice's head as the belief that her mother was in love with people who weren't in love with her and that she was not in love with her dad any more. Alice realised that letting Gina's demons out of her own personal Pandora's box would mean they couldn't be forced back in very easily.

As Alice sat curled up in the rather unpleasant beige armchair in the front room, a vision appeared on the TV screen that sent a frisson of something she had never experienced before through her body. A man wearing a necklace and a loose shirt, waving some gladioli about, was singing about not having anything to wear out that night. He was strange-looking, handsome with dark brows and a quiff. He seemed rather androgynous as he moved in a unique way around the small stage as if he owned it. Alice moved closer and turned up the volume.

Keith came into the room to see his daughter just a few feet from the television, transfixed by some oddball who to Keith looked like a skinny Irish Elvis.

'Alice,' he said.

Alice put her hand up to indicate she didn't want to speak and carried on staring at the screen. She felt as if she had been transported out of her tired and miserable life to a dazzling place of glamour and magic. She edged even closer and unwittingly put her hand out towards the screen to try and touch the man.

Oh bloody hell, thought Keith. This is all too familiar.

Alice watched in a trance, letting herself get lost in the swirling sound, and at the end when Mike Smith said that the band was called the Smiths and the track 'This Charming Man', she ran upstairs to get her diary and wrote the date, the name of the band and the name of the song.

At the end of *Top Of The Pops*, she dialled Karen's number. Karen's posh dad answered and rather irritably agreed to get Karen, although he preferred to keep the line free of chattering schoolgirls for more important things like arranging to meet his friends and massacre some animals. He never asked who it was, as teenage girls were all the same to him. Useless, screechy, expensive and a dead weight until some fool agreed to marry them and take them off your hands.

Karen's voice said, 'Hello.'

'It's me, Alice', said Alice. 'Did you see *Top Of The Pops*?'

'Sort of,' said Karen. 'I was doing my homework at the same time though.'

'Did you see the Smiths?' asked Alice, a little touch of excitement running through her as she said their name.

'Don't know,' said Karen. 'What did they look like?'

'Well, the singer, I don't know his name, had a loose shirt, a sort of necklace—'

'And a big bunch of flowers. Wanker. Yes, I saw him . . .'

There was a brief hiatus as Karen's sharp-eared mum spent a few seconds remonstrating with her daughter for her use of the word 'wanker'.

'Sorry about that, she's gone now,' said Karen. 'What were you saying?'

'Oh Karen,' said Alice. 'I know this sounds so stupid and I can't really describe it but as soon as I saw him, it sort of changed me. He was so wonderful, so odd, so beautiful . . .' She tailed off, embarrassed by the force of her uncharacteristic outburst.

'Bloody hell,' said Karen. 'He's certainly cast a spell on you but is he fuckable?'

This was typical Karen and normally she made Alice laugh with her outrageous statements. But Alice felt that Karen had somehow made the whole thing dirty and silly.

'Got to go,' she said and put the phone down.

With one of her best friends unable to see the unadulterated genius of the Smiths and the unique individual cavorting in front of the band, Alice phoned Mark.

'He's not here,' said Mark's mum. 'He's just gone out in the fields with his dad, giving him a hand.' Poor bastard, she added to herself as she put the phone down, convinced that her son was made for greater things than being a hulking great son of the soil.

The next day at school, life went on as normal. Alice had expected an excited buzz in the playground about this incomparable new band. But the same old kids she'd known for years were there doing what they always did. What did she expect?

'Who saw that poof on telly last night?'

Alice turned to see the school's resident homophobe.

'Put a fucking sock in it, Stephen,' she said.

'Ooh, hark at you, poof lover,' he said. 'You'd better watch it round here saying those things.'

'Leave her alone,' said Mark, not at all sure what he was defending.

'So you're one now an' all, are you?' said Stephen with more than a hint of disgust in his voice.

'I'm a what now?' said Mark.

'You know what you are,' said Stephen. 'An arse bandit.'

A few teenage boys grinned in a desultory way, sensing a ruck of some sort, and began to move closer to the source of the dispute in case fists started flying.

'Homo! Homo! Homo!' one of Stephen's henchmen began to chant at no one in particular.

The tension was resolved when an unwitting younger boy walked past carrying a lovingly prepared packed lunch artistic- ally wrapped by his mother and a chase began which ended when he was propelled into a scrubby bush, sandwiches sent flying.

'Did you see the Smiths on *Top Of The Pops*?' Alice asked Mark. 'God, I wish I could put it into words the effect they had on me.'

'I did,' said Mark. 'They were certainly unusual.'

Alice grinned.

'What?' said Mark.

'You sound like your dad,' she said.

'Not quite,' said Mark. 'What my dad actually said was, "Look at that limp-wristed little faggot. Turn over, son, there must be something decent on."'

They laughed.

Alice found it hard to concentrate for the rest of the day. Her mind kept replaying the image of the elfin Morrissey moving through a landscape of light and sound. She let herself be swooshed around in this world and it was only when a harsh voice said, 'Alice, repeat back to me what I've just said,' that she was propelled back into the reality of a very boring geography lesson.

'I don't know, Mrs Hurst,' she said. 'I'm sorry.'

'Well, perhaps a little extra work would help sort out your lack of concentration,' said Mrs Hurst. 'Come and see me at the end of the lesson.'

Nobody really understands how I feel, Alice thought to herself, along with lonely, unloved teenagers the length and breadth of Britain who were all beginning to fall in love with Morrissey.

'Dad,' Alice said some days later when they were settled having their tea in front of the telly while Gina smoked furiously in the kitchen and flicked through a magazine full of fashion she would never have any access to.

'Yes, dear,' said Keith, slightly stoned.

'Where would I find out more about some pop group I like?' She tried to say this as nonchalantly as possible because she didn't want her dad getting involved in his dad-like way.

'Who do you mean?' said Keith, trying to scrape the accumulation of several days' worth of grit off a piece of toast he had dropped butter side down on the carpet.

'Oh, just someone I saw on *Top Of The Pops*,' she said.

'Well, you could get a magazine and see if they're in there,' said Keith. '*Melody Maker* or *New Musical Express*. Try Doug in the shop.'

Alice didn't want to try Doug in the shop. He would definitely take the piss. She could hear him now.

'Ooh, little Alice, you're growing up, look at you, you're nearly a woman.'

Although Alice knew that Doug wasn't really like those pervy men who remarked on budding breasts and tight shirt buttons, she still couldn't face his attempts at a cheeky remark.

So the next morning she cycled to a further village where Mrs Akers, who looked eighty and had the lack of sight and hearing to match, stood guard over a vastly depleted little shop selling sweets and newspapers. Mrs Akers had a face like a flesh-coloured piece of crumpled paper. It was difficult to discern an expression on it but as she appeared to have only one mood, grumpy, the issue of how she was feeling on any particular day never arose.

Alice waited outside the shop until there was no one in there, embarrassed that she might make some sort of faux pas, like getting the name of the magazine wrong. Finally an elderly couple who had deliberated for what seemed hours over the relative merits of Ginger Nuts over Bourbons, came out and got into their old Morris Minor and bunny-hopped off down the road.

'Hello, young Alice, and what can I do for you?' asked Mrs Akers rather too loudly.

Alice began to scan the rows of papers and magazines and was presented with a blur of *People's Friend*, *The Lady* and *Bunty*.

'Do you have a *New Musical Express*, Mrs Akers?' she asked.

'Eh, what's that? Speak up,' said Mrs Akers.

'*New Musical Express*,' said Alice, flushing brightly.

'*New Musical Express*?' said Mrs Akers. 'What's that then? About musicals, is it?'

'No, it's a pop paper,' said Alice. 'You know, with pop groups in it.'

A tinkling sound heralded the arrival of another customer and there in the door like a gangly, spotty John Wayne stood Stephen Matthews.

Oh shit, thought Alice. The worst person possible.

'After you,' said Alice to Stephen. 'I'm still deciding,' willing Mrs Akers to keep her mouth shut.

'No, after you,' said Stephen. 'Age before beauty, ha, ha.'

Mrs Akers observed this exchange in silence. She had a short-term memory that rivalled a goldfish's so the *New Musical Express* was not mentioned.

'It's all right,' said Alice, 'you go.'

'No,' said Stephen, with an air of desperation in his voice. 'I said you first.'

'Forget it,' said Alice, angry at herself for being so weedy. 'I'll come back later.'

The door shut behind her.

'Ten Number Six,' said Stephen in as manly and unquavering a voice as he could muster. 'They're for me dad.'

Alice returned to Mrs Akers' shop three days later, having rehearsed over and over again in her head the speech she would make. Of course Mrs Akers' shop had never been graced by the *New Musical Express*, but eventually, after a few false starts and a potted history of the musicals

Mrs Akers had seen in her youth, it was ordered and Alice was instructed to return in several days to pick it up. Finally, by the next weekend, it was in her hands and, breathless with anticipation, she cycled home, ran straight up to her bedroom and began to go through it slowly and methodically, looking for any mention of the Smiths. Several pages in, there he was.

The object of her intense feelings was called Steven Morrissey, he was from Manchester and to Alice he looked like a combination of Keith and an angel. Alice knew that she wanted to write to this unhappy-looking person, to reassure him that his uneasy passage through the world thus far was mirrored by her own.

I wonder if his mum's ill like mine? she found herself thinking. Or perhaps his family is like the Wildgooses.

She looked at a picture of him and felt she was going to faint. She had to lie down on her bed. She'd spent so long trying to deny that she had any feelings, even to her family and friends, that she didn't really know what this was all about and why it had happened. Was she getting ill like her mum did with the weather forecaster? She shuddered at the thought.

'Do I love him?' she said out loud and then laughed at the sound of her words which were desperate and comical all at the same time. She could see herself reflected in the mirror as she spoke and she felt three years old. But she wasn't. She was fifteen years old. Two years older than Shakespeare's Juliet, as Mr Winston the mildly sadistic

English teacher had been at pains to point out in a thoroughly unpleasant way.

Do I want to have sex with him? she thought shamefully to herself and imagined herself alone in a flat in Manchester with him, laughing, and him saying to her, 'God, you're so funny and clever and so beautiful, come here.' She couldn't actually visualise what happened next. Maybe she didn't want to.

The *NME* was frustratingly pedestrian, lots of stuff about the paraphernalia of creating music, names of instruments, details about musical influences, all the sort of stuff she didn't really care about. She just wanted to know about Morrissey, what he wanted and what he was looking for. His quotes were oblique and difficult to put in a context she could understand but the underlying sense of them was loneliness and isolation and misunderstanding, all of which she knew intimately herself. He seemed accessible and yet so far away. Perhaps the best thing to do was to write and see if he picked something out of her letter and replied from his heart.

She went downstairs and found some scissors in the drawer and took them back up to her bedroom where she cut Morrissey's picture out of the *NME* (a picture in which he looked proud but damaged) and put it under her pillow. She'd have liked to place it over her bed like a religious icon, but knew this would result in some benign teasing from her dad and some not so benign mumbling from her mum. She decided, against all her instincts, to wait a few days before she wrote a letter, to allow the feelings whirling round her head to settle into something more formal than a jumble of ideas and romance. It had to be right or he would just laugh at her and throw the letter in the bin.

Chapter 7

Dearest Morrissey,

I am sure you get absolutely hundreds of letters from your fans, but I hope you will read this one because I think it's very important. I saw you on Top Of The Pops and although you will probably think this is stupid, I had such a strange feeling about you (I know – just from seeing you on TV!) that I felt I had to contact you and hopefully arrange to meet you and talk. The thing is, I can see from the way you looked, the way you sang and the way you acted that you are a person like me who has had a weird and hard life and I thought if we could talk maybe we could help each other to feel better. The first words of your song 'This Charming Man' seem to be about my dad Keith whose bicycle was left recently on a hillside with a puncture in it, and it really struck me that, without realising it, you are connected to my family in some way. I am a fifteen-year-old girl who lives in the deepest countryside in Herefordshire and sometimes (well, nearly always!) I feel like there is nobody here who knows what I am really like or how I feel. You see, although my dad is a really nice old hippy, I feel I can't talk to him because he has so much stress and pain in his life already and I don't want him to worry about me. This is because my mum has been ill with a mental problem for years now and it has really affected my dad and me. She has been in hospital twice and she has something which the psychiatrists think is de Clerambault's syndrome where she thinks she is in love with someone who is not in love with her. It's funny, isn't it, because here I am writing to someone who doesn't even know me. I'm not in love with you, by the way! But I do think you are so different and so intelligent that I straight away felt there was some sort of bond between us. Lots of nights I cry in my bedroom because I feel so sorry for my mum and for my dad who has to look after her. You see, my mum has been on drugs for ages which make her a sort of different person. My dad says when she was younger she was really good fun and full of energy and mischief, but now she just sits in the house smoking all day and staring out of the window.

I hope you don't mind me writing this.

Your greatest fan,

Alice xxxxxxxx

Alice didn't know where to send the letter so she addressed it care of the *NME* and got on her bike to go down to the village and post it.

It was a wild, windy November day and she had to toil quite hard against the wind going up the hill. As she entered the village, she saw Mark.

'Hi, Alice,' he called. 'Where are you off to?'

Alice was no good at lying on the spot, even though she didn't really want Mark or anybody to know she was writing to a pop singer she had seen on television.

'I'm going to post a letter,' she said.

'Oh. Who to?' said Mark.

Alice reddened.

'Not your boyfriend?' Mark said.

'Fuck off,' said Alice.

'Oh, come on,' said Mark. 'I'm only teasing, you don't have to tell me if you don't want.'

For the first time almost, Alice decided to trust Mark. Looking down at the front wheel of her bike, she mumbled, 'It's a letter to Morrissey from the Smiths.'

Mark was astonished. Alice had never seemed to be the type of person who would get weird about a pop singer. She rumbled about in her permanent semi-angry way with her thick mane of hair constantly out of control, falling out of a ponytail or escaping from a plait, with a frown on her face that was already starting to produce two lines in her forehead at the top of her nose.

'Do you think he will write back?'

'I really hope so,' said Alice with a determined look on her face. 'It's very important to me.'

Mark was slightly perturbed by the strength of feeling in her voice and steered things away.

'My mum and dad are going to the theatre in Birmingham tonight,' he said. 'Do you want to come over? I'll get a bottle of Woodpecker in the shop.'

'I'll ask Dad,' said Alice, although she knew Keith would say yes because he seemed so desperate for her to have friends that the spectre of drink, drugs or underage sex never even occurred to him in his eagerness to normalise his withdrawn and unhappy daughter.

Alice cycled up to Mark's at about seven o'clock. It was cold and wet and had been dark for some time. But she didn't mind. This was her favourite sort of weather and she felt the darkness and rain hid her from the prying gaze of the locals, who she knew called her 'the madwoman's daughter'. Stephen Matthews had been only too happy to inform her of this, another weapon in his depleted armoury of taunts and village gossip.

An owl sat in the middle of the lane, eyeing her nonchalantly, and only flew away with a huge flap of its impressive wings as she nearly ran it over. Despite talk in the village of a large cat that roamed the local countryside at night, she felt at her happiest. Mark had told her that his dad had discussed this local beast with fellow drinkers in the tiny pub in the village. He'd not been impressed when Andrew Overy, a local farmer prone to exaggeration, had said he'd found a savaged sheep on his land, the throat torn out.

'Could have been anything,' said Mark's dad scornfully.

'Yeah, but not halfway up a fucking oak tree,' Andrew Overy had replied triumphantly. 'Put that in your pipe and smoke it.'

Mark answered the big front door and led the way into the rather dilapidated interior, a shameful sight to Mark's mum who spent hours poring over *Homes and Gardens* in the hairdresser, dreaming of the day when her husband would let her tackle this rural jumble of styles.

They sat in the front room and Mark produced the bottle of Woodpecker which they drank from Manchester United mugs, a nod to the fact that Mark's dad still half-heartedly followed the romantic team of his youth.

Alice very rarely had any alcohol and to her it was a bit like taking medicine. The sweet sickly taste had to be ignored, Mark had assured her, to eventually feel the benefits of a warmth that couldn't be achieved in any other way. After a couple of mugs, she began to understand what he meant.

Their conversation, initially strangely stilted as if they hardly knew each other, became more relaxed and giggly.

Mark said, 'Can I ask you something about your mum?'

Alice never discussed Gina with anyone because she simply could not be bothered to battle the ignorance and hyper-interest that surrounded Gina and her illness.

'All right,' she said warily.

'Do you have to lock her up at night?'

It was an innocent question asked with no hint of a sadistic undertow, but it still made Alice really sad to hear it because it was the sort of question one would ask about an animal.

A tear rolled down her face.

'Oh, I'm sorry,' said Mark. 'I didn't mean to upset you.'

'I know,' said Alice, 'but she's not a fucking chimpanzee, you know.'

Mark looked in pain and it didn't take long before Alice realised he was using every muscle in his face to try and stop himself laughing.

This didn't make her angry, it made her laugh as well and before long the two of them were helpless on the settee, with tears cascading down their cheeks.

She had known Mark for years, from when he was an awkward five-year-old in ridiculously large jumpers to this gangly teenager with limbs that seemed as if they came from a rubber bendy man toy, and Alice finally realised that she had been holding back the personal areas of her life for far too long.

Her experiences with her mother flew out of her like one huge, cleansing vomit and Mark sat listening, occasionally laughing, like during the story of her mum on the roof, but not teasing or judging, both of which she'd feared.

'Thanks, Mark,' said Alice about an hour later and she raised her cup towards his to chink it. 'You're a good friend.'

Mark took the cup out of her hand and put it on the floor. He grasped her shoulders, his face looming towards her, and clamped his mouth on to hers.

It was quite unlike anything Alice had ever experienced and tempted as she was to pull away like a capricious heroine in a black and white film, she stuck with it to see where it would go and what would happen.

Normally I wouldn't like this probing tongue thing, she thought to herself, but it's all right, it's nice even, and she responded, so that their two tongues wriggled around, encased by their mouths in a wet drunken dance. Mark pressed closer to her so that his entire weight seemed to be on top of her. He took her hand and guided it towards his trousers, and almost without thinking Alice started to undo his zip. She'd never seen a penis before and was surprised at how big, benign and funny it looked. She'd have been quite happy just to sit and stare at it for a while, but Mark pushed her back and with the instinctive skill necessary at these moments managed to remove all the clothes on her bottom half in one move. As he slid on top of her, Alice realised she was going to lose her virginity and an unwanted image of Morrissey came into her head

'What are you doing here?' she said, not realising it was out loud.

Mark hesitated.

Oh Christ, he found himself thinking uncharitably. Is she nuts like her mum?

But Alice said no more and lay still, waiting for Mark to happen to her.

It didn't hurt, it was like being in a deep, hot well, out of which she looked up to see his face, an expression on it she had never seen before and wasn't sure she liked. She closed her eyes and images whirled in her head – Mark's parents arriving home and finding them, people gossiping in the village shop, Wobbly and Bighead grinning, Morrissey on a cross, her dad crying, a bull mounting a cow, trees being thrashed by the wind, her mother shouting and running naked through the garden, Marie Henty smiling shyly . . . and then with one great heave Mark seemed to collapse into himself and lay panting on her chest.

And then it was quiet. A voice on the television said, 'And now for the weather,' and they looked at each other and moved slowly apart until they were both sitting up on the huge settee. They shifted along to create what seemed like a mile-wide gap between them and looked down at the same time to behold an enormous patch of wetness between them on the sofa.

'Oh shit,' said Mark and jumped up, pulling Alice with him.

He hauled the offending cushion off the settee and turned it over as Alice slowly began to put her clothes on.

'I don't know what to say,' she said, 'except it was lovely and I have to go.'

Mark said nothing.

Alice snatched her coat which was lying on the table and let herself out of the door. Her bike lay on the ground like a big metal spider and she picked it up, got on and began the journey down the long, potholed track of the farm. In the distance she saw some car headlights – Mark's parents heading down the drive. Not wanting to explain what she assumed was her very visible, changed status, she jumped off her bike, threw it into the hedge and then lay on the verge behind a rotting log as the car whooshed past her, spraying her with dirty water from a particularly big pothole. Then she got back on her bike and rode home.

Chapter 8

She woke the next morning and lay, eyes open, for a tiny period of time before the events of the previous night came flooding back and her stomach lurched. She sat up in bed and twisted to get her picture of Morrissey from under the pillow. He looked more disappointed than he did yesterday and she wondered whether she should write to him again, but having just posted the first letter the day before, perhaps it might not be a good idea.

'Alice!'

Her stomach lurched again. It was her dad calling from downstairs.

'Come on, love, it's eight o'clock. I've put some Sugar Puffs out for you. Come on, they'll get soggy and you'll be late for school.'

'Coming!' Shit, Alice thought. School as well. How am I going to face that?

She rose slowly, went into the bathroom and turned on the bath taps.

'Alice!'

'Yes?' she shouted back.

'You haven't got time for a bath. Come on, hurry up, love.'

I don't want to go to school with Mark's sperm inside me, she thought. People will be able to smell me. She let the taps run.

'I'll be really quick!' she called down and plunged into the warm bath.

She really wanted to stay there all day but forced herself to have a cursory wash of all the bits that might present olfactory evidence to her classmates. She pulled on her uniform and slouched down the stairs, her head thumping and her heart beating. Would her dad be able to tell just by looking at her? She felt as though she was glowing like a hot coal but when she sat down at the table, Keith glanced up at her and then back at his breakfast. 'This Charming Man' was playing on the radio. Alice's heartbeat quickened. What did this mean? Surely it couldn't just be a coincidence? Was it a message? She looked over at her dad to see if it had had any effect on him.

Strangely, he didn't even seem to notice it.

'Hardly saw you last night,' said her dad. 'Did you have a nice time at Mark's?'

'Yes, thanks,' said Alice, her mouth full of cereal. 'Where's Mum?'

'Still in bed,' said Keith, a phrase he used every morning

and had done since Gina's first admission to hospital. 'She's going out to the shops with Nan Wildgoose later.'

Gina's mum often took her to the shops either in Ludlow or Leominster in an attempt to interest her in the surface paraphernalia of the everyday woman, but most of the time Gina dragged listlessly behind her, eyes downcast, not showing the slightest bit of a spark in anything that passed before her.

Alice must have looked in the mirror twenty times before she left for school to check whether her appearance was in any way changed. She still looked the same, the expression one she had seen on many mornings, and her hair messily drawn back into a fat ponytail. The frayed jumper with its bobbly surface still hung around her small chest like a rag and drooped to her thighs. The shiny, pleated skirt looked nothing like the neat, short mini skirts the other girls in her class hitched up once they got on the school bus, and her make-up-free face had a scrubbed and pink appearance.

She stood waiting for the school bus at the end of the lane and it drew up on time as usual. The doors wheezed open and she took a deep breath in anticipation of the children on the bus recognising and commenting upon her recently achieved adult status.

But nothing was different; the low-level buzz, rising in an occasional crescendo, was the same and so she began to look forward to the next ordeal, which was seeing Mark and gauging how their friendship stood.

She didn't have to wait very long. As the children were regurgitated off the bus and, as one, started the short walk through the school gates, Mark sailed past on his bike. Normally he stopped and got off his bike and walked in with her and Karen. But there was no sign of Karen this morning and Mark disappeared through the gates without even turning his head towards her. Alice opened her mouth to shout after him but the words faded and came out as a small squeak. Embarrassed by this, she stared hard at the ground and continued to walk.

She had double French first which Mark didn't do and so it was at break time that their second encounter occurred.

On the scruffy patch of grass outside the main block, Alice spotted Mark coming towards her. He seemed outlined by a thick black pencil as he dodged between other figures who immediately faded against his strong outline. Alice saw with some relief that he was grinning at her.

'Hello,' he said. 'You all right?'

'Fine,' she said, feeling a raging heat illuminating her face.

'Mark . . .' Alice began but was interrupted by Karen pushing in between them and grabbing them both by the arm.

'All right, you two?' she asked.

'Fine,' they said together.

'What did you do last night?' asked Karen. 'I nearly phoned for a meet-up but my mum made me help her with clearing out the garage. God, it was fucking boring. Did you go out?' She looked at Alice.

What can I say? thought Alice. Should we tell her now? Should I wait until I'm on my own with her?

As these thoughts ran round her head, she realised Mark had said, 'She came round to my place, we just watched telly, talked about bloody Morrissey for ages and had some cider.'

'Oh, you lucky buggers,' said Karen. 'Wish I'd been there.'

The bell rang and the crowd in the playground began to move towards the building.

'Can we talk later?' Alice said to Mark.

'Ooh, what's this?' said Karen, sensing something out of the ordinary.

'Oh nothing,' said Alice. 'I just want to ask Mark something about my maths.' This was dull enough to throw Karen off the scent.

'All right,' said Mark. 'I'll see you after school. You can walk back with me if you want.'

They walked into the building and became consumed by the crowds heading for lessons. Alice sat through geography trying to work out what she would say to Mark. This was difficult because she really had no idea what she thought about it all. The cider they had consumed had given the whole incident a surreal veneer and Alice kept trying to imagine that it hadn't really happened. But she knew it had and she wanted to establish the old familiarity with Mark before they drifted in different directions and became embarrassed by each other's presence. Or did she want to do it again? She wasn't sure. She loved the wild uncontrolled element of it all, because over the years her inner turmoil had disabled her from being what she felt was her true self. To her peer group and teachers she was distracted and monosyllabic, to her friends this layer was peeled off to reveal a sardonic sense of humour and a cynicism unusual in a fifteen-year-old. To her dad she was quiet but sweet, helpful and domesticated, always available to help with work in the house or keep an eye on Gina when her normally controlled mental state wobbled a bit. Alice wanted to be herself with someone and she was on the brink of doing that with Mark or with Morrissey, she didn't know which.

Mark seemed the obvious choice but Morrissey was so much safer. He wasn't liable to criticise her, to harass her, to make her fall in love with him and then leave her. Her head whirred with the possibilities.

After school, they met at the gates, Mark with his bike, and walked along the verge, one in front of the other much of the time as cars buzzed past them. This made it hard to talk.

The broken conversation that they managed to conduct amazed Alice who had gone over in her head what the various possibilities might be. She had predicted that Mark would either wish to be friends, or have a relationship with her, or break off their friendship altogether.

It seemed that none of these was the reality. Mark told Alice that for some years he had thought he might be gay and that although he had not had any physical relationships with men or boys, it was something that had sat constantly in his head since he was ten.

Alice thought, then what were you doing with me?

So she said it.

Mark thought for some time.

'I really don't know,' he said. 'You've always been one of my best friends. I love being with you, you're so different from all the other girls and you talk sense, you make me laugh, and I suppose I wanted some way of showing you and I got carried away.' He didn't say that sometimes he thought she was like a boy.

'What was it like?' said Alice. 'Did it feel wrong?'

'No, it didn't feel wrong,' said Mark. 'It felt lovely, but also weird.'

'It felt weird to me too,' said Alice, 'but I don't think I'm a lesbian.'

Mark laughed and the chasm that had existed between them since last night began to close.

'Alice,' he said, 'can I ask you something?'

'Go on then,' said Alice.

'You're not in love with me, are you?'

It was Alice's time to think.

'I don't think so. I don't know. Probably not, no, definitely not.'

Mark looked relieved. 'I don't want us to stop being close,' he said.

'Nor me,' said Alice and they shifted with the greatest of ease into their usual piss-taking, giggling relationship, the sort of half flirtation and half deep friendship that exists between two people who feel they are outside the main-stream for one reason or another and have to cling together against the tide of normality that threatens to overwhelm them into living lives controlled by others' expectations.

A car beeped behind them. It was Karen being taken home by her parents.

'Want a lift, maths people?' she said. They got in and were deposited at the tops of their roads, both Mark and Alice feeling relieved and positive.

Over the next few weeks Alice met the postman every morning in the hope and expectation of a letter from Morrissey. She had given him the minimum time to write back and then slavishly awaited Andrew the postman every morning. Still nothing came and the weirdness she felt inside she put down to a fluttering anticipation and a growing obsession with the singer in the Smiths.

After a month, there was still no word from Morrissey and Alice began to think he wouldn't bother to write. Normally this wouldn't really have upset her as her pessimistic outlook at least meant that disappointments were always anticipated, but she found herself tearful at the thought he wasn't going to write back and spent quite some time lying on her bed crying.

Keith was concerned about her. He understood that the maelstrom of teenage hormones could produce some strange behaviour but these last few days had been different. She seemed preoccupied with a particular problem and he longed to be able to sit in front of the telly with Gina and discuss their daughter's welfare. He could not believe that once Gina realised Alice was suffering, she would not join forces with him to make their daughter's life more bearable. So he tried. That night at ten fifteen, while Alice sobbed quietly upstairs, Keith said to Gina, 'I think Alice is unhappy. Have you noticed anything?'

Gina turned her face towards his, a good start.

'She seems fine to me,' she said and turned back towards the television.

Keith persisted but Gina was unable to come out of her private, strange world in which occasional murmured voices spoke about her, so muffled it wasn't really possible to hear them clearly but she still managed to pick up the tenor of their discussion which was negative and dismissive.

Keith tried for half an hour before he gave up, abandoning another piece of their relationship jigsaw, which would eventually tell him he was on his own.

Chapter 9

Morrissey remained incommunicado.

This threw Alice into a well of sadness. It was, she felt, one of the few possible joys she had to cling on to and she believed that if he didn't write back to her, there wasn't much point to anything.

She wondered if she might be turning into her mother and at what age this might start. Was it normal to spend hours on her bed staring at the ceiling mouthing the few Smiths lyrics that she knew, listening to their music, looking at Morrissey's picture, stroking it? Was it normal to walk through the fields in the dark, repeating his name over and over like a mantra? Or to withdraw from her friends, feeling slighted by their lack of interest in her obsession?

Eventually, after spending what seemed like hundreds of nights alone and feeling isolated, she booked an appointment with Marie Henty to see if she could discover whether she was becoming mentally ill. She was so often overwhelmed by such a rush of tears and emotion that she felt she really couldn't drag herself out of the protective womb of her bedroom. She felt physically ill too. She was so tired, a tiredness which she took to be some sort of depression, having worked out over the years of her mother's illness that individuals could be virtually brought to a standstill by their depression and remain catatonic and silent for months while they struggled with an all-encompassing blackness inside them.

Mark and Karen were worried about her too and it was to them that she wanted to take her feelings of despair and longing about Morrissey and her worries about her life and where it might be going. But she was worried about how they might react. She could hear Karen saying, 'Oh, for fuck's sake, Alice, forget the silly bastard and come out and get pissed with me and the girls,' or Mark shaking his head and saying, 'But I don't really understand.'

She wondered if she should try and meet Morrissey. If she could only stand next to him and let him see the sort of person she was, he might like her, want to be her friend. Perhaps he needed an assistant – she would be good at that. She would be loyal and trustworthy, unlike the arseholes she assumed had ingratiated themselves with him, who wormed around him, stroking his ego, laughing behind his back, not really being his friend, not being normal. Alice could be so normal with him, she knew she could, and he would feel comfortable with her, which was all she wanted. His songs swirled round her head from morning until night.

Gina sat silently smoking her fags and Keith sat worrying in the kitchen, slightly more stoned than usual. He began to feel desperate to break the deadlock and one evening after each member of the family had spent yet another night apart in separate rooms in the house, he called Alice down.

She came reluctantly, not wanting to be dragged back to real life, and she, her dad and Gina all sat in the front room feeling uncomfortable about being so close to one another.

'Alice,' said Keith, 'you've got to sort yourself out, love. You've barely been out of your room. What is it? Come on, I'm worried about you. Shall I get Uncle Bighead and Uncle Wobbly round to help?'

A smile flitted across her face. 'I wish I could talk to you, Dad,' she said. 'But you've got enough problems.'

'I'll be the judge of that, young lady,' said Keith in a comedy voice. 'I hardly dare ask but is it a boy?'

'Oh Dad,' said Alice. 'You know I wouldn't tell you if it was.' She looked at Gina.

'Sometimes I wish Mum could help.'

'Gina,' said Keith softly, 'Alice is feeling down.'

Gina farted loudly.

'Oh well,' said Keith. 'I suppose it's a start.'

Alice cancelled the appointment with Marie Henty, angry at herself for even having made it and hoping that Marie Henty would not come and seek her out. It never occurred to her that a rural doctor's surgery with its bunions, heart problems, farming accidents, cancers, old age, childhood illnesses and understaffing was just not equipped to pursue absentees who had cancelled their appointment.

On one of the days when Alice failed to make it into school, Mark and Karen sat together during break and tried to make sense of what was going on. They were aware of the Morrissey sadness and also Alice's fears about somehow becoming Gina in the next few years. Both had picked up shards of information from Gina's past, particularly about the incident with the weather forecaster, and although Alice had made them laugh by recounting the events of the day when Gina sat naked on the roof, they realised that Alice's fears of the illness manifesting itself in her were at the very least genetically possible.

'What can we do?' said Karen. 'We can't *make* this Morrison write to her.'

'Morris*ey*,' Mark corrected her.

Morrissey's rise had passed Karen by. She was a New Romantic through and through and found succour in the lyrics and performance of such bands as Duran Duran. Karen luxuriated in the words of 'Rio' and placed herself in her fantasies squarely on the deck of that yacht crashing through the water, imagining Simon Le Bon giving her a 'right good seeing-to' as it carved its way through tropical seas. She thought his almost chubby leonine looks were perfect and could not understand why Alice had allied herself to a fey, quiffed, droopy, bespectacled, miserable git who seemed obsessed with all things sordid and distasteful.

Mark, on the other hand, could see very easily why Alice's

heart lay squarely in Morrissey's palm. He could have allowed himself to become pulled into the movement which was gathering pace with every new piece of information and music the Smiths put out. He even admired their name, given his heartfelt socialist views, something unheard of in his house and something that his parents would have been horrified about. So he adopted an attitude of casual disdain for the highly charged lyrics of the man, coupled with a detailed knowledge of the group's performance dates, chart positions, musical styles, even news items referred to in their songs.

'What are we going to do then?' said Karen, who always wanted to do things to make people's lives better, not content with just allowing herself to be a steadfast support to friends.

'Not much we can do,' said Mark, 'except hope she comes through it and Morrissey writes to her.'

'Duran Duran are playing in Birmingham soon,' said Karen. 'Shall we take her?'

'Oh Jesus, no, that'll finish her off,' said Mark. 'No, let's just wait and see how things are.'

'All right,' said Karen, frustrated.

Three days later, while Alice lay in bed on a Saturday morning staring at the ceiling and listening to the blather of a Radio 1 DJ who was playing rubbish, her dad shouted, 'There's a letter for you!'

Her heart leapt then plummeted. It would be from Grandma or school or something. She dragged down the stairs. It was just a typical envelope but the postmark was

Manchester. She felt as if her head was going to explode. Not wanting her dad to see her weep any more, she ran up the stairs, two at a time, slamming her bedroom door behind her. She threw herself on to the bed and as delicately as possible, because she didn't want to lose even the tiniest atom of it if it was from Morrissey, she ripped the corner very gently and slid her finger into the hole, tearing along the crease.

It was one sheet of paper. She removed it from the envelope and opened it out.

It was from Morrissey.

She put it down, not even wanting to read it in case it disappointed her. She got up from her bed, went downstairs, through the door and out on to the lane from the scrubby front garden and began to walk.

It was a mild day with an all-enveloping light drizzle which tickled her face. All she could think of was *him* and that at some point in the last few days his dear hand had taken up a pen and written words to her. Her! It was astounding that someone like him should spend even a second thinking about her. He, Morrissey, had taken the time to write to her, Alice, a fifteen-year-old from Herefordshire with a mad mother. She then spent a delicious half an hour speculating what the letter might say. 'I am so happy,' she said out loud, looking round her at the familiar landscape, the big oak with its cargo of mistletoe, the hills with their shaven mottled look and the enormous dove-grey sky, and began to cry. Then she turned and started to run home.

Finally, in her bedroom, she unfolded the letter and looked at it.

The writing was big and had an old-fashioned look to it. All the letters were big and not joined together, childlike but so old, she thought.

There were two sentences.

Dear Alice (not just a photocopied fob-off letter sent to many then),

Your letter was so sweet (she felt faint and sick).

Thank you for opening your heart.

Morrissey

Better than she could ever have expected, and so poetic. She picked up the letter, carefully slid it back into its envelope and ran all the way to Mark's house with it, banging excitedly on the door.

Mark's dad, of whom she was rather scared, answered the door.

'Yes?' He always sounded as if he didn't know her. Little did she know this was deliberate. He wanted his son to hang around with Joanna, the daughter of Luke Wethersby, the master of the local hunt. Instead he'd decided to spend his time with this mongrel from the village. God forbid it should go any further. His heart fluttered. What if they ended up wanting to marry each other?

I almost wish he was a poof, he said to himself as Alice's back disappeared up the stairs to Mark's bedroom.

Mark was on his bed reading and listening to Elvis Costello. Alice shot into the room like a rabbit.

'Mark,' she shouted breathlessly. 'It's come!'

'What's come?' Mark looked puzzled.

'A letter from Morrissey! Look! Careful!' She thrust it under his nose.

Mark scanned the piece of paper.

'That's really nice,' he said.

'Really nice?' said Alice. 'Really nice? Try fucking brilliant or absolutely bloody amazing! He's written to me, I'm so happy.' She started to cry.

'Blimey,' said Mark, 'that happy?'

Through her tears Alice laughed and hugged him.

'Mark!' His mother's voice sounded from downstairs. She didn't like him being in his bedroom with a girl. Things could happen and the thought of being in any way allied to the Wildgooses made her feel slightly nauseous. Apart from the fact that it would wind her husband up beyond belief. 'Can you and Alice come down and feed the chickens?'

'All right,' said Mark. He turned to Alice. 'That should stop us having illegal intercourse,' he said with a wink.

Alice grinned.

They went downstairs and towards the field all but destroyed by the enormous gang of scratching hens.

While they were throwing out handfuls of feed, Mark turned to Alice.

'Can you help me?' he said.

'Sure,' said Alice. 'What do you need me to do?'

'I need you to use the Morrissey tickets that Karen and I have bought you for Leicester University on the sixteenth,' he said.

'My God.' Alice wobbled a bit. 'Oh Mark.' She hugged him really tightly. 'I can't believe it.' Her face darkened. 'Oh God.'

'What?' he said.

'What if it's not what I'm hoping? If I don't like it?'

'Shut up, you silly cow, and just go and enjoy it,' he said. 'Are you coming?'

'I can't,' he said, 'and Karen's parents won't let her. You'll have to get someone to go with you.'

Alice's brain flickered through the other possibities, few as they were.

'I'll ask my dad to go with me,' she said.

Excited, she ran slightly less fast all the way home.

Keith was in the garden.

'Dad,' she shouted as she kicked open the gate.

'Yes,' said Keith, thinking he hadn't seen her this cheerful for months.

'Mark's bought me some tickets for the Smiths in Leicester. Can I go? Can you come? Oh God, it's so exciting.'

'What about Mum?' said Keith. 'We can't put her in the boot.' Even though she might quite like it, he thought bitterly to himself.

Keith had absolutely no idea who the Smiths were and it didn't occur to him that Alice's mood in recent months may have been controlled or at the very least affected by the existence of these four boys from Manchester.

'All right,' he said. 'I'll get Nan Wildgoose to come down and sit with Mum. We'll have a lovely night out. I'll stand at the back so that people don't think you're with some horrible hairy old hippy twice your age.'

'Thanks, Dad, you're the best,' said Alice.

'After the Smiths,' he corrected.

Chapter 10

16 February 1984

The day that Alice had been waiting for finally dawned. She found herself in an almost hysterical state of excitement and had trouble eating any food all day. Nan Wildgoose was due at lunchtime. It was a school day but Keith had allowed Alice to have the day off sick; she only had PE in the afternoon anyway so it wasn't too bad a day to be skiving.

Nan Wildgoose was dropped off in the lane by Wobbly. As he departed with a roar of exhaust she limped up the drive looking a bit cold and tired.

Keith had not told Gina that her mother was essentially coming to babysit while he and Alice went out. It seemed safer not to. Gina's relationship with her mother was occasionally unpredictable but often operated along parallel lines. The two of them would sit in a room, with Ma Wildgoose gossiping about her neighbours, which did not interest her daughter in the least, while Gina occupied herself with the barely audible show going on in her head. This time, however, Gina was not pleased to see her mother and as soon as she stepped over the threshold, Gina spat out the words, 'What the fuck is she doing here?'

'Oh, don't be like that, love,' said Keith. 'Alice and I are going out for the evening and your mum's going to sit and watch telly with you until we get back.'

'Well, I don't want her to,' said Gina. 'She's evil, she'll try and kill me and I'll be all on my own.'

Keith was tempted to say, 'Come on, you could knock her out with one punch,' but he didn't want to encourage Gina. Instead he said as soothingly as he could, 'Don't worry, it'll be all right.'

Unfortunately this just proved to Gina that Keith was in on the conspiracy to finish her off.

'You both want to kill me,' she screeched. She picked up a book from the table and lobbed it in the general direction of her mother. It whooshed past her head and landed near the front door. Ma Wildgoose, who would have made a crap psychiatric nurse, picked it up and lobbed it back with the words, 'Take that, you silly little fucker.'

A full-blown punch-up looked likely and Keith positioned himself between them.

'Just tell her to piss off,' said Gina. 'She's not watching telly with me.'

Alice, hearing all this from her vantage point on the stairs, felt despair overtake her. She couldn't bear it if her mother ruined the evening. She got up and went into the sitting room.

'Please, Mum,' she said. 'It's really important. Can't you just get on with Nan for once, please.'

'Oh, so you're involved too,' Gina began.

'Oh, for fuck's sake,' screamed Alice. 'Why must everything revolve around you and your pathetic illness?' She kicked the chair nearest her and walked out into the garden.

'Right,' Keith heard himself say. 'Everybody calm down.'

To his complete surprise, everybody did.

Desperate for Alice not to miss what seemed to be such an important night, he turned to his mother-in-law.

'Will you go with Alice tonight?' he asked.

'Go where?' said Ma Wildgoose.

'To see the Smiths in Leicester,' he said.

'Who are the bleeding Smiths?' said Ma Wildgoose. 'Some friends?'

'No, they're a pop group,' said Keith. 'She's so desperate to go, please, I'll give you money for the train and cabs.'

'And a stout?' said Ma Wildgoose, ever conscious of the possibility of a drink.

'All right,' said Keith. 'Alice, love?' he called.

Alice came in, looking so sad and defeated, Keith couldn't bear it.

'It's all right, you can go,' he said. 'Nan's going with you.'

Oh, what a double-edged sword. Was the purest pleasure of the Smiths show worth the farting, swearing heap that was Nan Wildgoose? Alice decided it was. There was bound to be somewhere she could safely dump her near the gig and escape to meet the Smiths.

Keith deposited Alice and her nan at the station in record time and they both sat staring out of the window with their own thoughts for much of the journey. When they finally arrived in Leicester, Alice realised Nan had fallen asleep. She shook her gently. Nan woke with a grunt and her customary emission of wind.

'Where are we?' she said, bad-tempered as ever.

'In Leicester going to see the Smiths,' said Alice, the words giving her a little frisson of excitement.

They rose from their seats and trudged along the platform. Outside, taxis stood lined up and they joined the queue.

An Asian driver smiled and chatted amiably as they traversed the Leicestershire landscape, Alice praying that Nan Wildgoose wouldn't say something offensive.

'I want the toilet,' was what she came up with.

'We're nearly there,' said Alice.

'I want the toilet,' said Nan louder.

The driver looked concerned. 'She won't have piss in my car?' he said.

'No,' said Alice.

'I have,' said Nan triumphantly. 'I couldn't wait.'

'Oh my God.' The taxi driver launched into an unintelligible stream of a language they didn't understand.

The taxi stopped.

'Out please,' he said, barely keeping his temper.

'I'm sorry,' said Alice, 'she didn't mean it.'

'Give me all your money,' said the driver, 'to clean car.'

Alice regretfully handed over the thirty pounds Keith had given her.

They watched as he disappeared into the distance, having helpfully informed them it was 'bloody miles' to Leicester University.

Nan Wildgoose and Alice started to walk. There was a cold and bitter wind and shards of sharp rain whipped into them.

Nan was silent for a few hundred yards.

'I don't feel well,' she said.

'We're nearly there,' said Alice who could see the concrete jumble of the campus not far away.

She looked at her watch. Three-quarters of an hour to go. A bus shelter loomed in the darkness.

'Let's sit down for a minute,' said Alice, relieved. 'We've still got time.'

Nan Wildgoose sat heavily on the narrow plastic seat.

'What is it?' Alice asked.

'Pain,' said Nan.

'Where?' said Alice, guiltily feeling only irritable.

'Everywhere,' said Nan. 'I want to go home.'

Oh Christ, thought Alice. Don't be ill now, for fuck's sake, not today of all days.

Nan slumped over on to Alice's shoulder.

'Nan?' said Alice. Getting no answer, her voice rose with alarm. 'Nan! Nan!'

It was no good, there was no response. Nan Wildgoose was just a big heavy heap of flesh pushing her across the seat. Alice couldn't hold her and Nan toppled on to the wet, cold pavement.

Alice had absolutely no idea what to do. She'd seen nurses on telly put a finger to the artery on people's necks but she wasn't really sure what she was feeling for. Was Nan asleep? Unconscious? Dead? She had no clue. She tried to lift her but Nan's fourteen-stone frame wouldn't budge and so Alice sat on the pavement next to Nan Wildgoose and tried to decide what to do. A thought ran through her head that she could just prop Nan up in the bus stop, go to the gig and then sort it all out afterwards. She was so close to seeing Morrissey in the flesh and so desperate for that to happen, surely that would be all right. The thought exited almost immediately, to be replaced by the horror of sitting on a pavement in Leicester next to her grandmother who appeared to be dead. Regretfully she turned away from what had promised to be the best evening of her life. No one seemed to be about. No one to ask, to scream at, to tell. Alice pulled Nan into a sitting position and rested her gently against the side of the bus stop. She took off her coat and laid it over Nan just in case she was still there in the big tired body and ran up the road until she saw a phone box. Her cold fingers dialled 999.

On campus, in front of a huge audience of expectant fans, Morrissey called, 'Hello, Leicester!' and the band went straight into 'Pretty Girls Make Graves'.

A completely neutral, rather nasal voice inquired which service Alice wanted. The voice had no idea that while Morrissey was singing about Nature playing tricks, Alice was experiencing the biggest trick Nature could come up with. As the last breaths sighed from Nan Wildgoose out into the night air, Alice began to lose her faith in womanhood, along with Morrissey. She found herself angrily resentful that poor old Nan could not have hung on for one more night. And then she murmured, 'I'm sorry, Nan, I'm really sorry.'

As unruly girls and unruly boys swayed along to the song, she ran back to the bus stop to wait.

The strains of 'Back To The Old House' boomed round the hall and Alice, unable to hear anything except the sounds of the night, just wanted to go home.

The final song of the Smiths set, 'What Difference Does It Make?' was perhaps the most poignant. Nan had gone, and for years afterwards when Alice heard the line, 'and you must be looking very old tonight', an image of Nan Wildgoose's poor crumpled face entered her mind and the terror of the night came back to her.

A siren pierced the night as the ironic encore of 'You've Got Everything Now' was played and Morrissey shouted, 'Goodbye, Leicester! Goodbye!'

Chapter 11

Back at home in her bedroom the following day the whole incident seemed like a surreal drug-induced nightmare.

The ambulance had taken an hour to find them while Alice sat desperately holding Nan, trying to be positive in her head but knowing in reality there was no hope for her. She wanted to phone her dad but had no money and in her despair had forgotten she could reverse the charges. Besides, she didn't want to leave Nan alone and lonely under the rain that was falling faster and harder. They had had an encounter with a drunk who had mistakenly thought Nan Wildgoose was a member of his merry band of excessive drinkers.

'Bloody 'ell, she's had a few,' he said, hands on hips, staring down at Nan and Alice.

'Piss off,' said Alice, feeling the spirit of Nan behind her words.

'Only trying to help,' he said and sauntered off, wobbling and swaying until the darkness swallowed him.

Eventually the screeching of the ambulance heralded its arrival and it drew up at the bus stop. Two chunky men appeared, one carrying a bag, and knelt down beside Alice.

'Oh, you poor love,' said the older of the two.

Alice, who had held all her fears and distress inside, was unable to keep them under control because of these kind words and began to sob as if she would never stop.

'It's all right, love,' said the older one. 'What's your name?'

'Alice,' said Alice.

'I'm Del,' said the man. 'And who's this lady?'

'My nan,' said Alice. 'Is she all right?'

'Doesn't look like it,' said the younger harder-looking one.

The old man shot him a look, and more softly he said, 'No, I'm afraid not.'

'I knew it really,' said Alice and began to cry harder.

'Let's get you out of the rain,' said Del. 'We'll take you to the nearest hospital, then you can contact the rest of the family.'

They drove through the night and pulled up at a brightly lit casualty department. Nan was taken inside on a wheeled trolley and left in a side room, with Alice beside her. Eventually a tired-looking pubescent male doctor came in and asked her some questions and a kindly receptionist took Alice to a phone on which she could break the news to her dad.

'Alice?' His voice was relaxed and sleepy sounding. 'We were expecting to hear from you much earlier. Have you had a good time? I thought you were going to ring me at the station and let me know what time to pick you both up from Shrewsbury.'

'Dad . . .' Alice faltered. She didn't really know how to put it. Finally she said, 'It's Nan.'

'What?' said Keith, starting to sound worried.

'Nan's . . . Nan's . . .' She couldn't go on any further. She began to cry again.

The receptionist took the phone from her.

'Hello, to whom am I speaking?' she said.

Keith said something at the other end.

'I'm terribly sorry,' said the receptionist, 'but your mother has passed away.'

Keith was puzzled at the other end of the line and wondered briefly how his mother had managed to turn up at a Smiths gig in Leicester. At the same time, Alice was saying to the receptionist, 'No, it's not his mum, it's my mum's mum.'

'I'm terribly sorry,' said the receptionist. 'It's your mother-in-law who's passed away.'

'Can you put my daughter on?' said Keith.

Alice was handed the receiver.

'Alice, what happened?' said Keith.

'Nan just fell over at the bus stop,' said Alice, 'and I couldn't wake her up.'

'Oh, you poor girl,' said Keith. 'Hang on there and I'll be with you as soon as I can.'

Marie Henty was drafted in to sit in the little cottage while Gina slept fitfully, dreaming of being in heaven.

Keith drove like a maniac through the night and arrived in Leicester at two o'clock in the morning to find Alice with panda eyes and a face as white as a snowdrop. He picked her up and held her tight.

'I'm sorry this had to happen to you,' he said.

'And I didn't even see Morrissey,' Alice sobbed.

Keith let it pass and after some hellish bureaucratic interplay with the hospital staff, he and Alice left hand in hand and got into the van.

They arrived back at five thirty. It was still dark and raining and Marie Henty snoozed in a chair by the fire, dreaming of Keith kissing her feet.

Alice had fallen asleep in the van and Keith carried her, staggering, into the house, thinking back to when she was a baby and how he had done this so many times after days out at fairs and fetes.

He then woke Marie Henty who, looking up into his lovely, benificent face, gave a little squeak of pleasure as she woke from her dream.

'Thanks, Marie,' he said. 'You're released from your duties.'

'Is everything OK?' said Marie, now fully awake.

'My mother-in law died in Leicester tonight,' said Keith. 'Poor Alice was all on her own with her.'

'I'm sorry,' said Marie, secretly thinking to herself, one down and three to go. That'll make my life easier. 'Have you told the family?' she asked.

'Oh fuck . . . sorry,' said Keith. 'For swearing,' he added. 'No, I hadn't even thought of them. God, I'd better get over there.'

'You've had no sleep,' said Marie. 'Can't you leave it till the morning?'

'It *is* the morning,' said Keith, 'and I think it's a job better done in a state of semi-consciousness.'

'Shall I stay in case Alice or Gina wake up?'

'Would you?' said Keith. 'I feel like I'm asking you too much.'

'It's OK,' said Marie. 'I haven't got surgery till the afternoon. Go on, off you go, and I wish you luck.'

Keith drove the few miles to the Wildgooses' isolated cottage. The darkness was broken occasionally by a tepid moon peeping through the clouds but as he turned into the potholed track that led to the grimy cottage, it disappeared, leaving just the insipid headlights of the van to guide him.

The cottage was in darkness.

Keith realised that if he banged on the door he risked a shotgun blast of the 'ask no questions' variety, but he could not see any way round it. He tried to knock in as officious a way as possible so it sounded as if someone respectable had come to call for tea.

A light went on upstairs and a dog barked, causing some hens to start clucking in a panicked way.

'Who's there?' Bert's pinched face appeared at the tiny window.

Keith had always rather liked Bert who seemed,

underneath, to be a civilised man caught in a family of rabid animals. He looked so benign that Keith couldn't believe he didn't have a core of goodness hidden under the tacit approval of the extreme antics of his Stone Age sons.

'Bert, it's me, Keith,' said Keith.

'Missus run off with a train driver in Leicester, has she?' said Bert cheerily, expecting some banal news about his wife being too pissed to come home. 'Hang on, I'll be down,' he said.

The noise of bolts being drawn back and the door opening was more reminiscent of a medieval castle than a small cottage in Herefordshire, security put in place by Wobbly and Bighead because quite a few unsavoury types came looking for them.

'Hello,' said Bert and gestured for Keith to come in. Without Ma Wildgoose at his side he seemed smaller and more vulnerable than usual.

'What is it, boy?' he said when they got into the cramped sitting room.

'I'm afraid Violet has passed on,' said Keith. 'It happened in Leicester when they were walking to the show.'

Bert stared uncomprehendingly at him for a few seconds and then his face crumpled into that of a small boy and he bent his head, crying silently, the odd tear leaking out between his dirty uncut fingernails.

'I'm so sorry, Bert,' said Keith, wanting to put his arms round him but holding back because he was embarrassed. He wondered when Wobbly and Bighead would burst into the room and try and kill him. 'Are the boys around?' He tried to sound confident, as if he wasn't shit scared of them.

'They were out drinking last night. They won't be up for hours. I'll tell 'em, lad,' Bert said almost kindly.

He then asked Keith the sort of questions that revealed just what an innocent he was. He had absolutely no idea where to go from here, how to get his wife's body transported back to them, how to arrange a funeral or how to get his own breakfast. Keith found himself feeling sorry for him for perhaps the first time ever as he realised that as a package they were ferocious, but on his own Bert was just a sad, tired, lost old man who didn't know how to cope. Perhaps, on waking, his sons would restore him to his full intimidating glory but Keith doubted it. The spark had gone out of the Wildgooses and he wondered whether it could be relit.

'I'll ask May down the road about the arrangements,' said Bert. 'She lost 'er 'usband last year. She'll know what to do.'

'Call me if you need anything,' said Keith, but he knew he wouldn't; he suspected Bert had never lifted a telephone receiver in his life.

Back at home, Keith discovered a quiet house. Alice and Gina were still asleep upstairs and Marie Henty drooped over the edge of an armchair, looking very uncomfortable.

'Off you go,' Keith said, waking her. 'I'll look after everything here. And thanks, I really appreciate your help.'

Upstairs, Alice was penning another letter to Morrissey.

'Dear Morrissey, I came to see you in Leicester last

night with my nan (don't ask). I'm afraid she died on the way.'

Then she wrote, 'I didn't know she hated you that much!' and then put big black lines through it, screwed the paper up and put it in the bin.

She started the letter several times but it just didn't sound real, so in the end, she left her bedroom, kissing his photo before she went, and found her dad downstairs in a chair, staring at the wall.

'Are you all right?' she said.

'Fine,' said Keith, rousing himself and going into the kitchen to make their breakfast. 'But I don't know how your mum is going to be.'

Gina reacted to the news with her usual blank expression, uttered the word, 'Oh,' and went into the kitchen to make toast, where she sat munching several slices before she went back to bed.

Right, thought Keith. That's that for now.

Ma Wildgoose's funeral was arranged, with the help of May, for the following Tuesday. The small group consisting of Bert, Wobbly, Bighead, Keith, Alice, Gina and May stood in the little church while the vicar made heavy work of the funeral service. No hyms were sung as the vicar had made a unilateral decision that the number of mourners precluded any decent performance, so after a fairly short time the pall-bearers – Bert, Wobbly, Bighead and Keith – struggled outside and made their slow progress towards the freshly dug grave.

Keith had wondered whether the brothers would find some spurious reason for starting a fight, but they were unusually subdued as everyone stood round the grave and threw a handful of earth on top of Ma Wildgoose.

Bert shook the vicar's hand.

'Bit of tea back at ours?' he said. 'May's laid on a nice spread.'

'I'm so sorry,' said the vicar, 'I have another engagement, please excuse me.' And he escaped to the womb-like safety of his den in the vicarage and finished off *The Times* crossword.

May's 'spread' seemed to consist mainly of huge doorstops of bread, between which lay an unidentifiable slimy meat. On inquiry this turned out to be tongue. The sandwiches were accompanied by a huge amount of cider and a sad-looking bottle of sherry. May had also included a cake which looked as if it had literally been thrown into the room, its original shape completely lost after it had been stuffed by May into a carrier bag and then sat on by Bert who had taken up his usual seat in the kitchen without even noticing it.

Cider was poured into a selection of unclean glasses and Bert proposed a toast.

'To my old missus,' he said, 'who was often a pain in the arse but a good woman all the same. To . . .'

'Nan,' said Alice.

'Mum,' said Wobbly, Bighead and Gina.

Keith, after a split-second decision, said 'Mum' too and Bert whispered 'Darling' which was heard by no one and harked back to the day they had met at a funfair and her wild cackling and flashing eyes had inexorably drawn him towards her.

Alice felt sick. Her head was aching and spinning. Either the cider was so strong, one sip had altered her equilibrium, or she was ill. She sat down but didn't feel any better. Eventually she said, 'Dad, I don't feel well, can I go home?'

'Go on then,' said Keith. 'We'll see you there later.'

On the way home, Alice threw up in a ditch and covered it over with some stray branches. She went immediately to her bedroom, put on her Smiths album and lay on the bed thinking about how Morrissey would feel when she eventually wrote to him about the events on the night of his Leicester gig. He'll have to come and get me, she thought. He'll know how much I need him.

Keith, who had felt duty bound to stay at the wake until the bitter end, was beginning to regret it. Wobbly and Bighead were becoming more animated with every pint and had begun to tell each other dirty jokes. And then the atmosphere abruptly changed when Wobbly said, 'Of course, if poor old Mum didn't have had to drag herself all the way to fucking Leicester, none of this would 'ave 'appened.' His eyes glinted, showing the room some concrete evidence of his dangerous spirit.

'Aw, come on, son,' said Bert. 'It weren't their fault. Mum didn't have needed to go if she didn't want.'

'Who are these Smiths anyway?' said Bighead, yawning and scratching his hairy gut, most of which had lost the battle to be contained by his tight trousers.

'Well, just a group that Alice really likes,' said Keith. 'I don't really know much about them.'

'I've seen 'em in the paper,' said Wobbly, whose reading age was about nine. 'They say 'e's a poof who's a *vegetarian*.' To Wobbly, being a vegetarian was only marginally above being gay on the scum scale.

'Sounds like a right wanker to me,' said Bighead. 'Why can't your Alice like someone decent like Elton John or Barbra Streisand?'

Keith was desperate to point out that Elton John was not the full-blown heterosexual male the brothers assumed and that most of Barbra Streisand's fans also batted for the other side. Still, it was a wake, so he desisted, unwilling to return home with some physical evidence upon him that Wobbly and Bighead had abused him.

'Well,' said Keith, 'I'd better be going. Alice didn't look too well. Gina, are you coming?' He turned to Gina who had sat silently by the table guzzling cider and smoking for the last hour.

'No,' she said. 'I want to stay here with my brothers.'

'All right, love,' said Keith. He turned to the boys and Bert. 'Phone me when you want me to pick her up,' he said.

'All right, Keefy,' said Bighead in a high-pitched little girl's voice which scared Keith.

Once out of the door, he breathed a huge sigh of relief.

Chapter 12

Alice realised on waking the next morning that something wasn't right with the middle section of herself. Odd rumblings were occurring which felt strange and uncomfortable. She ran into the bathroom and vomited into the sink, immediately regretting that she hadn't gone for the toilet as it would have been so much easier to wash away.

It hit her like a punch.

Jesus Christ, she thought. I'm pregnant.

And so she was. The encounter with Mark in his bedroom had resulted in the tiny coming together of their genes which in some months from now would bind them forever. She found herself thinking that this wasn't necessarily a bad thing. Images passed through her mind of herself and Mark alone in a small house with a little gurgling bundle which knitted together their physical and emotional characteristics.

'Are you all right, love?' Keith had heard the noises in the bathroom.

'Fine,' said Alice. 'I think the food at the cottage yesterday was probably a bit dodgy.'

'OK,' said Keith. 'Are you all right for school?'

'I think so.'

Alice sat on her bed feeling less like school than she'd ever felt but it was important to stagger through the day as best she could without anyone noticing that she, as so many before her, carried the country girl's shame inside her.

Her mind whirred. She would need to find out for sure if she was pregnant and this would involve travelling to a far-flung chemist where nobody knew her, to buy a pregnancy test. Hereford was out of the question. She didn't know if she could sit on the rumbling bus without throwing up.

She conjured up an image of the transaction in her head. She entered an empty shop staffed by a friendly, weary-faced woman, asked for a pregnancy testing kit and left, unsullied by human dialogue. It all seemed so easy. She decided to go to Knighton on her bike after school. The fact that Knighton was in Wales, a different country, somehow set it apart, increased her anonymity. She just had the school day to get through.

She clasped the secret to her like a little package of woe all day.

The cycle ride to Knighton was lovely despite it being a journey towards potential catastrophe. When Alice arrived, she leaned her bike against the clock tower and entered the chemist. Of course, the scenario she had imagined had been replaced by a horrible reality. There was Mrs Percival from the farm near Mark's, chatting away to the pharmacist as if she was going to be there all day. They both turned their eyes towards Alice.

'Can I help?' said the pharmacist.

'Hello, Alice dear,' said Mrs Percival at the same time.

'Er, no ... I ...' Alice trailed off lamely. 'Hello, Mrs Percival,' she added.

The two adults continued their conversation, giving Alice a few precious seconds to account for her hesitation.

'My grandad wanted me to get him something and I can't remember what it was,' said Alice. 'Sorry.'

'What was it for, love?' said the pharmacist.

'Upset tummy,' said Alice, thinking that was probably general enough.

'Milk of magnesia's probably best,' said the pharmacist reaching behind him and getting a bottle.

'Thanks,' said Alice.

She paid the pharmacist and turned to embark on the well-worn walk of the teenager exiting the chemist bearing a product she neither wanted nor needed.

Mrs Percival turned to the pharmacist with a grin. 'Well, Bert Wildgoose has a cast-iron stomach and her other grandad lives over Birmingham way,' she said triumphantly. 'What do you reckon she was really after? Condoms or a pregnancy test?'

Alice arrived home, frustrated, sweaty and nauseous.

'Spag bol for tea,' said Keith as she lingered in the small dingy hallway, hoping she could avoid him.

'Right,' said Alice. 'I'll just go and change.'

She lay on her bed underneath her poster of Morrissey and was struck by an unfamiliar sensation, a hundredfold period pain ache accompanied by a somersaulting sensation.

'Something is happening, Morrissey,' she said aloud, 'and I don't like it.'

Whatever was happening to her, she didn't want it to happen in this small bedroom in the dark cottage; she felt she needed to be outside on her own.

She stood up and staggered a little, the change from lying to standing causing her blood pressure to drop. She walked gingerly downstairs, shouting to Keith as she went, 'I'm just going for a quick walk. Can you keep my tea warm?'

'Okey dokey,' he replied from the kitchen, feeling strangely miffed at her exit.

Alice walked quickly up the hill, her boots squelching on the mash of grass, oak leaves and brambles that lined the road. She opened the gate into the field that led up the small path into the wood. A dog-walker on the horizon above her raised a hand. She raised her hand and turned away, taking a less well-worn path which was nonetheless familiar to her in the gloom.

As soon as she was concealed by the trees from any passing strollers and their weak torches, she sat down on the earth and felt the wet and cold begin to seep into her as a warm rush of something poured out from inside her, accompanied by a great spasm, not so much painful as rolling and uncontrollable. The physical sense of loss was accompanied by a sharp pain in what she assumed was her heart as the tiny thing she had created with Mark began to fall out of her. She stopped a great roar which was rising in her throat for fear of attracting attention and just let it happen to her there in the darkness, with the drip of water from the trees pinging around her face.

It took hours and she knew that Keith would be worrying. Torchlight flickered beneath her at the bottom of the hill and she heard a voice calling her from below. It was her dad. More than ever she wished for a nice, comfy, all-enveloping mother but she knew that it was her dad who would always be the one to rescue her from the depths.

She stood up, her jeans soaked in blood, and wondered if she could hide it from him.

'Dad, I'm here!' she called and stumbled through the undergrowth towards him.

His worried face broke into a smile.

'Bloody hell, Alice,' he said, 'I thought it was going to be a short walk. It's half eleven.'

'Sorry,' said Alice. 'Can I not talk about it?'

'Are you sure?' he said.

'Yes,' said Alice

'All right,' he said and he put his arm round her. They descended slowly, neither of them saying a word, although Keith was humming a Bob Dylan song that Alice really liked and she began to sing the words as they got nearer the house.

He turned to her. 'Are you tangled up in blue?' he said.

'I'm tangled up in black at the moment,' she said.

In her room she took off her blood-soaked jeans and pants and put them in a carrier bag under her bed, not wanting to lose what remained of her first experience of motherhood. Then she put on her pyjamas over some big pants stuffed with a big wodge of folded toilet paper and went down at midnight to eat her dinner.

The Smiths album played continuously for the whole of the next day as Alice lay in her bedroom suffering the last physical knockings of her loss. Keith had nodded solemnly to her request to stay home from school. Gina had not returned from her family, so when Keith went off to work, his van limping up the lane firing salutes of dirty exhaust, Alice was completely alone with her thoughts and the music.

She felt as though the brief consciousness she'd had of being pregnant was surreal, almost hadn't happened, and she wondered whether to tell Mark and if it would ruin their friendship like their sexual encounter nearly had.

Morrissey looked pretty appalled by her behaviour and condition. Alice suspected he might not be the best person to comfort her during these desperate few days as he seemed somehow fastidious and disconnected from the scummy, earthy, bloody trivia of normal people's lives.

Nan's dead and my baby's dead, Alice found herself

thinking. Who's going to die next? In times of misery, shameful thoughts pop into the mind without the barrier of the superego batting them back into the unconscious because they are just too painful to contemplate. Alice experienced the words, 'I wish it was my mum next,' being said to her in her head and felt ashamed and shocked that her mind could come up with this. A tear trickled down her face as she thought of her unlovable mother, who must at one time have been lovable or Keith would never have fallen for her. But the drugs, the course of her illness, premature ageing from what seemed like the hundreds of cigarettes she smoked every day had combined to produce the pantomime ugly sister she found mumbling in the kitchen most mornings. Some days Alice wanted to withhold her mum's drugs just to see if any of the old Gina lay unchanged underneath, but she was terrified her mum might lose control altogether and kill her or kill somebody else. Other days Alice wanted to put her mum in a home where she could sit immobile by a window and telly all day, until one day she either set fire to herself or died of boredom. The ill Gina had been with them for so long that Alice had very little memory of the life force her mother used to be.

That evening, as these thoughts and others tumbled around in her head, Alice heard a knock on her bedroom door.

'Alice?' said Keith's kind, worried voice.

'Yes, Dad,' said Alice, biting back the tears that always came when she had any kindness directed at her.

'Can I come in and talk?'

'No, please,' said Alice. 'I'm fine, I'll be better tomorrow.'

The case of Alice's pregnancy and miscarriage was closed.

Chapter 13

1985

The season of winter and the dark cold nights of regret and
crying into her pillow whilst the inscrutable Morrissey looked
on turned into spring, summer, autumn and then winter
again. Alice existed in a kind of comfortable numbness which
externally manifested itself in the incompleteness of
someone who has had the joyous layer of living shaved off.
Only two people noticed this, Mark and her dad. Everyone
else whose knowledge of Alice was shallow and incomplete
saw the same teenager move through her life, unaware of
the emotional ghosts that flitted beneath the surface. Alice
had decided not to tell Mark about what had happened. She
reasoned that there was no point adding pain to his life,
given that the attendant comfort she gained would not
amount to much. She went automatically to school, did her
work, chatted to her friends, ate her tea, collected her *NME*

religiously from the shop and wrote in her diary every night as she spoke to Morrissey about the secret areas that no one else had access to.

Alice felt that she could not have survived the bruising pain of it all had she not had Morrissey to talk to. Despite what she read about his strangeness, inscrutability and arrogance, she believed that the face he put on for the world was a face to keep away the people who wanted to hurt him. She understood that for someone who is sensitive to the pedestrian gaze of lesser mortals, it is not possible to reveal one's true beliefs and thoughts for fear of being humiliated or ridiculed.

Had she been able to meet Morrissey, talk to him, share her thoughts with him, she knew there would have been many moments when their thoughts mirrored each other's. She knew he was a kind person, made bitter by circumstance, and she also understood that many people experience a cynicism which is not in keeping with their youth because they have been forced to grow up before they wanted to, or before they should.

As his voice coloured her bedroom with a warmth that did not match the rather spartan surroundings of a young woman who has eschewed the pinkness of femininity, Alice lay back on her bed with her eyes closed and imagined the two of them in all sorts of circumstances.

Her favourite fantasy was the pair of them together somewhere wild by the sea, perhaps Cornwall or Ireland during a storm, both wet and cold but both soaking up the poetry of the scene. They would talk about books, about history, about all the shit people in the world who make everyone else's life a misery. She would say things to him that then appeared in new songs and she would feel a secret thrill when she heard them or he phoned her and sang them down a crackling line to her. She could never feel anything sexual in her overwhelming attraction towards this unearthly creature; in fact he seemed to be slightly above physical needs, as if the mere pragmatic considerations of the fulfilling of the male sexual drive were something below him, something that tainted him and dragged him down.

I wonder if this is what all those crabby old ladies feel in church when they pray, thought Alice and then decided it couldn't be, because they didn't seem to have any joy in their lives and surely the object of one's religious devotion should make one happy and not grumpy.

Morrissey made Alice happy by his mere existence. Thinking of him made her feel better, more secure, and looking at his picture still sent a little shiver of pleasure through her, even though she must have looked at it hundreds of times. Alice also tried to examine herself. Was she just a foolish immature fan with something lacking in her as a person? Was she like those girls who had gone before, screamed over the Beatles, cried over David Cassidy, exploded over the Bay City Rollers? She wanted to think that she wasn't, that her attachment was more thoughtful, mysterious and spiritual, that it had a meaning above some adolescent quasi-sexual fantasy. But she wasn't sure. Perhaps everyone was laughing at her behind her back. Perhaps her dad and Mark thought she was an idiot, a child – like her mother and the weather forecaster.

But she didn't care and she knew that had Morrissey not existed or been taken away, she would be completely desolate and would have no reason to go on. And she didn't think that could be said for a mere Bay City Rollers fan. Alice also felt that with Morrissey behind her, she could tackle some pain in her life and the lives of those around her.

Chapter 14

1988

Alice looked out of the window at the grey soggy day and began to plot. Her mum, Gina, had not been free of so-called 'therapeutic' drugs for several years now and she had slumped into a blank-stared life of going to bed, sitting smoking, sitting looking out of the window and sitting looking at the wall. For a woman in her thirties who had been beautiful, formidable and unpredictable, every day of her life now slid into another with such minute changes in routine, they were not apparent to the naked eye. The far limits of her illness were contained by a cocktail of medication which included a monthly injection which ensured her brain had fogged into a primitive machine capable only of fulfilling her most basic needs and throwing out conversation that would have sat easily upon the lips of a five-year-old. Physically her rough and ready beauty had coarsened long ago behind a blanket of ageing, pallid mediocrity.

That's no life, Alice thought to herself, aware of the fact that, as far as her mum was concerned, she had begun to think in clichés. She longed for excitement for her mother, even a repeat of the incident when she'd sat in all her naked glory on the roof and been spirited to hospital in her dad's crappy old van. The psychiatric services were able to do nothing for her to increase the quality of her life and they, too, had fallen into an institutionalised pattern of containing Gina's behaviour so that she wasn't any trouble to anyone, least of all herself.

Had Alice examined her life in the intervening four years, she may have come to the same conclusion about her existence as she did about her mother's. It all seemed to have passed in an automatic way, with the rote of the day controlling what she did. She got up, she went to school if it was a school day and she didn't if it wasn't. Relatives and friends moved around her but she seemed to be somehow separate from them. On the surface she was still Alice, but inside she felt as though a different person was beginning to grow and just could not be allowed out yet. Her life was punctuated by Morrissey albums. *Hatful Of Hollow* saw her trudging to school surrounded by the unforgiving atmosphere of November. She hadn't done well in her GCSEs, apart from English, and Keith had tried to suppress his disappointment as they looked at her very average list of achievements. In February the following year, Alice surprised Mark by announcing to him that she had finally decided to become a vegetarian and she sat determinedly at home chewing on rubbery omelettes and forcing down chickpeas, the only motivation to keep this food on her plate coming from *Meat is Murder*.

Keith persuaded her to stay on for the sixth form even though she had wanted to get a job and travel round the country pursuing the Smiths.

She finished her second set of exams around about the time *The Queen Is Dead* came out and after eight months of waiting, the song 'There Is A Light That Never Goes Out' pervaded every aspect of her life. She played it over and over again and knew she wanted to experience an all-encompassing, mad affair that would generate the sentiments expressed in it.

Weight had fallen from her and she now looked more like Gina. The wildness in her was more pronounced. Her hair had grown longer and more uncontrollable and boys she knew at school had begun to include her in their list of possibilities, changed as she was from the growling, reluctant schoolgirl to a feisty young woman.

Having produced another set of reasonable but not impressive results in her A levels, Keith's attempts to persuade her to go to a university which would have her fell on deaf ears. Alice just did not know where to go or what to do. She felt there was so much unfinished business in her family that she needed to deal with before she moved on. Keith suggested she get a part-time job so she could pay her way until she decided what to do. Alice scanned the local paper and managed to find a quiet little bookshop in Hereford that wanted help three days a week. It was the sanctuary that she needed. Run by an elderly white-haired man called Ernest who shuffled around, silently smiling and quoting poetry at her, she found a comfortable quietness there which allowed her to spend happy days dealing with few customers and reading greedily.

At work, she thought about Gina almost as much as she thought about Morrissey, and wanted to change her unchanging, hopeless life.

Alice decided not to discuss her plan with Keith as she was worried that he might be dubious about unleashing Gina's illness upon the fusty little cottage. So she went to the hospital which carried out the so-called management of her mother's illness and asked to see Gina's doctor, still the young Dr Desmond who, having looked like a child some fourteen years ago, had just about managed to achieve a greasy adolescence characterised by lank hair and some angry-looking spots with big white heads.

'I want my mother's drugs to be changed or something,' said Alice. Dr Desmond noted that she looked like her mother but with somehow softer lines.

'Where is your dad?' he asked.

'At work,' said Alice. 'He knows I'm here but he's too busy and has told me to talk to you about it.'

'Well, I can't do anything without seeing your mum,' said the doctor, scratching his head, causing a faint down of dandruff to float on to his shoulders.

'Shall I bring her then?' said Alice.

There was a pause long enough for Alice almost to read Dr Desmond's mind and pick up that he was thinking: Oh fuck, do you have to? He'd been knocked around quite seriously in the early days of her illness and didn't want a repeat. Emotionally and medically he was contracted to maintaining the status quo. But he managed to bring the falsely cheery smile, more akin to a sex pest's leer, back on to his face.

'Yes, make an appointment with the receptionist and I'll see you then,' he said.

The receptionist was flicking idly through patients' notes, the contents of which she used to entertain the long stream of thuggish men who made their way drunkenly through her bedroom, a well-trodden sexual thoroughfare. It used to amaze her that grown men with heads the size of Hallowe'en lanterns could suddenly become so pathetically fearful of and fascinated by these sad little mad people who passed her desk.

'I'd like to make an appointment for my mum,' said Alice.

'Name?' said the receptionist without looking up as she was at a particularly interesting climax in someone's medical notes, in which they had locked their husband in a cupboard and run into the street screaming that Jesus was about to land in their village in a fiery chariot.

'Gina Wilson,' said Alice.

'Doctor?' said the receptionist.

'Dr Desmond,' said Alice.

'Eleven thirty on the twenty-third,' said the receptionist after much tutting and shuffling of paper.

'OK,' said Gina, as the receptionist handed her an appointment card.

Alice walked away marvelling at the lack of social skills possessed by this woman, which had meant that eye contact hadn't even been achieved, let alone a smile or a brief chat. She thought about lonely people who craved a friendly word or an acknowledgement of their existence from their fellow humans and surmised that this woman had probably been responsible for the odd suicide attempt.

Alice sat on the bus bumping through the valley and decided, finally, not to tell her father what she was doing. She was now nineteen years old and was sure she could fool the psychiatric services into making decisions based purely on her and her mother's say-so without any intervention from Keith.

The long journey, an hour and a half on the bus with a twenty-minute walk at the end, gave her ample opportunity to assess her current life and the yawning chasm between the reality of it and what she really wanted. She hadn't done well at school. Although teachers had endlessly told her she was bright and could catapult herself out of the drab, soulless existence the countryside offered many young women of her age, a combination of fear, apathy and laziness had so far prevented her from dreaming about big cities and university. Besides, every time she thought about moving away from Keith and her distant, trembling mother, a bolt of terror hit

the pit of her stomach and she turned her thoughts elsewhere. She clung to familiarity as if it was a wrecked ship
floating on the sea near to some rocks. It threatened to send
her under but was also her only chance of survival. Much
as her uncles, Bighead and Wobbly, repulsed and frightened
her, they were also major figures in her life, towering men-
acingly in the foreground but reassuring her somehow with
their presence. She knew that, thuggish as they were, they
really cared about Grandpap Bert and in their own unhygienic,
drunken way had steered him through the years since Nan
Wildgoose's death with some care. By their very existence
they protected Alice, because everyone in the area knew
them and therefore no one risked upsetting her or her dad
just in case Bighead and Wobbly came looking for them.

School had been disappointing ultimately, full of detached
teachers who had looked tired and angry much of the time,
loutish boys who seemed to control the course of the day
with their hormonal upheavals, and girls whose skirts
ascended minutely every day and whose thighs, pink and
mottled, became a major feature of their appearance along
with their badly made-up faces and witchy laughs. They
spent their time discussing their latest sexual conquests.
These were usually achieved in the woods after a session of
the sort of drinking that only British teenagers go in for,
reaching a state of disinhibition that, as well as placing them
in some considerable danger, encouraged testosterone-
fuelled spotty boys to come hunting in packs from
surrounding villages.

Alice felt like an alien handmaid to these hard-faced girls, who seemed only to be interested in drinking, cackling and being penetrated so hard they were almost unable to walk. Alice still sat in her room thinking about the things that Morrissey said in his songs and feeling that the groups of schoolfriends she had awkwardly circled during her time there would not have met with his approval.

Mark was also somewhat of an outcast although Alice couldn't quite put her finger on why. Some obvious traits sprang to mind, like his moral stance on the way in which local farmers conducted themselves and the hunts that took place across his father's land. They had remained close friends although for several months they had been slightly uncomfortable in each other's company, both feeling the weight of the air in the room which seemed to be pressing in on them and demanding some sort of resolution to the distance between two teenagers who have been in the most intimate of circumstances with each other. Ironically, neither could remember much about it because of the lubrication alcohol had afforded them. Alice had wondered for ages afterwards whether it would happen again and had wanted it to. Mark also wanted it to but was aware of so many stifling social conventions concerning his family's relationship with Alice, their contempt for her ill mother and snobbery towards the gentle but useless Keith, that he could not bring himself to openly conduct a relationship with Alice for fear of his bullying father's often physical disdain for his son's life choices. Mark had considered suggesting he and Alice conduct a sexual relationship secretly but he knew he would eventually have to own up to her that he was embarrassed by her and so in his ridiculous male way he kept her at arm's length. Their friendship settled back into its original pattern but with a layer of sweetness removed. This puzzled Karen, the third member of the triad, because neither Mark nor Alice had ever confided in her; something held them back. Retrospectively they were relieved they had withheld this most private piece of information as Karen began to look like and move towards the group of screeching girls that Alice was rather frightened of.

When, some weeks after her initial visit to Dr Desmond, Alice took Gina from their house to wait for the bus to Hereford, there was a frisson of scandalous utterings in the village. The local exchange lit up as the ranks of elderly curtain twitchers jumped immediately to their phones and began the long round of passing information to the whole county about the rare appearance in public of someone who, in their opinion, should long ago have been banged up in some institution where she couldn't cause trouble or over-turn social conventions.

Gina was like a docile animal and seemed drained of energy. Alice had got her ready that morning as you would get a child ready for school, except that she added some little touches of make-up and wound Gina's wiry hair into an intricate bun. Not many of Gina's clothes had escaped the telltale holes caused by cigarette burns, but Alice found a very pretty flowered dress in the wardrobe. She matched it with one of the hundreds of cardigans Nan Wildgoose had knitted during her life and some leather boots. Alice was surprised how good Gina could look when she'd been buffed up a bit.

In fact, Gina had the effect a local celebrity would have had on the village. Many people came out of their houses on the pretext of going to the village shop so that they could walk past the bus stop and have a good look. A couple of them, Annie Wilsher and May Budd, ventured a tentative 'Hello'. Gina completely ignored them as she had done most people, including her family, for years. In fact it was only Wobbly and Bighead's coarse way of interacting with their fellow mortals that seemed in any way to penetrate the chemical fog she inhabited. On the days when she visited the dark little family cottage she seemed like a real person and her face lit up as Wobbly and Bighead went through the motions of their thuggish comedy double act.

'How have you been then, love?'

The words cut through Alice's thoughts as she studied the bus timetable as if it was really interesting. She turned to May and Annie and the word, 'Fine,' slipped out of her mouth before she realised they weren't talking to her. 'She's OK,' she said, gesturing in Gina's direction helplessly.

'What have you been up to, love?' said Annie, obviously deciding to persevere.

'What the fuck do you think she's been up to, travelling round the world backwards on a unicycle?' Alice wondered if she'd said the words out loud or only thought them.

'Piss off,' said Gina, out of the blue.

The arrival of the bus pre-empted any blustering response from the two bewildered elderly ladies whose colourless lives were only lit on occasions like this. Alice thankfully stepped on, paid their fares and sat at the back with Gina, watching the little round figures disappear into the distance, deep in conversation and planning their next dispersal of information across the county.

Alice experienced that familiar feeling of sitting next to a stranger as the journey to Hereford progressed. The motherly smell of Gina which she could sometimes almost taste when she was a very young child had disappeared, to be replaced by a mixture of sweat and urine. It wasn't that Gina was incontinent, it was just that she didn't take a bath very often, her face filling with terror whenever Keith gently mooted the idea, as if he had suggested he slowly baste her on a spit. He had eventually given up the struggle and was reduced to giving her something akin to a bed bath every now and again when she was half awake and least likely to bite or punch him. Alice found herself wondering when Keith had last had sex with her mum, a distasteful subject at the best of times, and surmised it must have been years if not decades ago.

As the bus neared its destination, in his office Dr Desmond glanced anxiously at his watch. He checked his pulse and found it had speeded up considerably in the last ten minutes. It always did this when Gina Wildgoose was approaching.

The phone rang and made him jump. It was the receptionist telling him Gina and Alice had arrived.

'Send them in,' he said and took a deep breath.

The pair appeared at the door, Alice lovely in a pair of frayed bell-bottomed jeans with embroidery running the length of the legs, and Gina better than he had seen her look for ages, her hair now a tamed and almost respectable mop rather than the wild, scrubby toilet brush it had been the last time he'd seen her.

'Well, what can I do for you?' he said pleasantly, hating the sound of the patronising timbre he had adopted for his interactions with patients. It occasionally slipped out at home with his wife and normally resulted in a raging torrent of abuse, the content of which invariably included his lack of respect for her and pity for the poor patients he spoke to in this way.

'Well,' Alice said, 'my mum's just not really living like a normal human being and I want to see if there's anything you can do to bring back some of the enjoyment she used to have for life.'

This succinct and poignant sentence had been rehearsed, rehashed and repeated many times over by Alice in her bedroom and on the bus.

Dr Desmond had feared this might be the reason for their visit and his body slumped internally. Christ, these people, he thought. You stabilise their family member so they can function within the family and they're not happy with that, oh no, they want some quality of life for the poor cow.

What he actually said was, 'Right, so perhaps you are asking for a review of your mother's medication.'

Alice didn't know what she was asking for. It was hard to put into words the ache she and Keith felt when they looked at Gina. The loss of any spark, of a quick mind – of a future. She and her dad tried not to discuss it too much for they were at odds. Keith, having borne the brunt of the devastating effects of Gina's illness, thought that this current damped-down persona was the best they could hope for. Alice, although she could rationally see his point, wanted more for the once beautiful Gina and thought that if there was no more, she might as well be dead. But she didn't say this to Dr Desmond. She said, 'I don't really know if that's what I'm asking for because I don't know enough about how it all works, but we have to live with my mum and she doesn't really talk to us, she just sits there and I don't think that's much of a life, do you?'

She was right and Dr Desmond longed to throw off his professional mantle and chat to her like a friend. She seemed so sweet and earnest, but over the years his humanity had crept further and further inside him and the hard shell of his professional pronouncements had become as automatic as getting up every morning.

'Look, let's try a couple of things,' he said. 'I'll change your mother's oral drugs and we'll reduce the volume of her injection a bit and see if that improves things at all.'

A flicker of hope passed across Alice's face.

'OK,' she said. 'When will we do that?'

'Well, let's start today,' he said, encouraged by the softening expression on her face.

Almost simultaneously it occurred to them that they had ignored Gina completely during this exchange and they both turned to her.

'How do you feel about that?' Dr Desmond asked her.

Gina was looking out of the window at an elderly lady being all but dragged by two members of staff towards a door and listening to two voices discussing how shit she was at tennis.

'What?' she said.

'We'll change your medication a bit,' said the spotty little creep of a doctor who had been responsible for locking her up once and now for some reason was smiling beatifically at her as if he was her saviour.

'Piss off, I'm fucking brilliant at tennis,' Gina mumbled.

'Well, it's better than fuck off,' said Alice cheerfully.

'I'll write to Dr Henty and tell her to halve the dose,' said Dr Desmond, 'and I'll write your mum up for some different tablets. Let's review it again in a month and see how we're doing. Obviously if there are any problems you can bring her back before that or take her to your GP.'

He scribbled on a piece of paper.

'Take that to the pharmacy,' he said, handing her the prescription, and Alice rose, gently pulling Gina up with her.

Chapter 15

'What did you do today, love?' said Keith.

'Oh, just messed around at home,' said Alice.

'I went to Hereford,' said Gina from her usual position in the corner.

Oh shit, thought Alice. She's going to land me right in it.

'Yes, love,' said Keith, not really even registering what she had said, so accustomed was he to her pronouncements having all the authenticity of a cheap romantic novel.

Alice now had to work out how she was going to square things with Marie Henty who, she had realised over the years, was probably a bit in love with her dad. Little glances, slight breathlessness, redness of cheeks and an over-willingness to help out at any time of day or night were the symptoms she had diagnosed in the awkward GP.

Of course, as soon as there was a whiff of anything to do with Keith, it was likely Marie would insist on talking to him directly, in the vain hope that something might happen between them. Keith, in all his unashamed blissful naivety, hadn't got a clue, even after all this time, that Marie Henty had an unrelenting crush on him. He just thought she was a bit weird. Alice had picked it up when she was quite young, in an instinctive female way, and had immediately felt protective towards her dad. It was not that she couldn't understand that he might want to look elsewhere for some love and comfort, she just could not help feeling censorious towards those potential feelings because Gina, after all, was still her mother.

Alice decided on the tack she was going to take with Marie Henty, which, if it paid off, would work like a dream and if it didn't would land her well and truly in trouble.

The following morning found her sitting in the little surgery, flanked by two elderly ladies who had what sounded like exactly the same cough. She flicked through the dog-eared copies of *The Lady*, fantasising about being a nanny to some family who lived half the year in America and travelled round the world for the rest, although she suspected the reality might be tiredness and irritation with a bunch of precocious little poltergeists and their equally precocious parents.

'Alice, what a pleasant surprise. What can I do for you?' said Marie Henty.

'Well, it's what I can do for you that is probably more important,' said Alice, immediately grabbing back the elevated position in their duet.

'What do you mean?' said Marie Henty, intrigued and wondering against hope if Alice was going to offer somehow to get rid of Wobbly and Bighead.

'Let's not beat about the bush,' said Alice, 'and I don't want to embarrass you, but you really like my dad, don't you?'

Marie Henty was so shocked by this statement, rocketing as it did from beneath the big comfortable blanket of social convention, that her central nervous system nearly forgot to make her blush. But blush she did, as she wrestled with an appropriate and professional answer with which to counter this ever surprising eighteen-year-old's inquiry.

'Um, yes,' she said. 'I do like your father very much, he is a very nice man, but I'm not sure that this is an appropriate topic of conversation for us in a medical consulting room.' Her voice had subtly changed pitch into the vaguely dictatorial yet assured tones favoured by her colleagues when faced with having to deal with an enormous emotional quagmire.

'Well, we can discuss it elsewhere if you want,' said Alice, 'but it is linked to someone's medical care. Not mine,' she added swiftly.

'Is your dad ill?' said Marie Henty, a tiny edge of genuine concern creeping into her voice.

'No,' said Alice. 'I want to talk to you about my mum.'

'Right,' said Marie Henty. 'What does that have to do with my . . . apparent feelings for your dad?'

'Well,' said Alice, 'I'm not happy about what a sad life

my mum is living and I want to try and improve things for her.'

'I'm in agreement so far,' said Marie Henty.

'So,' Alice went on, 'I want to see if scaling down her medication a bit will help and I know Dr Desmond is going to write to you to cut down her depot injection, but I'd like you to stop it for a couple of months altogether.'

Marie Henty looked worried. Like Dr Desmond, her aim was an uneasy preservation of the status quo with regard to the psychiatric patients under her care and any threat to this made her stomach start to churn slightly.

'Oh Alice,' she said, 'it's quite risky, you know, because it could bring on another . . .' she searched for a neutral word, 'attack.'

'I know there's a risk,' said Alice, 'but I can't bear to think this is her for the rest of her life. She's like a big, stranded whale with all the fun and laughter sucked out of her and I can't believe she'll never have fun ever again.'

'I know it's difficult,' said Marie Henty.

'No, you haven't a clue what it's like,' said Alice. 'You don't see her often enough. She's my mum and she's a dirty, filthy, stinking, cigarette-smoking alien in our house who sits there day after day doing fuck all. I've half a mind to put a fucking pillow over her face because I can't bear to see her be this stranger who has no emotions any more.'

Marie Henty didn't really know how to cope with this because she was in complete emotional accord with Alice, but she thought about how her colleagues, friends and the General Medical Council might view a decision that could spell professional suicide.

'Look,' said Alice, 'I promise I will do everything in my power to push things forward between you and my dad. I'll tell him how lovely you are, I'll engineer opportunities for you to see each other, go out together. I'll make him fall in love with you, if you just give me this one thing and let my mum off that fucking medication for three months, give her some life. Christ, you're a doctor, aren't you? Surely it's not just about stopping her being a nuisance, is it? Is it?'

Marie Henty's head was swimming.

'Calm down, Alice,' she said, because she genuinely could not think of anything else to say.

Alice stood up. 'I will not fucking calm down.' By now she was half crying and half shouting. She banged her fist on the desk. 'It's your decision.' Then she turned and walked out of the door.

Immediately the phone began to ring.

'Are you all right, Marie?' said the receptionist's voice.

'Fine,' said Marie Henty, recovering her poise. 'Yes, don't worry, Joy, just some teenage angst.'

'Oh good,' said Joy, 'because Mrs Devonshire has just shit herself, I'm afraid.'

Marie Henty wondered if there was some sort of training course Joy could go on.

Alice walked home very fast and went straight up to her

bedroom, banged the door and put on 'There Is A Light That Never Goes Out' on the highest volume setting and played it over and over again for about an hour. She still hadn't got bored with the tune or lyrics and desperately wanted someone to be with who would be happy to be run over by a bus, as long as he had her.

The next morning she found a little handwritten note on the mat.

Dear Alice,
Come and see me after morning surgery. About 12?
Marie Henty

The next morning Alice cycled up to the village again and slunk into the surgery, well aware that the eyes of Joy, the garrulous receptionist, were upon her. She waited for well over half an hour before Marie Henty's door opened and Marie motioned her in.

'I've thought long and hard about it, Alice,' she said, almost as if she was continuing the same conversation with no break, 'and I'm prepared to try your mother without her injection for three months but no more.'

'Oh, thank you,' said Alice, 'thank you, Dr Henty, and I promise I will fulfil my part of—'

Marie Henty put her finger to her lips. 'I don't think we need to discuss that any more,' she said. But her face said something altogether different.

On the way home, Alice met Mark.

'Not at work?' he said to Alice.

'And I presume you're skiving off college.' Mark's father had persuaded him to go to a local agricultural college where his peers were attempting to erode any sensitivity that was left in him, which had the effect of increasing his determination to stay the same.

'There's no one at mine,' said Mark. 'Do you want to come back for a coffee?'

'Yes, all right,' said Alice and they walked together through the village, Alice pushing her bike.

'Hunt this weekend,' said Mark.

'Oh yeah,' said Alice, not really interested.

'I'm going up there,' said Mark.

'But you hate hunting,' said Alice. 'We both do.'

'I'm not joining the hunters,' said Mark indignantly.

'What do you mean?' said Alice.

'I'm going with some protesters,' said Mark matter-of-factly, but his flushed cheeks betrayed just what a huge step forward this was from being on the sidelines seething with resentment yet socially handcuffed by his father's bullying and eminent position in the county as one of its most rabid fox hunters.

'But what if your dad catches you?' said Alice.

'I'll just tell him to listen to that Morrissey song "Meat Is Murder",' said Mark. 'That'll turn him.'

'Yeah, right,' said Alice.

'You coming?' said Mark.

'I don't know,' said Alice.

'Put your money where your mouth is, you recently converted vegetarian,' said Mark, poking her in the arm and laughing.

'Will there be trouble?' said Alice.

'Don't know,' said Mark. 'It could be good fun.'

'But really,' said Alice, 'what if your dad does see you?'

'He won't see me, I'll be covered up. He won't know it's me. I've arranged to swap clothes with someone. Come on, Alice, you know you want to.'

'All right,' said Alice, 'I'll come, but only to keep an eye on you.'

Mark grinned. 'Bring a balaclava,' he said, 'or something that covers you up and makes you disappear into the crowd. There'll be a lot of people there that we both know and we don't want to be recognised by anyone.'

'All right,' said Alice, thinking it was probably time she supported her friend in his endeavours.

At home, she listened to 'Meat Is Murder' again and couldn't get the phrase 'unholy stench' out of her head. Keith, passing her room on the way to the toilet, called in, 'How did that man know I was on my way for a poo?'

'Dad,' said Alice reprovingly.

They met early on Saturday morning and lingered just outside the small town centre where the hunt was meeting. A compact group of so-called 'hunt saboteurs' were there, maybe fifteen or sixteen, a high number of whom did this all over several counties and were poised ready for the fight.

Alice was aghast to see quite a few of them appeared to be concealing rudimentary weapons, like homemade truncheons, under their clothing.

'Is it going to get nasty?' she said, turning to Mark who had a determined look on his face.

'Don't know,' he said. 'It has done a few times.'

Oh God, thought Alice. Out loud she said, 'If it all goes off, I'm legging it. I can't stand violence of any sort.'

'Fair enough,' said Mark. 'I'm not expecting you to knock anyone out.'

When the hunt was fully assembled and had gone through much patting of each other and the raising of glasses of unidentifiable alcohol, it left the square and began to head out towards the fields. Mark and the rest of the little gang lay in wait in a lane which led down towards the woods and, as they passed, the beagles yelping and playfully nipping at each other's paws, the gang appeared from the camouflage of several large trees and implemented their plan which seemed to be shouting a lot of abuse at this early stage.

'Fuck off, you bunch of towny fairies,' shouted one of the huntsmen, who turned out to be Mark's dad. He obviously had absolutely no idea that his son was concealed amongst these well-wrapped and heavily disguised students. Another of the huntsmen took a swing with his whip at one of the girls who stood by the side of his horse, shouting something slightly more conciliatory and more constructive than most of the others.

The whip caught her on the side of the face and she screamed out in pain. Someone shouted, 'We've got one of the bitches!' causing the hunters, including some relatively young children, to cheer at the top of their voices.

Very quickly, everything became uncontrolled and chaotic. There was some shouting and scuffling around the legs of the horses, some of whom became frightened and started to rear up, others to bolt. At this point, the huntsmen, fed up with their morning's entertainment being interrupted, decided to split into smaller groups and pursue the protesters. They almost seemed to have a plan, as pairs of riders each isolated one or two saboteurs and began to chase them through the woodland or along the muddy, rutted paths that ran beside them.

Alice didn't have enough time to slip away unnoticed and divest herself of her disguise. Instead she found herself running as fast as she could alongside Mark as they were driven further into the darker part of the wood. Alice could hear her own heart thumping in her ears and felt as if her lungs were bleeding. She knew it was ridiculous to try and outrun a horse and prayed they would come to a small river they could wade through or a fence they could climb. They did finally hit a barbed-wire fence and exchanged frightened glances as they attempted to scramble over. It was no use, though, and the more they tried, the more entangled they became until two huntsmen appeared behind them wearing sadistic grins and shouting abuse. They pulled Mark down and one of them produced an evil-looking lump of wood with which he battered Mark until blood began to seep out of the scarf wound round his head.

'Stop, for Christ's sake, stop!' screamed Alice and looked up to see Mark's father in a frenzied rage standing over his son, about to deliver yet another blow.

Chapter 16

Alice realised that the two furious huntsmen had no idea who they were and pulled off her balaclava and the scarf hiding her face.

'Now will you stop!' she screamed, as Mark's father paused for a moment, weapon in mid-air, and looked at her, nonplussed. Rather than the shock followed by sympathy that she had expected, a sneer appeared on his face.

'I might have known it would be you with the fucking mental mother,' he shouted in her face, spittle flying from his mouth. 'I've told my son to keep well away from you and your mad family and I'm glad I did, you stupid little tart. And who have you got with you then? Some cretinous posh wanker from Birmingham, I expect. Well, a beating never went amiss with those sort of arseholes, eh, James?'

He turned to his comrade who chuckled and nodded. 'Let's have a look, shall we?'

He bent down towards Mark and pulled off the bloodied balaclava and scarf to reveal his son.

A greyness filled his face for a spilt second and then he was comfortably back in his unfeeling skin.

His friend, however, looked as if he might faint. Mark groaned, blood coming from his nose and from a cut on his face, and he curled into a foetal ball.

'Jesus fucking Christ, Mark,' shouted his father. 'What the hell do you think you're playing at? I'll never live this down in the village, you stupid little arsehole.'

'He's really hurt,' said Alice. 'Shouldn't we take him to hospital?'

The friend nodded in accord and Mark's father grunted and sat his son up. He pulled him across his body and managed to get Mark's slim frame over his shoulder. Once Mark was secured in the manner of a fireman's carry, his father turned to James and Alice and searched their faces with a venomous expression.

'No one is to hear about this, do you understand?'

James, who was obviously terrified of him, nodded and mumbled his agreement. 'Yes, Phil, I promise, wouldn't dream of it.'

'Right,' he said, looking slightly disgusted by James's grovelling capitulation. 'And you?' he said, turning to Alice as if she was a prostitute he'd just used, which he did frequently in the grimmer part of Hereford.

Alice stared defiantly at this brutal man, a rather more upmarket version of her uncles, and nodded her head. She didn't want to make things any worse for Mark.

'Right,' said Phil. 'This is the story. Me and Jim found you in the woods and you'd been attacked by two blokes who could have been with the hunt, you're not sure. The police will not be involved, but that is the story you will tell people. Do not elaborate on the incident, decline to give descriptions and we'll leave it at that.'

Then he turned and began to move through the tangle of the woods like a man in his twenties, at such a pace that Alice could hardly keep up. She and James threw glances at each other every time Mark groaned and Alice realised that James was a coward, the sort of man who clings like a frightened animal to whoever is winning. She noted a tiny glimmer of sympathy in his expression and smiled reassuringly at him. But this was too much of a betrayal for James and he gave her a hard glare.

When they reached the road, Phil flagged down a Land Rover belonging to Stan, a smallholder from the edge of the village. James helped Phil into the car with the semi-conscious Mark. As Alice tried to climb up too, Phil turned to her and under his breath said, 'Not you, you can walk home.'

'Is she not coming?' shouted Stan from the driver's seat. 'She's welcome, you know.'

'It's all right, I'd rather walk,' said Alice and despite Stan's protestations she headed off up the lane without a backward glance.

As the Land Rover disappeared round a corner, the shock of the attack overcame Alice and her legs started to buckle. She sat down on the verge and began to cry.

Some hours later she arrived home to find a quiet house. Keith was asleep in front of the telly and her mum was upstairs in the bedroom. Alice calmed her shaking body. She didn't want to tell Keith about the scene that had just occurred in the woods unless she absolutely had to.

'Hello,' shouted Alice up the stairs, more out of habit than any expectation that her mum would answer.

'Hello!' came back the reply.

Alice raced up the stairs two at a time, not quite believing what she had heard. Her mum was not in her bedroom but in Alice's room where Alice found her staring at her big poster of Morrissey.

Gina looked her normal dishevelled self and although there had been no miraculous transformation into the old Gina, something about her facial expression told Alice that a sense of interest in her surroundings had begun to re-emerge.

'Who's that?' Gina asked.

'It's a singer called Morrissey,' said Alice.

'Oh,' said her mum and retreated back into her normal silence.

When Keith woke up and shouted up the stairs, Alice raced down to meet him.

'Mum answered me!' she shouted as she ran triumphantly towards Keith and hugged him.

Keith simultaneously managed to think how wonderful this was and also how tragic that the mere answer to this question should elicit such joy.

'So, what's different?' he asked.

Alice looked a bit defensive and said, 'Nothing really.'

Alice wondered if it was time to tell him about Gina's new regime of medication. She felt shaky and damaged after the incident with Mark's dad and a longing to confess nagged at her.

'Alice?' He only needed to use a certain tone of voice and out came every piece of relevant information he needed about what had been going on. Alice detailed the two visits to hospital, and her meetings with Marie Henty, although she left out the bits about promising to facilitate a romance between Marie and her father.

'Alice.' This was an angry voice laced with a tiny shred of concern.

'I'm sorry, Dad,' said Alice, 'but I can't stand it for Mum. And I don't suppose she can stand it either.'

'I know, love,' said Keith wearily. 'All right, we'll try it for a couple of months and we'll see how it goes. If not, she's straight back on her injections.'

'OK,' said Alice. 'Marie Henty's been great, though, Dad. She really does care, you know.'

'Yes,' said Keith, somewhat surprised by this positive reframing of Marie Henty, who for years had seemed to irritate Alice.

'Yes,' Alice went on. 'I had a really long talk with her and she wants the best for Mum like I do – well, she wants the best for all of us, you know.'

Keith's expression of increasing bemusement stopped Alice in her paean to Marie Henty. Realising she was laying it on a bit thick, she said, 'I've got some work to do upstairs, I'll see you later.'

'Okey dokey,' said Keith. 'I'll make us some food. Cheese and toast OK?'

'Fine,' said Alice, smiling to herself. Poor Keith struggled to come up with ideas suitable for a recently spawned vegetarian. Alice climbed the stairs again to find her mother still sitting in her bedroom staring at the poster.

'Tell me some more about Morriston,' she said as Alice came into the room.

'Morrissey,' Alice corrected her. 'Well, why not listen to some of his music and see what you think?'

'OK,' said Gina.

The pair sat on the bed and Alice put on the first Smiths album and they listened all the way through, neither saying a word until Keith came into the room.

'Well, I never,' he said. 'Mum's listening to that Morrissey, is she?'

'I like it,' said Gina. 'He's saying something to me.'

Keith and Alice exchanged half-worried, half-bemused glances.

'Come on then, let's eat,' said Keith and they all went downstairs together like a proper family and sat at the tiny kitchen table with Keith and Alice trying to ignore the fact that Gina was eating like a toddler and managing to get more dinner on her clothes than in her mouth.

About nine o'clock the phone rang and Keith answered it. He held the phone up towards Alice.

'It's Mark,' he said.

Mark was ringing from a call box in the village. Alice took the phone out into the hall and sat tugging the lead as far as it would go while she talked to him.

'I've left home,' said Mark.

'What, forever?' said Alice.

'I haven't really thought that far ahead,' said Mark and he explained that after a trip to casualty where he had been checked over, X-rayed, had a few stitches and his wounds dressed, he had gone back home only to face an avalanche of abuse from his dad, the content of which concentrated mainly on what a disgrace and embarrassment he was to his family.

'What did your mum say?' said Alice.

'Not much,' said Mark. 'She's scared of my dad so although I know she's on my side, she doesn't actually say anything to support me in case it winds him up.'

'Do you want to stay here?' said Alice. 'You can, you know.'

'I'd better not,' said Mark, 'it's the first place my dad'll come looking for me. I'm going to sleep in the woods tonight. Is there any way you can meet me up there and bring me some food? I left the house pretty quickly.'

'Sure,' said Alice. 'Do you mind if I tell my dad about it?'

A silence.

'Not sure,' said Mark. 'Will he cave in and tell my dad where I am?'

'Not a chance,' said Alice.

'All right then,' said Mark, 'but no one else, OK?'

'Not even Karen,' said Alice.

'Especially not Karen,' said Mark. 'She can't keep any sort of secret, as you know.'

'All right,' said Alice. 'Where are you going to be?'

'Do you remember where we built that shelter in the woods round the back of McCabe's farm?' said Mark.

'Course.' Alice's heart somersaulted. It was where she had gone the night of the miscarriage.

'Meet me there in half an hour or so,' said Mark.

'What shall I bring?' said Alice.

'Food, drink, a sleeping bag, torch and a waterproof sheet of some kind if you've got one?'

'I'll see what I can do,' said Alice and went back into the sitting room.

'Dad,' she said, 'Mark's left home for a bit.'

Keith nearly said, 'Sensible boy.' Instead he said, 'Why, what's going on?'

Alice explained, feeling relieved that she didn't have to keep this secret too. Although Keith's face didn't betray any feeling, inside he seethed with hatred towards Phil whom he had always believed to be an ignorant bully.

'He can always come here, you know,' he said to Alice.

'Thanks, Dad,' said Alice, 'but he doesn't want to put you under pressure in case his dad comes here looking for him.'

'I can handle Mark's dad,' said Keith; compared to Bighead and Wobbly, Mark's dad was a lightweight.

'Well, I'll talk to him,' said Alice. 'I said I'd meet him up behind McCabe's.'

'Is he sleeping out?' said Keith.

'Yes,' said Alice.

'Better take some extra blankets,' said Keith and turned back to the telly.

Alice was used to scrunching about in the woods in the dark. She had never felt the fear that many people do of all the unexplained rustlings and calls from birds and foxes, and although a person from a well-lit town would describe the countryside as pitch black, it was not long before she could see where she was going and turned off the torch to conserve the batteries.

As she neared the meeting place to see the father of her lost baby, a huge longing came upon her to tell Mark what had happened, but she knew that this was not an appropriate time, given his other more pressing problems.

'Mark,' she called softly.

'Here,' came the reply and Mark's dirty, slightly tear-stained face appeared from behind a beech tree.

'Give us a hug,' he said. 'I bloody need one.'

They stood there hugging for several minutes and a kiss wasn't too distant a prospect when Mark pulled away and tensed at the sight of a pair of headlights flooding the lane nearest McCabe's, which led down to Alice's cottage.

'Shit, I wonder if that's my dad,' he said.

It wasn't.

Keith had steeled himself for a nasty encounter but the door opened to reveal Marie Henty.

'Is Alice in?' she said.

'No,' answered Keith.

'Great,' said Marie Henty. 'Can we talk?'

Keith motioned towards the sitting room.

Gina sat upstairs in Alice's room and softly crooned 'This Charming Man' to herself.

Chapter 17

Marie Henty just wanted to see Keith. She arrived at the cottage on some spurious pretext, having told herself she must maintain Alice's confidences. She found herself, however, somewhat disappointed that Alice had told Keith everything.

'I think Alice is quite angry with Gina's lot in life,' said Marie, feeling simultaneously that she wanted to put her arms round Keith and rock him backwards and forwards in the squeaky rocking chair, and – rather unsettlingly for a girl from a family of prudish agnostics – that she wanted to fuck his brains out. Even the phrase going through her head strangely excited her and she looked up in alarm towards Keith in the hope that he hadn't picked any of this up.

Of course he hadn't. He sat looking benignly at her face.

'What are the chances of her ever making a recovery?' he said after a few minutes, even though he knew the answer.

'I'm sorry, Keith, they're pretty slim,' said Marie, who had been reading up on Gina's condition. She knew from letters that had been sent to her from the hospital that the doctors in charge of her care had never been sure whether she suffered from paranoid schizophrenia or De Clerambault's syndrome. The fact was that Gina's symptoms had now been so dulled by the amount of chemicals coursing round her system that it was very difficult for anybody to tell what was going on with her.

Poor Gina, Keith found himself thinking. Standing in a huge pit of fog, unable to think, to sparkle or to be what she had been when he first met her. Just like Alice, a part of him wanted Gina to have another chance.

'I can really sympathise with Alice's feelings,' he said to Marie. 'She wants her mum back. She can hardly remember the old Gina but it would be so wonderful if she had the chance to see just what a great woman her mum is.'

Marie's heart started to sink gently. Did he mean that for himself or just for Alice? Did he want his wife back? She would have to try and find out.

Right, she thought to herself. I've loved this man for years, he's had a shit time with his ill wife, bringing up his daughter on his own virtually and there's so much I could give him. I'm going to kiss him because I've got to know one way or the other whether he wants me or not.

She got up, moved towards him in the darkened room.

'Keith,' she said.

'Yes, Marie,' he said.

She couldn't think of anything to say. Instead she put her hands on his face and just managed a glimpse of his nonplussed expression before she pulled his head towards her and touched his mouth very gently with her lips.

'You cunt!'

Gina stood in the doorway clad only in a very scruffy diaphanous nightdress which outlined her figure against the miserable electric light in the hallway.

Keith wanted to say, 'Which one of us are you referring to?' for a joke but knew this might encourage some sort of violent episode, so he said very quietly to Marie, 'I think you'd better go now.'

Marie thought the same and as she walked, trying to look purposeful, towards the door, she realised she would have to run the gauntlet of Gina to get out. Holding her head up in a semblance of innocence, she got her hand on the door handle before she felt a sharp pain in the back of her head. She didn't look back but pulled the door open, ran to her car and drove blindly through the lanes, not even allowing herself to think until she was safely in the emotionally sterile area of her small cottage.

Gina, meanwhile, was laughing hysterically in the bedroom, Morrissey turned to full volume, while Keith sat downstairs thinking about Jane Eyre, waiting for Alice to come in and pondering the implications of the evening's proceedings.

He liked Marie Henty, even quite fancied her, but his feelings over the years had become almost as dampened down as Gina's because he'd had to live for so long denying himself the pleasure of being able to relax and just be content with his life. And had it not been for Gina's illness, he would have been perfectly happy. He loved the brooding, dark nature of the Herefordshire countryside with its bloody history, he liked his undemanding job, his home and his family, and he could have stayed contented for the rest of his life living out an uneventful day-to-day existence full of pleasure at the lack of pressure. Instead, the duress he felt from having to be father, mother and housekeeper to his child had pushed his naturally humorous optimism to the back of his being to be replaced by a weary resignation.

He looked at the clock. Ten past ten. He had supposed Alice would be back a long time before now given that it was cold and slightly damp. Perhaps he should go and look for her and ask Mark to come and stay and bugger the consequences. He wondered if Gina would burn the house down if he went out. He wondered if Marie Henty had gone mad. There was a knock at the door.

Oh God, is it Marie back? What shall I do? What the fuck will Gina do is more to the point, he thought bitterly to himself.

He opened the door to Mark's father.

'Hello, Phil,' he said as neutrally as he could manage. 'What can I do for you?'

'Just tell me if my son is here,' he said wearily.

'No,' said Keith. He wanted to keep the conversation as brief as possible with this alien being.

'I don't believe you, Keith,' said Phil.

'Nothing I can do about that,' said Keith. 'Now excuse me, I'm busy.' He started to shut the door but Phil put a hand up to stop him.

'I want to have a look in the house,' he said.

'Be my guest,' said Keith, opening the door, thinking he wasn't taking a battering from this thug tonight.

Phil stepped into the hall and then Gina, with perfect timing, came to the top of the stairs, now wearing only a very small towel and, for some reason Keith could not fathom, an old hat of his.

'Is it Morrissey?' shouted Gina down the stairs.

Phil looked up at her with an expression of pure terror. He turned to Keith.

'It's all right,' he said, 'I believe you.' He turned and disappeared, calling behind him as he went, 'Let me know if you see him.'

'Not Morrissey,' Keith shouted to Gina, 'more like Meat Loaf.'

Gina seemed happy with that answer and disappeared back into Alice's bedroom and tried to turn the volume up even higher.

Keith was just climbing the stairs to ask her to turn it down when he heard the door go. It was Alice.

'I just saw Mark's dad's car,' she said. 'You didn't tell him, did you?'

'Course not,' said Keith, putting his arm round her. 'How is he?'

Alice didn't really know whether to tell her dad the whole

truth. That Mark was damp, cold, tearful but determined to shun offers of help and comfort.

'He's fine,' she said. 'He'll decide in the next couple of days what to do. I said I'd keep him stocked up with food and drink.'

Much as he hated to hear himself say it because it was an adult thing to say and he didn't really mean it, Keith said, 'Don't you think he'd be better off going home?'

'Dad.' Alice's expression said everything.

'S'pose you're right,' he said.

'How's Mum?' said Alice.

'Slightly odd,' said Keith.

'As opposed to really fine most of the time?' said Alice.

'Oh, you know what I mean,' said Keith. 'Different. More alive. Slightly out of control. She hit Marie Henty.'

'Marie Henty's been here?' said Alice.

'Yes, just to chat about how Mum is,' said Keith, denying the tiny electric ping in his brain.

'That's all?' said Alice. 'No other reason?'

'Like what?' said Keith.

'Oh, nothing,' said Alice, knowing he wouldn't tell her if anything had happened anyway. 'Christ, that's loud,' said Alice, realising she was having to raise her voice. 'Has she been playing it all night?'

'Yes,' said Keith, 'and it's getting on my bloody nerves.'

'Dad, how can you say that?' said Alice. 'It's gorgeous, he's gorgeous, and it's the first thing Mum's shown any interest in for years.'

'Yes, you're right,' said Keith. 'Sorry to be a grump.'

'I'm going to bed,' said Alice. 'I'll see you in the morning.'

That night in bed, Keith lay looking at the ceiling while Gina snored beside him, feeling a little stirring inside that he had not experienced for so long. He felt slightly dirty because of it. He tried to imagine Marie's face and relive the moment she had kissed him so softly on the mouth he had barely felt it. But he just could not conjure up her face and remembered with some shame that when he had first fallen in love with Gina, he could never imagine her face either.

Keith could not deny that Gina seemed to be more alive, more in touch, more alert and more human. But he feared that the consequences of her re-entry back into the human race would be a huge deterioration in her behaviour and ability to control herself. Various clichés arrived in his head – 'a double-edged sword', 'an iron fist in a velvet glove'.

Alice lay thinking of Mark and Morrissey until in her half-waking state the two merged, Morrissey lying pained, crying and lonely in a dark wood without anyone to help or hold him. She began to weep softly and decided she would rescue him and hide him somewhere less dank and inhospitable.

Phil sat up watching television, asking himself over and over again in his head what he had done to deserve such a wet son. 'Probably homosexual too,' he muttered to himself as his wife, devastated by the loss of their only boy, seethed with hatred beside him.

Gina dreamed of Morrissey, astride her, like a great animal grunting and sweating, and called out in her sleep. Keith stroked her arm and murmured, 'It's OK, love,' and she moved out of her dream cycle and down into a deep sleep.

Marie Henty was still awake, endlessly replaying the three seconds it had taken for her to walk across the room and kiss Keith. Each time, a wave of anxiety swept over her and the more she tried to visualise Keith's face, the less she was able.

Chapter 18

Over the course of a few weeks Keith and Alice noticed a marked deterioration in Gina's behaviour. Keith had known this would happen. There was simply no way round the fact that an illness such as Gina's could not be controlled without strong drugs. As her personality struggled out from under the tranquillising effect of her pills, the illness which had hidden beneath the enormous ingestion of chemicals inevitably came with it. It was a relief to both of them in some ways to see the fiery and idiosycratic Gina begin to live again. For many years she had spent endless hours in bed or sat gloomily staring out of the window at the mean little garden; now she rose early, did some things which resembled taking care of her appearance, put her old wellington boots on which hadn't seen the lanes of Herefordshire for years, and began to appear all over the village and at her father's little cottage on regular occasions and without warning. Wobbly and Bighead were not quite sure what to do with her when she turned up because if they were honest with themselves they felt slightly frightened of her, as if she was some contemporary witch with medieval power who could lay a curse on the house and bring them to their knees. She seemed happier but there was no doubt she was madder too.

Despite many reassuring signs of the old Gina, worrying new developments in the way she talked and behaved were an unavoidable accompaniment. She had been to the cottage on three occasions since her medication had been cut down and with each appearance her conversation seemed wilder and more unintelligible, leading them to think that either she was drinking or, in their parlance, 'becoming fucking mental again'.

As children, a constant low-level niggling had gone on between them all, which frequently bubbled over into chaotic violence. Wobbly and Bighead had fought on many occasions, once or twice injuring each other quite badly with hastily picked-up pieces of wood from the garden or anything suitable from the big toy box. The pecking order was established when Gina was about seven. Wobbly was top dog because during one of these fights he had delivered a glancing blow to the side of Bighead's face, drawing blood. It had almost necessitated a visit to the local hospital but Nan Wildgoose's instinct was to let the boys deal with any injuries on their own. Gina had mainly been a bystander when these fights occurred but had somehow felt it important even at that young age that she make her mark and establish some credibility as a family member. So one bright crisp morning when they were standing at the edge of the pond in the clearing up past the dark wood, she pushed the pair of them into the freezing water. They went in with an enormous splash. Neither of them were swimmers and with the shock of the cold water, they were both immediately in trouble.

'Fuck, bollocks, Christ!' shouted Bighead. 'Help us, you shitter!'

Gina moved towards a large strong branch she had prepared earlier for the task.

'All right,' she said. 'I'll let you both grab this if you promise to be nice and not hit me again or put my dolls in the cow shit.'

'Yes!' screamed Wobbly as he disappeared under the water and came up again spluttering and gagging.

'I could push you further out,' shouted Gina, quite enjoying the moment and not really aware that they were a few seconds away from drowning.

'Gina!' Bighead had started to cry in the water. 'I'm going to die!'

'Promise then!' she shouted back.

'We promise,' they screeched together and she man-oeuvred the branch towards them. They climbed shakily on to the bank, both too weak and shocked to grab Gina and give her the beating they wanted to.

With a shriek of delight and a cry of, 'Got you!' Gina ran for it, leaving the shivering pair to make their way home, both too ashamed to admit that their younger sister had got the better of them and even prepared to risk a number ten walloping from their mum rather than admit their humiliation.

From that day onwards they treated Gina with a grudging respect and very seldom bullied or whacked her. If she was prepared to drown them to move up the pecking order, Wobbly and Bighead weren't going to mess with her.

This very memory coursed through Wobbly's head as he saw Gina walking purposefully up the rutted dirt track towards the cottage. Bighead, who was out the back chopping some logs, had also seen her. He tended not to have memories like his brother. Wobbly was the more sensitive of the two. Bighead tried not to think about the past at all because he did not like the sensation of nostalgia and regret that flooded over him and made his eyes moisten. In Bighead's book, men didn't behave like this, they did things but they didn't have feelings. Feelings were for homosexuals and women. Consequently he very rarely let slip any sign that he had experienced an emotion at all, unless it was anger or frustration, something well up the manly end of the spectrum.

'Gina!' he called. 'What you doing up this way?'

'I've come to talk to you about someone called Morrissey,' said Gina.

'That poof fucker,' said Bighead. 'What about him?'

'You know him?' said Gina, surprised.

'Course I bloody do,' said Bighead. 'It was 'im what Alice went to see the night with Mam when she died.'

'Really?' said Gina, as if this was news to her.

'For Christ's sake, Gina,' said Wobbly, coming out of the front door. 'Don't you remember?'

Gina stood thinking for a bit.

'Not really,' she said. 'When was that?'

'Be about four years now,' said Bighead, not one for anniversaries.

'Really?' said Gina again as if her mother's death was something akin to a slight mishap instantly forgotten.

The implications of Gina's reaction to their words hit both brothers; up to this point they hadn't really taken on board just how much damage Gina's so-called illness had done. Neither of them was overtly sentimental about their mother but they had loved her in an instinctive way and were both shocked Gina seemed so unconcerned.

'Mum's dead,' said Wobbly.

'I know, you said,' said Gina irritably and that was the last mention of their mother that day.

Luckily Bert had heard none of this as he would have been heartbroken to think his mad daughter's madness had progressed this far. He lay snoozing upstairs waiting for Wobbly or Bighead to bring him some tea the colour of oxtail soup and their customary huge chunk of badly buttered bread and jam.

'Anyway,' said Gina, 'Morrissey would be well pissed off with you two calling him names. All right, he looks a bit weird and too feminine, but he is very intelligent and his songs are all directed towards me, you know.'

'How does that work?' said Wobbly, genuinely interested in how Gina could have come up with this statement.

'I don't know how it works,' said Gina, 'but I just feel that he's trying to tell me something.'

'You and a million others,' said Bighead. 'He's trying to tell you he wants your fucking money.'

'*No!*' Gina screamed. 'You don't understand, you stupid thick bloody tossers. Christ, is there no one I can talk to about this without getting a load of shit back?'

'I would've thought Alice would talk to you about 'im seeing as she likes 'im too,' said Wobbly.

Gina's eyes narrowed. 'That's exactly why I can't talk to Alice, you knobhead,' she said. 'Alice wouldn't like it if she knew about our special bond.'

Because Gina was a good six inches smaller than her brothers, they were able to converse in soundless sentences over the top of her head.

'She's talking bollocks,' mouthed Bighead.

'What the fuck shall we do?' replied Wobbly.

'Send her home then we can talk.'

They came up with some spurious reason why Gina couldn't stay. She went along with this, if rather disgruntled by the fact that neither of them was prepared to discuss the centre of her universe with her. Wobbly walked with her down to the gate.

'Do you think I've got a chance with him?' she asked, turning to face Wobbly.

'Dunno,' said Wobbly disinterestedly, but inside he was

saying, 'Jesus fucking Christ.' He realised he preferred the damped down Gina, whose sole ambition in life, it seemed, was to make her fingers yellower with nicotine.

The brothers' discussion consisted of saying to each other, 'She's mental,' a few times.

Finally Wobbly said, 'Shall we talk to Keithy boy?'

'Do we have to?' replied Bighead. 'Let's leave it a few weeks and see what happens.'

'All right,' replied his brother. 'Shall we go to the pub then?'

'Yeah,' came the reply.

Similar turmoil was occurring in Mark's life. He had lasted three nights in the open and finally been defeated by sheer boredom. Visiting him on the third day, Alice noticed a considerable downturn in his mood.

'You can't stay here, Mark,' she said. 'What are you going to do?'

Mark honestly didn't know. He was fed up with having to even think about his situation and just wished he could turn back the clock and slip once more into the uneasy dishonest relationship with his father, protected most of the time by his mum. He wondered whether he should leave college and get a job. Mark had fantasised about walking into an army recruiting office in Hereford and being immediately accepted by the SAS as it would be apparent to them straight away that he was a fine specimen, rugged and capable. He knew the reality was different, though, and someone who was sensitive, liked reading and could only last three days on his own in the woods probably wasn't what they were looking for. The only thing he was sure about was that he didn't want to go crawling back home like a guilty dog to be further abused by his master.

'Come round to our place for a decent meal,' urged Alice, 'and then you can stay tonight and we can sit and discuss a plan.'

'What about my dad?' said Mark. 'Isn't he likely to turn up?'

'He's not been round since my mum scared him off,' said Alice with a rueful laugh. 'I think you're safe.'

So they tidied up Mark's makeshift camp and headed down the hill towards Alice's house. Keith was still out at work and Gina was not there. Strolling round the countryside talking her nonsense to anyone who will listen, thought Alice.

'It's really weird,' she said as they sat down with a cup of tea. 'My mum has really got into Morrissey since she came off her drugs,'

'Does that make her madder or saner?' said Mark, hoping that Gina would stay out all evening and he wouldn't have to face this woman about whom he'd heard so much.

'Saner in my book,' said Alice. 'She's still a bit odd but since she stopped her injections she's got some of her old self back, though she sometimes talks rubbish and does weird things.'

'What sort of weird things?' said Mark, not really wanting to know but at the same time fascinated.

'Well, she keeps trying to hide her Morrissey crush from me.'

'Perhaps she's embarrassed,' said Mark.

Alice made a snorting noise. 'My fucking mother has never been embarrassed in her entire life,' she said. 'I have my suspicions that maybe it's something going on inside, you know . . .' She pointed to her head.

Mark was on shaky ground here. He didn't know anything about mental illness, let alone any specifics about schizophrenia; like most people he thought schizophrenia was a multiple personality condition.

'I'm sure she'll get better,' he said, more in hope than anything else.

'Fucking hell, Mark,' said Alice bitterly. 'She'll never get better. People with this never do. I've read about it. The best we can hope for is to find some sort of happy medium between her being a fucking blob and a maniac.'

'I'm sorry,' said Mark. 'I don't know what I'm talking about.'

'I'm sorry too,' said Alice. 'I didn't mean to snap. I don't think most people are ever going to understand because they're too scared or uninterested. Anyway, let's talk about what you're going to do.'

'Well, I'm not going back home,' said Mark. 'That would mean I have to be the sort of person my dad wants me to be and I just don't know if I can live like that, listening to all the shit he talks about politics, about women – about everything.'

'You'll have to get a job then,' said Alice. 'You'll have to give up college.'

'Yes,' said Mark. 'For now anyway. A friend of my mum's runs a shop in Ludlow, they're always looking for people to help out there.'

'So we'll have to work out a way for you to get hold of your mum,' said Alice.

Alice waited outside the village shop the following morning and when she saw Mark's mum's little blue car approaching, she steeled herself because she didn't have any idea what reaction she'd get. The car drew to a halt and Mark's mum got out. Normally she was immaculately turned out with spotless clothes and a face which had had at least half an hour spent on it. But that veneer had vanished in the three days Mark had been away, for not only was she mourning the loss of her son but she'd had to weather the unpredictable rages of her husband as he oscillated between 'leaving the bastard to get on with it' or 'calling that fucking useless excuse for a policeman to go and look for him'.

'Hello,' said Alice.

'Oh Alice.' She began began to cry. 'Have you seen him? Is he OK? Where is he? What's he doing?' The desperate questions spewed out almost in relief.

'He's OK,' said Alice. 'I need to talk to you. Shall we walk?'

Alice went through what she had agreed she would say. By the end of the conversation, Mark's mother had agreed she would talk to the friend in Ludlow, not tell Mark's father and drop off some cash for Mark to survive in a cheap B and B for a couple of weeks until he found a job.

'Can't he come home?' she asked sadly.

Alice shook her head. 'I don't think so. I'm sorry.'

'His dad's not as bad as you think, you know,' said Mark's mum. But they both knew that wasn't really true.

Alice agreed she would call Mark's mum as soon as Mark was settled and at that point they could negotiate between themselves as to whether they might meet.

Mark and Alice went to Ludlow that weekend and met the friend of Mark's mum, who predictably offered him a part-time job in the little shop. The two then sat in a cafe with the local paper and ringed all the possibles in the accommodation section.

Within two days a very small, grimy room had been found; it was the kind of room that would make Mark's mother burst into tears but it was affordable.

Alice spent Mark's first day at his new accommodation with him to try and banish the gloom and grime. She bought scented candles and covered the walls with a few Morrissey posters, despite Mark's protests. After cooking him a celebratory vegetarian breakfast of scrambled eggs and beans, they decided to head forth into the nice bit of Ludlow and browse around the market. As they approached, they heard laughter and noticed a large crowd gathered round someone.

'Oh God, please don't let it be a juggler,' said Mark in mock alarm.

Alice smiled and the pair squeezed in between the laughing, fascinated crowd to see what the attraction was.

The attraction was Gina, who had somehow acquired a guitar from somewhere and was sitting on a stool dressed in a loose white shirt, NHS glasses, a bunch of gladioli stuffed into the back of a pair of Keith's trousers, and her hair in a pretty bad attempt at a quiff. She was making a very bad fist of 'William It Was Really Nothing' and Alice was put in mind of stories she had read in history books of mental hospitals where the public paid to go and look at the mentally ill for entertainment.

'What do you want to do?' whispered Mark.

'Just disappear,' Alice said hoping that no one in the crowd had made the connection between herself and the obviously disturbed woman on the stool with the guitar. But it was too late. A face she knew well from school turned with a sneer towards her. Stephen Matthews, the school's most accomplished bully, looked at her with a mixture of sadism and amusement.

'Still cracked, I see,' he said and the group round him joined in with his loud laugh.

Chapter 19

Mark threw a punch at Stephen and Stephen's yobby friends attempted to make short work of Mark in return. Alice got stuck in and put herself between Mark and the group of evil-smelling ne'er-do-wells that Stephen counted as his friends, in the expectation that they would not hit a girl. Either they were blinded by excitement or less moral than Alice had hoped because a fist hit her in the stomach and another one caught the side of her face. A few stallholders decided that a girl being used as a punchbag by a gang of youths was socially reprehensible and joined in and, hey presto, a fully fledged fight began.

For once Alice hoped for the appearance of Bighead and Wobbly who were remarkably accomplished at this sort of thing. Unfortunately they were still in bed at home following a night out in the pub and both snored on, oblivious of the distressed maiden Alice felt herself to be.

Eventually a few languid policemen spilled out of a car on the fringes of the scene and peace was restored. During the fight, Gina had managed to slip away unnoticed. As policemen turned to various culprits to ask them what had started it all, they pointed vainly around, trying to locate the strangely dressed woman. Some policemen began to think she may have been a figment of their imagination. Gina slunk through the alley beside the Butter Cross building, divesting herself of the more extreme elements of her costume, realising even in her disturbed state that it was advisable perhaps to merge into the background of shoppers and traders.

Eventually Stephen and his friends were cautioned after Alice and Mark said they didn't want to press charges, and their departure from the scene was supervised by an overweight policeman with a stubby beard just in case ill feeling caused another outbreak of belligerence. An old woman coming out of the chemist's jumped and let out a little squeak as she nearly stepped on what she thought was an injured kitten. She bent down to take a closer look and realised it was an inanimate object. She held it up to her bespectacled eyes, wondering how on earth an Elvis wig could possibly have found its way to this sliver of pavement in the centre of Ludlow.

Mark and Alice wandered back to the grimy room, feeling shocked and hurting. Alice bore the beginnings of a black eye and Mark was feeling distinctly put out that he had been beaten twice in a couple of weeks. But as they sat in front of the small black and white portable TV that Alice had brought from her bedroom, Gina was the sole topic of conversation.

'Where do you think she's gone?' said Mark eventually after they had sat staring at the local news for some minutes.

'Christ knows,' said Alice, 'but we'd better find her soon because I've made a mistake and she's really ill again.' She started to cry. 'All I wanted to do was give her a taste of real life,' she said through her tears. 'Oh God, Mark, I must have been mad.'

'Well, *she* definitely is,' said Mark, trying to lighten the situation. It only made Alice cry harder.

That night, under a full moon, a woman called Grace was driving through the Shropshire countryside on her way from London to see her parents for a few days. She'd had a stressful week. Her job as a social worker in child protection had left a trail of unfinished work, angry clients and even angrier bosses. But as her car struggled up Clee Hill in the moonlight, her spirits began to lift. She knew that once she crested the hill, she would freewheel down into an area which to her was untouched by modern life. She could leave her burning, negative thoughts at the top of the hill and soak up the therapeutic rustic rhythms of the countryside down in the sheltered valley.

Sheep stood dead-eyed along the road and she slowed to make sure she didn't hit one as it ambled across the deserted ribbon of tarmac in search of more interesting grass. She passed through the sprawling village noting the landmarks, the viewing point, the chippie, the high-set Edwardian villas which gazed towards the Black Mountains. She often arrived at this very late hour in an attempt to avoid sitting in traffic on the beleaguered motorway. She became aware of some movement ahead of her. She blinked her tired eyes, having forgotten her driving glasses, and wondered if she was so exhausted she was hallucinating. She wasn't hallucinating. A seated figure appeared to be bouncing towards her in the middle of the road. An invisible hand clutched her heart and a welter of fear shot through her. Almost unconsciously, she pressed the little button on the car door, locking herself in, in case her progress was somehow halted by this strange apparition. As the figure bounced closer, she realised it was a woman, wild hair streaming out behind her, dressed in men's clothes. Impossible to tell her age, though. She dropped her speed down to twenty and as she drew almost level, she realised the laughing figure was sitting on a spacehopper, one of those big, orange, rubber, bouncy balls with ears to hold on to, something she'd had when she and her brothers were younger.

And then she was past it. She checked her mirror, but even with the help of the moon, it revealed nothing but a black rectangle, with no clue that she had passed anything alive.

Bloody hell, what the fuck was that? she said to herself, in an attempt to steady and comfort her nerves.

She then began a dialogue in her head as to what action

she should take. What on earth was someone like that doing out at this time of night, let alone dressed in men's clothes and on a spacehopper, for Christ's sake? Was she pissed or mad? Pissed probably, found a spacehopper in the garden at a party and decided to have a bit of a laugh. Yes, that was it.

Still, as she drove on, her thoughts began to niggle at her, making her feel anxious. There hadn't been any evidence of a party, all the houses seemed to be sleeping with their occupants. What if the woman was ill? What if one of those massive trucks that thundered down that road in the middle of the night didn't see her and hit her? She had a vision of the woman and the spacehopper flying up in the air. A phone box approached on the side of the road. She found herself pulling in. 'Better let the cops know,' she said aloud and her voice frightened her. It was now very dark, as the moon had concealed itself behind some cloud, and her childhood imagination took root and began to flower. She saw herself trapped in the phone box by a murderer, a werewolf . . . Anything could be out there.

She pressed down on the accelerator and pulled away, trying to still the guilty voice inside her that accused her of not giving a shit.

Keith sat huddled in front of the television and glanced at the clock. Two a.m. and still no sign of Gina. Alice had phoned him from a call box in Ludlow and told him what had happened in the market square and how worried she was. Keith had driven over there in his van and scoured the environs of Ludlow, touching the many areas he knew Gina loved, High Vinnalls, the castle, Ludlow racecourse and Clee Hill, but there had been no sign of her. He wondered if he should call the police. Perhaps he should call Marie Henty. Maybe even Wobbly and Bighead. He shuddered at the thought of getting those two great wanton behemoths out of their beds. He was worried that the police would laugh at him, Marie Henty would see it as a come-on and Wobbly and Bighead would hit him. But he was so desperate for someone to talk to, eventually he plumped for Marie and bugger the consequences.

'Keith,' a sleepy voice said in response to his initial apology about waking her.

'I'm worried about Gina,' he said.

Marie had been dreaming about being kissed by Simon Le Bon, not someone she'd ever really taken any notice of, and was glad to be pulled away from this slobbery and unpleasant experience.

'Shall I come over?' she said.

'Well, she's not here so there's no point really,' said Keith.

There's every point, thought Marie Henty, but didn't say it.

They chatted for several minutes, running over recent events, the improvements and yet concurrent deterioration in Gina's mental state, and agreed that they would meet the next day and work out a plan of action to get Gina back into hospital and stabilised.

As Keith put the phone down, he realised that talking to

Marie had made him experience a mixture of good emotions: reassured, less anxious, happy even. He sat for half an hour longer in the chair, running images of her and their encounters through his mind until, smiling, he fell asleep with the television on and the applewood in the grate still fizzing and crackling.

Gina lay in a barn just off the A49, covered with sacking and shivering. An owl hooted and seemed to say, 'Go home.' The voices in her head became more animated. 'She doesn't want to go home,' one said. 'They hate her there.' 'Tell her to stay away from home,' said the other voice. 'They want to lock her up.'

For once Gina didn't have to push her hands over her ears and scream at them to shut up. Exhaustion and hunger were blessedly snuffed out together as she dropped into a sleep which carried her through a few more painful hours on earth.

In the morning when she woke, stiff and cold, her uppermost feelings were physical. She had a pee in the corner of the barn and set off towards the village, desperate for something to eat.

It will have to be Doug's shop, she thought grimly to herself. It's the nearest.

The two voices set up a little round of singing in her head. 'She's going to Doug's shop,' they sang tunelessly. 'Silly bitch! Silly bitch!'

It was seven o'clock in the morning and Doug was laying out the papers in neat rows along the shelf.

The door opened to reveal Gina in a state of disarray.

With his practised eye, Doug did not see just a mad, scary woman, he saw an emotionally disturbed, frightened unmedicated outpatient who desperately needed to be an inpatient.

'I'm hungry, Dougie,' said Gina in a child's voice. 'Help me please.'

Doug thought he could buy time by making some breakfast and trying to get on the phone to Keith while Gina was eating. He took her through to his little back kitchen and sat her down, popped two slices of white bread into the toaster and flicked the kettle switch down.

'Where have you been, Gina?' he said pleasantly, as if he was asking her about her holidays.

'Dunno,' said Gina, staring at the toaster and wanting it to disgorge its booty.

'Does Keith know where you are?'

'Dunno,' said Gina. 'Where's my fucking toast?'

The bell on the shop door tinkled.

'Hang on, Gina,' said Doug. 'I'll just see who that is.'

'Better not be the fucking Gestapo,' said Gina, whose hunger was still overriding the urgent voices in her head telling her to get out of there.

It was Mrs Langforth from the little cottage on the outskirts who managed a brisk walk there and back every morning, despite being well into her eighties.

'There you go,' said Doug, handing her a *Daily Mail* and thinking, enjoy having all your prejudices reinforced, you old bag.

He walked back into the kitchen where Gina seemed to have lapsed into catatonia and buttered the toast.

'Marmalade or jam?' he asked politely, continuing the fantasy that she'd come round for a social breakfast.

Gina didn't answer but rose, grabbed the two slices of toast from his hand and tried to stuff all of it into her mouth at once.

'Bloody hell,' said Doug, 'you must be starving. Sit down, I'll make you some more – and some tea,' he added, noticing her dry, cracked lips.

He put some tea bags into the teapot and put more bread in the toaster.

'Just going for a piss,' he said cheerfully.

He ran into the little front room and dialled Keith's number. Keith answered immediately.

'Keith, she's here,' he said. 'Come and help.'

'On my way,' said Keith and Doug heard the receiver crash into its cradle.

He walked back into the kitchen, only to find an empty seat and an open door.

'Shit,' he said and ran outside, looking desperately in both directions. In front of Mrs Langforth, running for all she was worth, was Gina, heading for Wales.

Doug broke into a run, passing Mrs Langforth, whose progress back home was always at half the speed of her outward journey.

Despite all the years of major tranquillisers and no exercise, the memory of the days when she could run faster than not only all the girls in her class at school but the boys too had stayed with Gina. However, Doug, whose bulky body constantly let him down, was fired with the adrenalin of his work memories and knew that he had to grab her now or they might not see her in one piece again. He managed to grab the tail of Gina's jacket, causing her to trip and fall to the ground, half in and half out of the hedgerow.

Doug pounced and landed on top of Gina as she tried to grab a tree stump and pull herself up.

Mrs Langforth, about twenty yards away, gaped at them shortsightedly. Doug looked like some marauding, pillaging Norseman intent on getting his woman. She began to increase her speed, shouting as she went, 'Stop it, young man, stop it!'

Gina and Doug were rolling on the ground, Gina screaming, 'Get off me, you fat fuck! Piss off and leave me alone.'

Mrs Langforth reached the thrashing pair and brought her walking stick, fashioned with the silver head of a pheasant, cracking down on Doug's head.

'I told you to get off her!' she shouted by way of explanation.

As Doug lay stunned and throbbing in the ditch, Gina made her escape and a smile of satisfaction spread across Mrs Langforth's face.

'What did you do that for?' said Doug. 'She's not well, I'm trying to hold on to her until her husband gets here and we're going to take her to hospital.'

'Oh, why didn't you say?' said Mrs Langforth. 'I could have helped.'

Doug swore under his breath and looked down the road. Gina had disappeared. She must have got to the crossroads. Which way had she gone? Anybody's guess.

Keith drew up in his van as Doug was heading back to the shop.

'Sorry,' said Keith, winding the window down. 'Bloody van wouldn't start, had to get some WD40.'

'She's legged it,' said Doug. 'Couldn't stop her, and that old bird Langforth cracked me on the head with her bloody walking stick, thought I was attacking Gina.'

'Sorry,' said Keith again, but this time because he was starting to laugh.

'Yeah, yeah, very funny,' said Doug, rubbing his head ruefully.

'Shall we get after her then?' said Keith.

'Shit,' said Doug. 'I've left the shop unattended. Let me get someone to cover. You have a look now, she can't have got far, and come back and get me in half an hour.'

'All right,' said Keith. 'You haven't got a shotgun, have you, Doug?'

Doug looked slightly alarmed. 'What for?'

'Thought I'd finish off Langforth for you.' Keith grinned and pulled away.

For the next couple of hours, Keith and Doug zigzagged backwards and forwards between Shropshire and Herefordshire in a vain search for Gina, who despite her disturbed state was proving extremely adept at hiding.

Eventually, Doug turned to Keith and said, 'Shall we have a pint and make a plan?'

'Okey dokey,' said Keith. 'And I'll call Marie Henty to come and join the discussion.'

Marie Henty arrived at the pub within five minutes and ordered herself a Dubonnet and lemonade.

'Drinking on duty?' said Doug, one eyebrow slightly raised.

'Shut it, Doug,' said Marie. 'Extenuating circumstances.'

'Right,' said Keith. 'We need someone to wait at the cottage in case she comes back, someone to go and tell her brothers she's on the loose and to hold on to her, and someone to drive round looking for her. OK, any volunteers to wait at the cottage?'

'Yes,' said Doug and Marie together.

'I think perhaps Marie,' said Keith. 'No disrespect but we probably need a bit of brute strength when we catch up with her.'

'OK,' said Marie, 'but what about Alice, couldn't she do it?'

'She's not there,' said Keith, 'but obviously when she gets back, you can come and join in.' He turned to Doug. 'Do you want to go and see Wobbly and Bighead then?'

'You're fucking joking, aren't you?' said Doug. 'They'll kill me.'

'They'll kill me too,' said Keith gloomily.

'Tell you what,' said Doug, 'let's go together and then we'll go and look some more.'

'Should we tell the police?' asked Marie. 'I mean, it might be useful for them to keep a lookout.'

'S'pose so,' said Keith. 'All right, Marie, can you call them?'

'Will do,' said Marie.

Keith's van rumbled up the track towards the Wildgoose smallholding and as he always did at the sound of anyone approaching, Bighead appeared to see who it was.

As they pulled up, he went over to the car.

'Well, bugger me if it isn't Butch Cassidy and the Sundance Kid,' he said. 'Although neither of you's exactly butch, are yer?'

Doug giggled nervously like a schoolgirl while Keith tried to maintain the demeanour of a grown-up.

'What's happened to your 'ead?' said Bighead, looking at the ostentatious sticking plaster Doug had applied.

'Mrs Langforth hit him with her walking stick,' said Keith without thinking, and then seeing Doug's thunderous look and realising the endless possibilities for piss-taking, he mouthed, 'Sorry.'

Bighead let out a huge throaty laugh which degenerated into an explosive phlegmy cough that nearly doubled him up.

'Oi, Wobs!' he shouted when he caught his breath. 'Come 'ere, we have a victim of extreme violence.'

Wobbly appeared from the outside toilet, pulling up his trousers.

Bighead pointed to Doug's head and spluttered, 'Langforth done that with her walking stick!'

'Yes, all right,' said Doug. 'Can we get on with why we came?'

'Some fighting lessons?' said Bighead. 'How to pound an old lady? Wrestling a baby? How to keep a teeny weeny little kitten under control?'

The brothers laughed heartily, holding their crotches to communicate to Doug that they were in danger of pissing themselves.

Keith and Doug gritted their teeth and waited for them to finish pulling faces and punching each other in the arm and doing impressions of old women.

'We've come about Gina,' said Keith at last.

'Oh, right,' said Bighead. 'What about 'er?'

'She's really not well and we need to get her into hospital again.'

This time the brothers didn't protest, given Gina's recent behaviour and their total inability to fathom it, let alone deal with it.

It was decided that Wobbly and Bighead would also go out and search for Gina, and local areas were allocated to them.

'Bring her to our cottage if you find her.'

'OK,' the brothers chorused meekly, which was probably the first time in their lives they hadn't been combative towards Keith.

Gina, meanwhile, was becoming ever more distressed. She had been wandering about on the outskirts of the village for some time, confused and frightened, and had decided that the only two people who could save her were Jesus and Morrissey. A pilgrimage to Manchester seemed out of the question even to Gina, so she slipped quietly into the church to try and find her saviour. But the church was empty, dark and cold. Her footsteps echoed round its huge expanse. The relief she had expected to discover there was nowhere to be found. She called, 'Help me, Jesus, please come here and help me.' Echoing silence. Maybe something louder was needed. Gina climbed the bell tower to the little chamber where the ropes were neatly hooked to the wall. She snatched a rope free and began to pull on it with all her might, expecting help to come. The bell had been left in the down position and a professional ringer would have brought it up to rest on the wooden stay in readiness for ringing. But Gina didn't know this and the harder she pulled, the higher she flew with the rope until she was a good twenty feet in the air. Something about this was exhilarating and she screamed with excitement, lost in the rhythm of it all, until she became aware of the figures of Doug and her husband staring in disbelief at her swinging form. She couldn't hold on much longer and let go . . . landing on the pre-positioned heap of Doug and Keith.

'Gina,' said Keith. 'Time to go home.'

Chapter 20

Alice was sitting by the fire when Keith and Doug arrived with Gina who was alternately protesting vehemently and singing hymns and Morrissey songs. They brought her into the house between them like two security guards.

Marie Henty was on her way and had called an ambulance to meet them at the house. The ambulance centre had told her there would be a wait of about two hours. When he heard this, Keith's heart sank. How would they contain Gina for that length of time? Doug offered to stay in case there were any escape attempts and the four sat together in the sitting room, with Gina glowering at them.

'Gina,' said Keith. 'Dr Henty has organised an ambulance to take you to hospital. We're very sorry this has happened, because in a way it's our fault. We just wanted to see how you were without too much medication and it hasn't worked and we wish it had.'

'Reel around the fountain, smack me on the patio,' sang Gina.

'It's "slap", Mum,' said Alice, unable to let this minor slip go.

'Reel around the fountain, fuck me on the patio.' Gina upped the volume to an almost unbearable level.

'Mm, that's a nice song,' said Doug. 'Who's that by then? Des O'Connor?'

Gina glared at him and then stood up and started to scream.

'Oh God, can we cope with two hours of this?' said Keith quietly.

'I have to cope with a whole fucking lifetime of it!' Gina shouted in his face. 'Just let me be on my own.'

'Do you want to go in my bedroom, Mum, and listen to some Smiths?' said Alice, desperately thrashing around for some way to calm her mother.

Gina nodded like an acquiescent five-year-old and put her thumb in her mouth.

'Come on then,' said Alice. 'I'll come with you,'

'No, I want to go on my own,' said Gina.

Alice's stomach churned minutely when she thought of all the precious Morrissey objects in her room.

'OK,' she said tentatively. 'I'll bring you a cup of tea in a minute.'

Gina climbed the stairs and disappeared into Alice's room and then there was silence.

'Oh God, this is worse in a way,' said Keith. 'What do you think she's doing?'

'Go and have a look through the keyhole, Dad,' said Alice. 'I don't want her to ruin anything.'

'All right,' said Keith. He tiptoed up the stairs and knelt to place one eye against the keyhole.

Alice and Doug stood at the bottom of the stairs waiting for news.

'She's eating something,' said Keith in a stage whisper.

'But there's no food in there,' said Alice. 'What does it look like?'

'A piece of paper,' said Keith. 'Maybe a letter?'

'Oh Jesus!' Alice took the stairs two at a time and flung open her bedroom door to see the final scraps of her letter from Morrissey disappearing into her mother's mouth.'

'Oh Mum,' she shouted. 'How could you? My most loved and precious thing.' She launched herself at Gina and grabbed what paper she could from her mother's mouth. Gina began to laugh hysterically.

Keith stood helplessly in the doorway as Alice sat on her bed and cried, clutching a tiny saliva-covered piece of paper with some writing on it, and his wife stared out of the window, laughing uncontrollably.

'Fuck, Dad,' said Alice through her tears. 'She's eaten the only thing that means something to me.'

Keith wanted to laugh, even though he was desperately sad for Alice.

'Never mind, love,' he said as if she'd grazed her knee in the playground.

Gina turned to them. 'He's inside me now,' she said, 'and no one can get him out.'

At a loss to know what to say or do next, Keith was relieved to hear a knock on the door. He went downstairs, followed by a disconsolate Alice. It hardly mattered what her mother did now, it couldn't be any worse than what she'd already done.

Please let it be the ambulance, Keith said to himself as he opened the door.

'Surprise!' His parents were standing on the doorstep, his mother with her arms outstretched. 'We came out for a drive in the country, love, and Norman said we should make a detour to see you, didn't you, love?' She turned to Keith's dad with a flourish as if they were in a play and it was now his turn to speak.

'Yes, dear,' said his dad.

'Mum, Dad,' said Keith, 'it's lovely to see you but I'm afraid it's not a good time. Gina's very ill and we're waiting for an ambulance to come. This is Doug, a friend of ours who's been helping. Say hello to Nan and Grandad, Alice. Maybe another day, Mum?'

But Jennifer was not to be deterred. Sailing into the cottage like a nylon armada, as if the last and only time she'd been there wasn't sixteen years ago, she said, 'We won't be any trouble, honestly. I'll just put the kettle on and make Norman a sandwich, he hasn't eaten for a couple of hours and you know what his digestion's like.'

Keith didn't, thankfully, and he realised that his mother

was not going to be put off by the mere presence of a seriously disturbed woman.

'Have you got any liver pâté?' said Jennifer, continuing her progress towards the kitchen. 'Norman loves that.'

'I do,' said Norman, patting his stomach.

As Keith foolishly asked himself the fate-tempting question, 'Can this get any worse?' Wobbly and Bighead exploded through the front door.

'Is she here?' said Bighead.

'Yes,' said Keith, retreating into monosyllables.

'Keith, this bread is days old,' said Jennifer, re-emerging from the kitchen massaging a perfectly good loaf. 'And where's the Hoover, dear? Oh heavens.' The sight of Wobbly and Bighead stopped her in her tracks. 'How lovely to see you two boys.'

Their expressions betrayed the fact that they had absolutely no idea who this woman was, having met her only once at Gina and Keith's wedding, during which Wobbly and Bighead had only taken notice of those guests they could have sex with or beat up.

''Ow do,' said Wobbly, and Bighead released a very loud fart.

'Better out than in,' said Norman.

Jennifer looked as if she might faint.

'Too right, mate,' said Bighead and slapped Norman heartily on the back, making him fear for the continued well-being of his ribs.

'Right, who wants tea? Hands up,' said Jennifer, rallying bravely.

Everyone raised their hands.

'Would Gina like one?' said Jennifer.

Jennifer's response to any crisis was to make a cup of tea, whether it was for a visiting friend or a daughter-in-law with chronic schizophrenia in the acute phase of her illness. Norman had always assumed that given half a chance Jennifer would have popped into Hitler's bunker and offered him a cup of PG Tips.

'Hmm,' said Doug quietly to Keith. 'Tea as a cure for schizophrenia, it might just work.'

'No muttering amongst yourselves,' said Jennifer. 'Come on, lay the table, Keith, and I'll knock up some rock buns to go with our tea, as you don't appear to have any biscuits in your tin.'

And she did. Within twenty minutes tea had been made, cakes had appeared on plates and everyone stood around as though life was completely mundane.

'I'll just pop a cuppa up to poor Gina,' said Jennifer. 'In bed, is she?' as if she had flu.

'I'd better do it,' said Keith. 'She's in Alice's room.'

'No, it's all right, dear,' said Jennifer. 'Haven't seen poor Gina in an age, we'll have plenty to chat about.'

Bloody hell, thought Keith. Absence does make the heart grow fonder. I wonder if my mother has early-onset Alzheimer's.

Jennifer tripped up the stairs like a teenager, humming a tune from *The Sound Of Music*.

'Hello, Gina dear,' she called. 'Tea.'

She entered Alice's room. Gina had torn the big Morrissey poster from the wall and stuck her head through it.

Jennifer decided to ignore this and put the tray on a chest of drawers.

'So how are you?' she said.

Gina sang, 'It's time that the tale were told of how you took a boy and you made him old.'

'Nice tune, dear,' said Jennifer pleasantly, 'but I think you'll find that you're the one who's made my poor Keith old before his time. Do you ever spare him a thought in all this . . . this . . . this . . . disorderliness, dear?'

Gina snorted and launched into the chorus.

'We'll talk later,' said Jennifer. 'Try a rock bun, Gina. Everyone at the bridge club swears by them.' She left the room, shaking her head.

Gina did try a rock bun – as a missile. She had spotted Marie Henty's car arrive and as Marie climbed out of it, a couple of rock buns whistled past her ears.

'Piss off,' shouted Gina. 'We're having a nice time without you.'

This cut right to the heart of Marie Henty's deepest fear, that eveyone did have a better time without her and people said things like, 'Oh shit, here comes Marie Henty, now the party'll take a nosedive.'

She nearly got back into her car, but as she turned she saw an ambulance crawling up the road, seemingly in no hurry.

'After all, it's only a fucking nutty bird,' as Gil the driver had remarked to his partner, Shaz.

The ambulance stopped a few inches behind Marie Henty's car and Gil wound down the window.

'Nutter patrol,' he said cheerily, saluting Marie.

'That's rather unprofessional,' she said. 'I could have been a relative or indeed the patient herself.'

'Sorry, love,' said Gil. 'Only having a laugh.'

'You'd better come in with me then,' said Marie. 'I'm Gina's GP.'

Gil noticeably stiffenened in his seat and muttered, 'GP,' out of the side of his mouth at Shazzer, who mentally put on her professional hat too. The pair descended from the ambulance.

Keith opened the door and relief swept over his face when he saw the trio.

'Great,' he said. 'Let's get going then.'

Jennifer appeared behind him.

'Hello,' she said. 'I'm Keith's mother, Jennifer.'

'Marie Henty, GP,' said Marie.

What a lovely young woman, Jennifer found herself thinking. If only Keith could have married someone like her.

Keith and Doug went up to Alice's bedroom and found her still wearing the Morrissey poster.

'Come on, love,' said Keith. 'The ambulance is here, we need to go.'

In the deepest part of her Gina knew it was the right thing and if she was honest with herself, the fight had gone out of her. She pulled the poster off and stood up. Keith handed her a little bag containing some toiletries and clothes he had packed for her. He put one of his old jackets round her shoulders and she smelt him sitting round her like a protective cape and smiled as a part of her remembered how it had been right at the beginning. Then she was assaulted by how it was now and tears began to roll down her cheeks.

'Don't worry, sweetheart,' said Keith. 'Let's try and get things back on an even keel.'

'To die by your side . . .' sang Gina.

'I know,' said Keith, 'I know.'

Alice volunteered to stay at home. Secretly she had no wish to go in the ambulance, since the last time she'd been in one it had carried her and the recently departed Nan Wildgoose to hospital.

Keith saw this and nodded in agreement. He, Doug and Marie Henty went towards the ambulance with Gina.

'Shall we strap her in, guv'nor?' said Gil too cheerily and too loudly.

'No,' said Keith with a thunderous expression, all his contempt, misery and anger in that one word.

'Shall we come?' shouted Bighead as the trio propelled Gina into the ambulance.

'No, you're all right,' said Keith, and then mischievously he added, 'Stay and have a cup of tea with my mum and dad. I know they'd be interested to hear all about your lives in the country.'

Jennifer heard this and blanched. She gazed very point-edly at her delicate, expensive-looking (she thought) lady's wristwatch.

221

'Norman, dear,' she said. 'I believe some football you might want to watch is on tonight and we should be making tracks.'

Nonplussed, Norman nodded, hoping against hope that the afternoon's proceedings had evoked an empathy in his wife which presaged a rosier future together.

As they stood and waved the ambulance off as if it was going to war or on holiday, he was rapidly disabused of this belief when Jennifer turned to him and said, 'Well, I had to say something to get us away from these pungent bump- kins. There's an extended *Corrie* tonight.'

His heart sank in rhythm with the sun, which disappeared behind the hill, flooding the countryside with black.

In the ambulance, a subdued Gina turned to Keith and said, 'I know I'm not very well, Keith, but Morrissey will make me better.'

That the one and only time Gina had ever shown any insight into her illness should be tempered by this ludicrous belief made Keith despair.

Chapter 21

Gina's arrival at the hospital was a slightly quieter affair than her previous admission. Keith was surprised at how calm and compliant she seemed and wondered what lay behind it. After a brief interview with the duty doctor, he, Doug and Marie accompanied Gina down the usual paste-coloured corridor to the admission ward. At the door Keith kissed Gina goodbye and told her to call him if she needed anything. Gina nodded in assent and then walked into the ward as if she was off for a two-day break at a health farm.

'They've no idea what she's planning,' whispered one of the voices in her head.

The other voice laughed in agreement.

In the taxi on the way home, Marie sat next to Keith in the back and Doug sat in the front.

'Thanks, guys,' said Keith and gave Doug a pat on the

shoulder and Marie a squeeze of the hand which woke a few sleeping butterfies in her stomach.

'You're welcome,' they said together and laughed at the sound of their chorus.

Doug was deposited at his shop and the taxi continued on its way with Keith and Marie.

'I'll collect my car at yours,' said Marie, 'and then I'd better be off. I've lots to do at home.'

The years had taught her that as a woman whose physical charms put her some way down the universal list of beddable females, it was always better to appear to be busy, to be on your way somewhere, to not care whether someone invited you for further contact or not. Each time she made one of these self-protective statements, she awarded herself a point which pushed her, in her own eyes, up the scale of independent women who did not give a toss about whether the male in their life cared or not.

At the cottage Marie followed her rules and did not hang around to see what Keith would do, particularly given that she had so spectacularly broken her rules recently by kissing him. She headed for her car and was about to unlock it when Keith called out, 'Do you want to come in for a drink?'

She knew a few strategic refusals might bolster her chances with many men but something instinctively told her that this was a milestone for Keith and that she should accept. Shouldn't she? Maybe he wanted to talk wife, medication, daughter or – horrors – some physical problem he was suffering from.

'OK,' she found herself saying, and turned back to the cottage.

Alice was in front of the television, staring gloomily at it but not really seeing it.

'Hello, Dad, Marie,' she said miserably.

'Don't worry, love, Mum's in the best place,' said Keith, assuming the failure of her plan to free her mother from the yoke of long-term medication was the reason for her gloom.

'It's not that,' said Alice. 'She ate my bloody letter from Morrissey. The one thing I've got that's truly from him, and it was such a beautiful letter as well.'

Keith, whose raison d'être was to make everyone's life better, said, 'I'm sure I could—'

'What, get it back? Get him to write a copy? Oh, for Christ's sake, Dad, that's one thing you can't do,' said Alice angrily, one of the few times in their relationship when she'd turned on him. 'I'm going to bed.' She got up and walked out of the room, with Keith's hurting, helpless heart following behind.

'Oh dear,' said Marie. 'Poor Alice, she's had a rough time of it lately.'

'Yes,' said Keith. 'I really wish there was something I could do to cheer her up.'

'Well, how about getting her some tickets for Morrissey?' said Marie. 'I'm sure he must be playing somewhere reasonably near and perhaps you could write to him and ask him if she could go backstage and meet him afterwards.'

'You're a bloody genius,' said Keith. 'That never even occurred to me. Let's celebrate with a beer and a smoke.'

Marie Henty was a little bit naive about drug consumption and assumed Keith was going to produce a packet of Number Six. She didn't smoke but she grinned encouragingly because she didn't want to appear too much of an innocent.

Keith came in from the kitchen with two cans of Heineken.

'Sorry,' he said. 'It's not exactly posh.'

'It's fine,' said Marie, taking the can and waiting for him to hand her a glass. But he didn't, so she opened her can and began to drink, thinking her mother would be more than disapproving if she saw her daughter behaving in this loutish country way. Keith disappeared and returned with an old tobacco tin, out of which came Rizlas, a rolling machine, filters and a tiny lump of cannabis. He set to work rolling a joint while Marie observed the process with fascination, having bypassed drug experimentation and piss-ups at medical school in favour of dinner parties and behaving like a middle-aged church-goer from the Home Counties.

Should I say something, she wondered, about never having done this before? Should I point out it's illegal?

Keith seemed to have guessed her thoughts.

'It's all right,' he said. 'I won't tell anyone if you don't.'

He lit the joint, had a few big draws on it and then handed it over to Marie, who took it rather gingerly.

She had only once had a puff of a roll-up at school and it had caused her to throw up in a bin by the hockey pitch, so she was slightly worried about what it would do. But in the spirit of the hour she drew in a huge amount of smoke and then found herself coughing, gagging and laughing all at the same time.

'Steady on,' said Keith. 'I've only got a little bit, you know.'

The 'little bit' extended to five joints, by the end of which Marie felt distinctly weird. She and Keith were chatting easily about Gina, about the village and about Keith's parents when Keith turned to Marie and said, 'I'm sorry to ask you a professional question amongst all this, but my dad, Norman, who was here today, was complaining about his haemorrhoids. Is there anything you can suggest?' He looked very serious.

Marie felt an uncontrollable urge to laugh. She attempted to hold her features in an expression of concern but the effort proved too much and she let out an explosive guffaw, soaking Keith's elderly Aztec-patterned tank top with a mouthful of lager.

Keith looked horrified and then his features began to crumble and he let himself be overtaken by a fit of the most adolescent giggling he could ever remember.

This only made matters worse for Marie and through her tears of laughter she suggested, 'How about poking them back up with a sharp stick?'

'He hasn't got a stick,' said Keith simply, which was possibly the funniest thing Marie had ever heard in her life and her laughter became a torrent of hiccupping, scattergun cackling which she could not rein in.

'He's got some golf clubs,' said Keith and this set them both off again until Marie felt there wasn't enough oxygen in the room to supply their breathing.

'I recommend a nine iron,' she said, at which point Keith sank on to the floor and pummelled the ancient Axminster rug with his fists, shouting, 'Oh stop it! Stop it!' between cascades of laughter.

Marie got up to help Keith off the floor, wobbled and then keeled over on top of him, both of them still laughing. And then out of all the ridiculous, uncontrolled jollity came a moment when they stared directly at each other and their expressions changed.

Even in this state of advanced intoxication, Marie found her inner self telling her outer self, 'Don't pounce, whatever you do, don't pounce.'

She didn't need to because Keith did. Fuelled with two cans of Heineken and five joints, the realisation dawned on him that Marie Henty was the most captivating, most entertaining, most articulate and most intelligent woman he'd ever met. They kissed each other like drunken teenagers and every now and then broke their embrace to stare at each other, giggle and then kiss again.

Upstairs, Alice started and woke out of her miserable sleep. She heard a thump downstairs and wondered what could be going on. Surely her dad couldn't be stumbling around at this time of night and there wasn't a burglar in the county who could find anything remotely interesting to steal in their mean little cottage.

She went downstairs and, attempting to hold her nerve just in case the noise was an intruder, threw open the sitting-room door to witness her father standing in the middle of

the room, trousers round his ankles, in a compromising position with her GP who was kneeling in front of him doing
something to him that he was obviously enjoying.

There was absolutely no point in Keith attempting to
make it look like anything other than what it was.

'Oh bloody hell,' he said as he spotted Alice. Marie, intent
upon her task, took this to be verbal encouragement and
upped her pace. There was an excruciating moment when
Keith attempted to communicate to her that they were being
observed.

Then Alice turned her back and headed upstairs.

'Oh my God, Marie,' said Keith. 'That was Alice, she just
came down and saw us.'

'What shall we do?' said Marie, pulled out of her lovely,
real dream.

'Carry on?' said Keith, and began to laugh.

'Right you are,' said Marie and they did.

Chapter 22

It was difficult to say, the next morning, which was worse, the emotional or physical devastation. Marie raised her head with a groan from the settee and surveyed the havoc that two middle-aged drunk, stoned people could wreak on a small room. Keith was close to her snoring on the floor, with a cushion she had put under his head and a rug thrown over him from the small chair in the corner.

She realised what had woken her. It was Alice in the kitchen, putting the kettle on. Marie got up and put on some items of clothing that were draped around the room like washing.

'Hello,' she said tentatively.

'Hi,' said Alice, rather more brightly than Marie Henty could have hoped for.

Marie formed the word 'Sorry' with her mouth, but before the sound came out, Alice cut through it.

'It's all right, Marie,' she said. 'My dad deserves some fun in his life.'

'Thank you,' said Marie.

'I just wish I hadn't seen it,' said Alice with a grin.

'Yes,' said Marie, feeling a red-hot flush flood her face.

'Tea?' said Alice. 'Toast?'

'Yes please.'

Keith appeared at the door, his hair so charmingly awry that both women gazed at him with an almost palpable fondness.

'Morning,' he said, the bravado on his face starting to slip as he watched Alice standing by the kettle distributing cheap tea bags amongst the group of mugs.

'It's all right, Dad,' said Alice, 'but if she's pregnant, there'll be hell to pay.'

Keith and Marie's laughter echoed round the tiny kitchen, evoking a thought in Keith that there hadn't been too much laughter in recent years.

'What time is it?' asked Marie, realising her watch had escaped during last night's sexual tornado.

'Nine thirty,' said Keith.

'Oh bollocks. I've got surgery at ten.'

Keith and Alice looked at her admiringly. They didn't know she could swear.

'It's all right,' said Keith, 'you've got twenty-five minutes. It'll take you five minutes to get there. Relax, have some breakfast and you can get yourself together in five minutes in the bathroom.'

Marie almost cried with relief. It wasn't often that she spent the night with someone who then treated her with respect the next day and even invited her to stay longer. The last man who'd got into her bed after a few too many spritzers at a medical conference was a drug rep called Malcolm, who left the room in the morning with indecent haste, without so much as a backward glance at Marie.

'OK,' she said. 'That would be lovely.'

The three sat round the little table in the kitchen and chatted easily. The ghost of Gina seemed to be there but in a benign rather than malevolent way, as if somehow her spirit had allowed Keith a little emotional leeway.

This slightly skewed family breakfast was interrupted by the telephone ringing.

'I'll get it,' said Alice.

She picked up the receiver, said, 'Yes,' once and then listened intently for a few seconds, her face reflecting the sombre news being fed into her ear.

'Is everything OK?' said Keith.

Alice raised her hand to silence Keith and listenened for a few more seconds, eventually saying, 'Thank you for letting us know, we'll be in touch in a little while.' She turned to Keith and Marie. 'Mum's escaped from hospital.'

'Oh, for Christ's sake,' said Keith. 'How the hell could that happen?'

'The doctor wants us to go and see him and discuss what we're going to do. They've informed the police and they think they'll find her pretty quickly.'

The morning's relaxed atmosphere was shattered. Marie got up and headed to the bathroom, realising after a few steps that she didn't know where it was.

'Top of the stairs,' said Keith helpfully.

In the bathroom, Marie examined what her mother had always called 'a plain but nice face', and tried to catch some of the urgent discussion going on downstairs. When she went back down five minutes later, Keith and Alice were putting on their coats.

'We're going over there,' said Keith, 'see what's happening.'

'OK,' said Marie. 'Will you let me know?' although she really wanted to say, 'Can I move into your house with you, can we get married and I'm probably not too old to have a baby.'

'Of course,' said Keith.

They drove in convoy up the small lane and when they hit the main road, they set off in opposite directions from one another.

Marie looked in her mirror to see Keith's hand stuck out of the driver's window, waving frantically.

She did the same until her car nearly went off the road and the van had disappeared into the distance.

The drive to Hereford took about half an hour and as they entered the hospital, Alice half expected to see her mother shuffling along the corridor, fag in hand. They were told to go to the doctor's office and within five minutes the familiar face of Gina's doctor appeared at the door.

'Good morning,' he said, as if he believed that saying it

brightly might pre-empt any flak that was coming his way. There wasn't much. Over the years both Alice and Keith had become used to contemplating the worst possible scenario, although it had to be said that Keith was probably at his most indignant and unhappy, which was most other people's best.

'What on earth happened, Dr Desmond?' he said. 'How could you let someone in Gina's state walk out of the door?'

'I'm so sorry,' said Dr Desmond. 'As you know, initially she came in willingly but as time went on she started to say that she wanted to go because she had to see this Morrissey chap.'

It was apparent that he had not known who 'this Morrissey chap' was until some of the younger, more aware staff had filled him in.

'Yes,' said Alice, 'she has become rather obsessed with Morrissey over the last few weeks.'

'So . . .' said Keith.

'Well,' said Dr Desmond, 'we decided we would put her on a temporary section to keep her here, given that it was the weekend, while we waited for the ward round on Monday and got ourselves organised. We kept her off medication so we could get a chance to observe the true Gina.'

'And?' said Alice.

'Well, I'm afraid she became increasingly upset and just before we were about to move her to a ward that was locked so we could contain her, she walked out. When she was challenged by a male nursing assistant, I'm afraid she kicked him in the testicles and ran for it and by the time the emergency team arrived, she was off the premises and away.'

'So, what time was that then?' said Keith.

'Last night at about seven,' said Dr Desmond. 'Any idea where she might have gone?'

Alice resisted the temptation to say, 'Morrissey's house?' Both she and Keith shook their heads.

'Well,' said Dr Desmond, 'we have told the police and I'm sure Gina won't last very long out in the big wide world because she is so ill. People will notice her and I hope they'll give her some help or contact the authorities.'

'Not much else to say then, is there?' said Keith, looking at his feet. 'We'll get home and make a plan our end and obviously we'll inform each other if we find her.'

'Indeed,' said Dr Desmond, a word he'd started using a lot lately because he thought it made him sound very mature.

Pompous little twat, thought Alice.

As they drove home, Keith and Alice discussed a plan.

'I'll get Bighead and Wobbly out looking round here,' said Keith reluctantly.

'I know this might sound daft, Dad,' said Alice, 'and I don't know if she has the capability of doing it, but I think she'll head for Manchester to try and find Morrissey.'

'Oh Alice,' said Keith, 'she'd never make it.'

'I don't think we should underestimate her tenacity, Dad. If she's determined enough, she'll make it.'

'It's December,' said Keith. 'She'll have nowhere to sleep and no money. The police will pick her up long before that.'

'Let me go to Manchester,' said Alice. 'Mark could borrow a car off someone. We could go for two days and really scour all the areas she's most likely to be. I won't even miss work. Anyway, you can't stop me even if you wanted to.'

Keith knew that was true and he also knew how unbearable it was just sitting at home waiting for news.

'All right,' he said in a resigned way. 'Two days, but straight back after that.'

Alice nodded. 'I'll go everywhere and I'll find her.'

Keith felt a small glow of fatherly pride. He knew lots of men who despaired of their teenage daughters because of the distance between them, but Alice seemed to have all the good qualities of Gina and none of the bad ones. She seemed so convinced that she would find Gina in Manchester that all he could do was wish her well.

As soon as Alice arrived home she phoned Mark at work. The woman who answered responded to her request to speak to Mark with a snooty, 'Our part-time employees are not permitted phone calls at work, madam.'

'I'm so sorry,' said Alice, trying to keep her temper. 'I wouldn't normally do it but it is an emergency.'

'Very well,' said the woman, 'but please make the call as short as possible.'

'Hello?' said Mark, sounding understandably worried.

'Mark,' said Alice, 'I'm sorry about this but I need you to come to Manchester with me for two days to look for my mum who's escaped from hospital. Can you get a car and the time off?'

'Blimey,' said Mark. 'I feel like I'm in *Mission Impossible*. Well, I finish in an hour, so with any luck I'll be over at yours in a couple of hours. Not sure about the car, though.'

'Whatever you can manage,' said Alice. 'We need to go today.' She put the receiver down.

'I'd better phone Marie,' said Keith. 'Just to let her know what's happening,' he added in response to Alice's raised eyebrows.

Marie Henty's unhelpful receptionist eventually put him through.

'What's happening?' Marie asked immediately.

Keith explained the current state of play.

'I can't really talk now,' said Marie. 'Why don't you pop round later?' She crossed her fingers behind her back so that the flu-infused patient in front of her couldn't see.

'OK,' said Keith.

Mark arrived at one thirty in possibly the most ridiculous orange car Alice had ever seen.

'What the bloody hell do you call that?' she said. 'It's like a baked bean tin on wheels.'

'It's a Honda 600 Z coupé,' said Mark, 'and it costs about three quid and does about four thousand miles to the gallon.'

'Where did you get it?' said Alice. 'Borrowed it off a leprechaun, did you?'

'Don't take the piss. It's got to get us to bloody Manchester, this has. It belongs to my mate's brother, he's away for the week.'

'So he doesn't even know you've got it then?' said Alice.

'No,' said Mark, 'and I'm not insured to drive so we'd better be bloody careful.'

Keith roared with laughter when he saw the car.

'Yes, all right,' said Mark. 'I know.'

Alice had packed a small bag and brought her Morrissey folder with her. This collection of scrappy articles and pictures would give them some idea of where to look. She knew Gina had been through them many times – there were some tiny comments in Gina's hand in the margins and the occasional splodge of coffee or butter from her rather chaotic breakfasting behaviour.

'Be careful, you two,' said Keith, pressing thirty pounds into Alice's hand, 'and drive carefully in that bloody Noddy car,' he said to Mark.

'Do you want a lift to Uncle Bighead's?' said Alice.

'No bloody fear,' said Keith. 'They'd execute me on sight. Call me tonight,' shouted Keith as they drove off, waving furiously. 'Let me know you're safe.'

'All right,' shouted Alice, but the wind carried the words, away before they reached Keith.

Keith steeled himself to go and see Wobbly and Bighead. On the way he dropped into Doug's shop to tell him the news.

'Bloody amateurs,' said Doug. 'Wouldn't have happened in my day.'

'I'm going to see Bighead and Wobbly,' said Keith. 'Want to come and be my bodyguard?'

'Ooh, yes please,' said Doug sarcastically.

'Oh, one thing I nearly forgot,' said Keith. 'I was going to get Alice a ticket for the next Morrissey concert. Can I have a butchers at that *NME* and see when he's on?'

'Be my guest,' said Doug.

Keith discovered that Morrissey was playing in Wolverhampton in about a week's time and that all those who arrived with a Morrissey T-shirt would be let in free.

'Now I just have to get a Morrissey T-shirt,' he muttered.

'You'll have to go to Brum for that,' said Doug.

'Great,' said Keith. 'Doesn't look like I'm going to get any work done today.'

He hared off to Birmingham and managed finally to locate a T-shirt. On his way home he detoured via the Wildgoose cottage to talk to Bighead and Wobbly.

'Don't tell me,' roared Wobbly, who'd had a few barley wines, 'she's fucking scarpered!'

'Well, yes, she has actually,' said Keith.

'Oh bollocks. Dad! Wobs!' Bighead shouted over his shoulder. 'She's escaped from the bin!'

He looked at Keith as if he was a piece of fishing bait.

'Wanna come in, Keithy?' he said.

Keith made a quick calculation involving time of day, amount of alcohol consumed and level of social disinhibition achieved, and turned down Bighead's offer.

'We should have a search tomorrow, though,' he said. 'Shall we meet in the morning?'

'Dunno,' said Bighead distractedly. 'All right, we'll come to yours in the morning.'

'OK,' said Keith and walked away, thankful once again that he was physically unscathed.

Marie got up to answer the ring at her door.

Keith stood there grinning.

'Want to come to ours?' he said. 'Alice is calling me later so I've got to be in.'

'All right,' said Marie, picking up her bleep and her handbag.

Keith held his breath as they drew up at the cottage as it suddenly occurred to him that Gina might have come home.

There was no sign. I wonder where she is? he thought.

Gina was in a lorry doing seventy on a dual carriageway heading north. She had promised the driver sex if he took her to Manchester.

They overtook a tiny bright orange car.

'Jesus,' said the driver. 'What the fuck is that?'

Chapter 23

Alice and Mark arrived in Manchester about six o'clock. Neither of them had been there before and didn't really know where to begin.

'Let's start with a map, shall we?' said Mark, parking the car on a single yellow line. 'There must be a crappy newsagent's near here that's got one.'

There was. They bought a street map of Manchester, two Twix bars and a can of Coke each and then sat in the car, Alice with the contents of her folder spread out on her knees.

She produced a little notebook and a tiny blue pen, the type that come from a bookies. At some point it must have been in the possession of one of her uncles, she mused.

'Shall we start with the Salford Lads' Club?' she said distractedly to Mark. 'It's where that great photo on the inside of *The Queen is Dead* comes from and it seems to be a bit of a mecca for Moz fans.'

'Whatever you like,' said Mark. 'Have we got a strategy?'

'Just go there, hang about and keep our eyes open,' said Alice. 'I'm afraid that's all the strategy I can manage at the moment.'

'What about Morrissey's house?' said Mark.

'That's in Stretford,' said Alice, 'King's Road, but we'll do Salford first, we might meet people there who can help.'

They drove, chewing their chocolate, for quite some time until eventually they found themselves in Salford. They passed the Salford Lads' Club and could see a few people hanging around outside in the rain and cold. A gaggle of Japanese tourists was obviously trying to re-enact the photo which had appeared on the inner sleeve of *The Queen Is Dead*.

Alice approached a small group who looked like students, three boys and one girl.

'Hi,' she said. 'I'm sorry to bother you but I'm looking for my mum.'

'Morrissey fan, is she?' said one of the floppy-haired boys with a slight sneer.

'Patrick,' said the girl. 'Don't be horrible.' She turned to Alice. 'What does she look like?'

'Oh, about five foot five with wild black hair, a bit odd-looking,' said Alice. She put her hand in her pocket and produced a picture of Gina taken about four years ago. Her features were slightly flattened by the progress of her illness but there was definite evidence of the wild witchiness that had dominated some years before.

'She looks amazing,' said the girl. 'Why are you looking for her?'

This was the first potential stumbling block for Alice, something she had wrestled with in the car on the way up. She had no idea how much she should tell the people she met, but she supposed her questions would anyway alert them to the oddness of the situation so she went ahead and said, 'She's not very well . . . mentally, you know, and she needs some help . . . and yes, she does love Morrissey and we thought she might come to some of the places that remind her of him.'

'Wanna lock her up and give her some of this?' said the sneery bloke, putting both his hands to his head and simulating ECT.

'I'm sorry,' said the girl, 'he's a bit anti everything conventional, can you tell? I haven't seen anyone like that but if you want to give me your phone number, we come here quite a lot and if I see her I could call you.'

'Thanks.' Alice tore a page out of her notebook and wrote down her name and number. 'We'll just hang around for a bit and see if she turns up,' she said, almost as if she was asking permission.

'OK,' said the girl, almost as if she was giving it. 'I'm Lou, by the way. Nice to meet you.'

They shook hands with an embarrassed laugh. The boys were glowering at Mark who was returning their gaze with equal ferocity. Alice wondered why teenage boys had to do this and why they couldn't just relax and get on with each other.

'Any suggestions about where we could look?' said Alice. 'We were obviously planning to go to Stretford.'

'Of course,' said Lou. 'Well, I suppose you could try Canal Street and round there too.'

'Yes,' said Alice. 'I suppose it's worth a try.'

Mark and Alice stood in the rain for an hour, Alice truly convinced that if they waited long enough, her mother would appear magically from round the corner. There was occasional communication between her and the students about Morrissey but Alice found that the almost machine-generated facts spewing from the sneery one's mouth sat uneasily with her emotional attachment to Morrissey.

Do I really care, she thought, what sort of guitar someone has or what key a certain song was written in? That's not going to get to the heart of the man.

It got darker and colder and eventually the little groups who had been there when they arrived melted away and left the two of them alone.

Eventually, Mark said, 'Let's move on, shall we?'

Alice didn't want to go.

'Just another fifteen minutes,' she said.

'All right,' said Mark, not wanting to express what he was truly feeling, which was a sense of utter hopelessness about the task they had set themselves.

After fifteen minutes no one had arrived and they were wetter and more demoralised.

'Come on then,' said Alice. 'Let's go to Canal Street. At least we can get a drink. I'd better phone my dad first,' she added.

They found a phone box and as Alice listened to the ringing tone, she wished she could see what Keith was doing. Was he pottering around in the kitchen? Watching sport on the television? Or lying on his bed dreaming and listening to Bob Dylan, as he often did when he was tired?

Keith was lying on his bed but it wasn't Bob Dylan who was there with him, it was Marie Henty.

They had started the journey to the bedroom in a very contained fashion, discussing the current situation with Gina and why Alice had gone to Manchester, although both of them weren't really thinking about that. Marie was considering just coming out with a request for sex and seeing what happened, and Keith was wondering how long they needed to talk before it was socially acceptable to stop and go upstairs for sex. The conversation ambled everywhere for a good twenty minutes. Eventually Marie said, 'Keith.'

'Marie,' said Keith.

And just speaking each other's names was the catalyst they needed. Keith grabbed Marie's hand and pulled her up the stairs with him into the bedroom and there in the dark, each with their own issues of fidelity, lust and love niggling somewhere in the back of their minds, they undressed each other in a furious tangle of awkwardness and laughter. Just as Keith's pants flew across the room and hit the window, their progress was halted by Alice's call.

Keith looked at Marie.

'I don't want to answer it,' he said, 'but I can't ignore it because I know it's Alice and I just want to check she's

247

OK. Is that all right?' and he walked backwards out of the door, trying at the same time to hop back into his pants, some ancient rule of decorum telling him that you cannot have a phone conversation with your daughter without your pants on.

Marie lay on the bed trying to avoid the thought that this was the marital sanctuary of two of her patients and listening to Keith's voice downstairs.

Eventually he returned.

'She's fine,' he said. 'They got there safely and they've been to look in one spot and now they're on their way some-where else. I'm sure they're not going to find her but I know she feels she's got to do something.' He looked at Marie. 'Has the moment passed for you?' he asked.

'Has it for you?' said Marie.

'No,' said Keith. 'Far from it.'

'Me too,' said Marie, and the pants flew off again.

As Keith allowed himself to be sucked into the whirlpool of Marie, he spared a brief thought for his wife and the pit of his stomach gave a little lurch as he wondered where she was and what she was doing.

Gina was at that very moment lying in the back of a lorry belonging to someone called Dunk, or Duncan to give him the name he was christened with. Dunk was seventy-one years old, came from Chester ('Only complete Roman town wall in England,' he had already informed Gina twice) and couldn't quite believe that a woman under the age of forty had agreed to have sex with him. He was a widower, whose wife Jennie had died four years ago, leaving him lonely and bored. His children, Mary and Tom, had both emigrated, one to Canada and one to Australia – he frequently forgot which one was where. Having been a lorry driver all of his life, he had decided to go back to work with a small, busy haulage firm who were quite happy about the fluidity of his age, given that he often forgot what he had told people.

To Gina, this was a small price to pay for being delivered to the home town of the man of her dreams. In hospital she had occasionally succumbed to young male patients who were locked in and deprived of their usual supply of sexual partners, and who paced the ward like panthers ready to pounce. It had in no way entered Gina's head that the supplying of sexual favours was anything other than a neutral arrangement, designed to empty them of their frustration and thus make their stay on the ward a little more bearable. Some of the nurses had an inkling of what was going on and either ignored it or had a quiet word with Gina. One of them said to her, 'Come on, you don't want to become the ward bike, do you?'

Gina rather did.

Dunk finished his grunting business reasonably swiftly and put the radio on in his cab. It was Radio 2 and some unidentifiable musical mush drifted around them as Gina fumbled in her bag for some Rizlas and tobacco.

'Thank you, that was nice,' said Dunk, totally sincerely.

'S'all right,' said Gina as her yellowed, dirty fingernails poked and prodded at the roll-up.

'Fancy some grub?' said Dunk, not exactly an invitation to dinner but as near as damnit.

They were in the lorry park of a motorway services near Manchester and when Gina nodded her assent, Dunk climbed down from the cab and went in search of a Ginster's pie and a cup of tea for them. Gina lay back humming along to the music and pleasantly surprised at the slight dimming of the voices in her head. She gave not a thought to her family; she increasingly found that when she was away from them, they ceased to exist for her, and each renewed contact with them after a period of incarceration or liberty from the little cottage was a bit like meeting them for the first time.

'Here you are, love,' said Dunk, pushing a pie and some tea in a polystyrene cup into her hand.

Gina grunted something unintelligible which Dunk with his poor hearing took as an expression of gratitude. He was well aware that Gina wasn't what he'd call 'the full shilling' but she seemed in need of a little TLC, and although Dunk felt vaguely uncomfortable that he'd exploited her for his own ends, he was resolved to show her how thankful he was to have had a bit of female contact. His wife Jennie hadn't been too keen on it for the last ten years of their marriage, so to find a woman who had assented so readily to his suggestion was like a gift from heaven.

'Can you take me to Manchester then?' said Gina.

'Righto,' said Dunk cheerily. 'Where do you want to go?'

'Can we go to the Salford . . .' She stopped. 'Shit, I've forgotten what it's called.'

'Well, what is it?' said Dunk. 'What sort of place?'

'Do you know Morrissey?' asked Gina, as if she was asking, 'Do you know Jesus?'

'Don't believe I do,' said Dunk. 'Who is he?'

'He's my saviour,' said Gina, 'and I've got to go to him.'

'Blimey,' said Dunk, 'that sounds quite serious.'

Gina started to sob loudly. 'It is serious, more serious than anything ever in my life,' she said. 'I first heard Morrissey sing in my house. So I came to Manchester.'

'That doesn't really make sense,' said Dunk, who was not an expert on mental illness and hadn't come across any examples of knight's-move thinking before, in which the sufferer misses out the second logical step of a thought process, thus arriving at what seems to be an illogical conclusion.

'Are you going to take me?' said Gina in her little girl's voice, an affectation that had survivied the turmoil in her mind caused by her illness.

'Of course, love,' said Dunk and turned the key in the ignition. 'We'll head for Salford and then on the way you might come up with a bit more info on where you want to be.'

As they approached Salford, Gina said, 'Salford Boys' Club, that's it . . . that's where I want to go.'

What on earth for? wondered Dunk, but he didn't gainsay Gina who, he had correctly assessed, had a right temper on her.

Dunk pulled in to the side of the road and asked someone for directions to the boys' club. He was immediately corrected by the indignant passer-by. 'It's fooking Salford *Lads'* Club,' he said. 'Ain't you heard of it, mate?'

'Course I bleeding haven't,' said Dunk, 'or why would I be asking?'

'That way, mate,' said the passer-by, pointing.

'Ta,' said Dunk and roared off.

Gina became animated. 'There it is! There it is!' she chanted over and over again.

Dunk, who was becoming increasingly uneasy about Gina's mental state, tried to soothe her.

'All right, all right,' he said softly.

But as they drew level with the building, Gina's expression changed.

'Fuck, fuck, fuck,' she shouted. 'Quick, drive, escape, go, faster, go!'

Without thinking, Dunk put his foot down.

'What's the matter?' he said.

'I fucking knew,' said Gina. 'I fucking knew.'

'Knew what?' said Dunk.

'Can't say, it's a secret, after me, want to get me, lock me up.'

'Where shall I drop you?' said Dunk uneasily.

'Don't know, got to think, nowhere to go now they're here, shit,' said Gina.

By this point Dunk had realised that Gina definitely wasn't 'right in the head'. He could see she was vulnerable and needed protecting. But do I really want to lumber myself with a nutter? he asked himself.

Then he thought of the sex, then he felt guilty, then he felt altruistic, then he felt revulsion, then he felt ashamed.

'You better come home with me,' he said.

Gina brightened. 'Morrissey's home, that's it. Let's go there.'

Chapter 24

Mark and Alice did not have a comfortable experience in the gay district of Manchester.

The heaving, colourful and fascinating sights of Manchester stood largely unnoticed as they concentrated on their pursuit of Gina. They had very little money and after some discussion outside one of the pubs, they agreed that if they were going to have a drink and something to eat, it was probably not possible to afford a bed and breakfast for the night. So they decided they would sleep in Mark's friend's little car.

The mass of people milling past afforded them a bizarre, theatrical entertainment, their own miniature carnival. Occasionally, Alice saw someone in the crowd who looked a bit like Gina, but none of them was Gina and as each fresh hope was dashed, their spirits sank lower.

Eventually, they felt brave enough to go into a pub. Inside sat a selection of gay men of all ages.

Alice felt she was in a zoo for exotic birds.

Mark, still struggling with the manly side of himself, which was expected of the sons of hardy country folk, felt simultaneously uncomfortable and fascinated.

'What do you want to drink?' he asked. 'I'll go to the bar.'

Alice asked for half a lager and he left her sitting at a table and pushed his way through the crush.

'What are you doing here, Alice?' said a voice Alice could only describe as 'fruity'. It belonged to a man at the next table who appeared to be a flamboyant mixture of Oscar Wilde and a builder.

'How do you know my name?' she said, surprised.

'Oh, I don't, dear,' he said. 'It's just that you look like Alice in Wonderland with that expression on your face in amongst all these mad hatters.'

She had to agree that there was an amazing selection of strange headgear on display.

'I'm looking for my mum,' she said. 'She's a big Morrissey fan and she's run away from hospital and we think she might be here in Manchester looking for him.'

The man extended a hand, the nails of which, Alice observed, were obsessively well-manicured and painted with black nail varnish.

'Molly's the name,' said the ostentatious character.

'Hello,' said Alice.

'Hello, Alice,' said Molly. 'What does she look like?'

Alice described her mum.

'Fuck me sideways, dear,' said Molly. 'She'd stand out like

a sore thumb in here. I certainly haven't seen anyone answering that description but I'm happy to ask around for you.'

Despite the uncomfortable feeling that Molly would be using her and her family as the centrepiece in a stand-up routine, Alice thought this was a small price to pay for getting some information on Gina's whereabouts.

'Thank you,' she said.

'And who's that very tasty young man you are accompanied by?' said Molly. 'Is he spoken for?'

'No,' said Alice and then wondered if she'd made a mistake. Would Mark be the target of some sort of romantic assault from Molly and friends?

Mark was doing equally uncomfortably up at the bar. Having ordered two halves of lager and turned down the offer of a free cocktail from the immaculately dressed and coiffed barman, he thought he'd better turn the talk to the Gina situation.

'I'm looking for a woman,' he ventured.

The barman guffawed.

'Bloody hell, love, this isn't the right place to start.'

Mark felt his face flushing bright red, although it was concealed by the flashing red lights positioned round the bar.

'No,' he said. 'My friend's mother has gone missing from hospital and we think she might be wandering around Manchester.'

'The words "needle" and "haystack" spring to mind,'

said the barman. 'Manchester's a fucking big place, you know.'

'I know,' said Mark irritably, feeling he had been cast in the role of country cousin.

Just as he was preparing to deliver a wounded speech about being perhaps a little more in control and knowledgeable than maybe he looked, a hand belonging to someone behind him began to very gently stroke his left buttock. Alarm shot through him at this unwarranted assault on his person and he spun round to see a smiling, good-looking man staring at him in a humorous way as if this was a perfectly natural thing to do and had been carried out in lieu of an introduction. Any remaining doubt that Mark had about his sexuality has extinguished as his instinctive response to the man's touch closed that book for him once and for all.

'White wine spritzer, please,' said the smiling man.

'I'm sorry,' said Mark, 'I don't have enough money to buy you a drink.'

'Hope your arsehole's as tight as you are,' said the man, giving the impression that this was a well-worn line.

The predatory nature of his expression and his assumption that this sort of behaviour was perfectly acceptable made Mark feel as if he was from another century. He turned back to the bar, paid for his drinks and then turned with what he thought was a neutral yet vaguely threatening expression on his face and headed back to the table where Alice sat waiting.

He put the drinks down and whispered, 'I hate it here, can we leave after this?'

Alice, conversely, was enjoying herself immensely; it was so rare that she was able to sit in a pub without there being at least one allusion to her appearance and her suitability as a sexual partner. A whole room full of men, none of whom either did or didn't fancy, her was an absolute joy.

'Some bloke felt up my bum,' said Mark.

Alice could not help laughing. Mark's expression was one of hurt outrage and Alice scolded herself for not taking something seriously that she would want taken seriously if it happened to her.

'I'm sorry, Mark,' she said. 'It's just such a surreal place compared to what we're used to. I didn't mean to be horrible. All right, let's drink these quickly and go then.'

Molly seemed highly disappointed by their intention to leave.

'Come on, luvvie,' he said to Mark, stroking his hair. 'Stay and have a few more, it might relax you.'

Mark didn't want to be relaxed. He stood up.

'Let's go,' he said to Alice.

Alice downed the dregs of her half and they nodded a goodbye to Molly and exited with some speed.

'Thank Christ we're out of there,' said Mark as the cold air hit them. 'Can we go home? I know we said we were going to stay but I don't know if I can.'

'I'm sorry it's been hard for you, Mark,' said Alice. 'Please can we just pop down to Morrissey's mum's house, do one last drive past the Salford Lads' Club and then go?'

She fixed him with such an imploring gaze that it made his heart jump a little.

'All right,' he said wearily. 'Let's do that, but I don't like this place, it's too big, too weird and too frightening.'

They got in the car and Alice directed him to the house where Morrissey had grown up, a surprisingly surburban street, not the scene of decay, desperation and splintered dreams that Alice had expected. Again, there were a couple of groups of student types standing quietly outside. The curtains in the house were drawn for the night and the containment of light and warmth inside the house served only to underline the isolation and frustration of the few hopeful fans lurking there. This time there was no friendly woman to approach so Alice decided against asking any of them about Gina, a foolish decision as Gina had left the place with Dunk some ten minutes before.

It was now nearing eleven and a brief sail past the Salford Lads' Club completed their unsuccesful search for Alice's mother. Alice stepped briefly into a call box to let Keith know that the search had thrown up no leads and they were on their way home.

'Never mind, sweetheart,' said Keith down the line. 'It'll be all right, you'll see . . . and I've got a nice surprise for you.'

The little car made its way out to the west of Manchester and eventually they hit the A49 and headed south, skirting Whitchurch and Shrewsbury.

The pair realised they were hungry and pulled into a service station to buy something to sustain them until they got home.

'Where do you think she is?' Alice said to Mark, not really wanting to think too deeply about this question herself but just wanting to hear some reassurance.

Mark was not hopeful. He knew enough about Gina to understand just how vulnerable she was and even though his sheltered, reasonably wealthy lifestyle had cocooned him to a certain extent, he was well aware that there were plenty of men out there prepared to take advantage of Gina's inability to make sound judgements. But he knew Alice didn't want to hear this.

'I reckon she's all right, you know,' he said. 'I think she's found herself somewhere warm and cosy and she's OK.'

Alice smiled and patted Mark's knee in the dark.

'Thanks,' she said.

Gina was snoring soundly, tucked up in bed with Dunk in his grubby little flat on the outskirts of Chester. Having lived on his own for so long, free from the shackles of being compelled to order his life in the pristine way his wife wanted him to, he revelled in the most enormous mess imaginable. Washing-up sometimes stood for weeks, the carpet was a chequered memorial to all the snacks he had consumed over the last few months, and the neglect in the bedroom bore witness to the fact that it was a place used purely to lie down in then leave until the next time it was required.

After their tour round the Morrissey monuments of Manchester, Dunk had managed to persuade Gina she needed sleep and food. He felt an immense fondness for her already; she was the antithesis of his departed wife, whose primary purpose in life in the few years before her death seemed to be to berate him about everything. Gina was totally non-judgemental, it seemed. Life just flowed past her, without her in any way wanting to alter its course, apart from satisfying her passion for this Morrissey person.

Sure, he thought to himself, she probably is a bit cracked with this pop singer business but she's no trouble and I like her. She hadn't even complained about the long row of empty beer bottles decorating the perimeter of the kitchen but had just fetched herself a glass and began to examine the bottles one by one, adding their contents to her glass to create a flat beer cocktail as a prelude to bed.

Mark and Alice reached Alice's house at two thirty in the morning, both exhausted.

'You might as well stay here,' said Alice, 'seeing as you're so knackered.'

'Where shall I sleep?' said Mark, wondering whether a night on a settee would really offer him the opportunity for a decent night.

'With me or my dad,' said Alice cheerily. 'Your choice.'

'Tempted as I am by a night with your dad,' said Mark, 'I choose you.'

A curled cheese sandwich was waiting for Alice in the

kitchen and they shared it between them with a glass of milk each. After that, they climbed the stairs, divested themselves of the outer layers of their clothes and lay down together under the blankets in the cold room. Within seconds they were asleep in each other's arms for practical reasons rather than romantic ones.

The next morning, having sneaked Marie out of the house like a teenager, Keith shouted up the stairs, 'Breakfast!' and Alice padded down in her dressing gown to inform him of Mark's presence in her bedroom.

'Well, I hope you didn't get up to anything,' he said with a grin.

Karen would have said, 'I fucked his brains out,' thought Alice, but she just said, 'Oh Dad,' and smiled.

Over breakfast with a tousle-haired Mark, who felt like a condemned man even though there was no reason to, Keith produced his surprise.

'A Morrissey T-shirt,' said Alice. 'Thanks, Dad. Lovely.'

'Not just a Morrissey T-shirt,' said Keith with a flourish of the tea towel. 'This will get you into his gig in Wolverhampton in five days, on the twenty-second.'

'Oh my God!' she said. 'I'll finally get to see him. How incredible.' She jumped up and hugged her dad.

'And I've arranged for you to stay the night with Grandma and Grandad,' said Keith.

This was a bit of a depressing thought, but she would have stayed with Wobbly and Bighead in a haunted house if it meant she could see Morrissey. She was flooded with happiness and all her worries about her mum suddenly seemed lighter. Alice lay awake in bed that night, with Morrissey crooning on her record player, and blissfully contemplated the transcendental experience of being in the same room as the lovely man.

Chapter 25

Keith found himself thinking about Gina many times during the days that followed her exit from his and Alice's life. He didn't know whether to trust his instincts that all was well and that somewhere Gina was safe and being cared for by a good, patient person. In his mind's eye he saw some nuns in a small rundown city convent ministering to Gina in a cosy cell-like room while she recovered. He knew this was solely a result of his fervent wishes rather than reality but the strong feeling still existed that somehow everything was fine for Gina.

One day, without even thinking about it, Keith sank to his knees in the little sitting room and found his hands touching each other in the manner of a prayer.

'Please keep Gina safe, God,' he found himself saying. His own voice sounded very strange to him in the empty room. He laughed. 'Sorry, God, for laughing. I'm not really used to this and I'm sure you're mighty fed up with those of us who experience a little tragedy in our lives and turn to you because we can't think of anything else to do.'

Keith had always thought God was fundamentally a good bloke who had a sense of humour and was pretty laid-back about human weakness. This he had gleaned from an upbringing in the Church of England and the inability of the vicar in his local church to be anything other than a charming and feckless libertarian. His unspoken acknow-ledgement to the children of the parish, whom he saw mainly at weddings and harvest festival, that church services were meaningless and dull for anyone under the age of ninety had endeared him to all the local children, whilst simultaneously making a few elderly matrons suspicious of his motives. But, to Keith, the vicar had always sat in his head as the repre-sentative of a benign institution to which he could turn in times of crisis and from which he could receive some sort of spiritual relief.

Gina, meanwhile, remained with Dunk in his crummy little abode outside Chester.

Gina's mental condition was not something Dunk was particularly uncomfortable with. His own mother had been prone to what the rest of his family had called 'funny little turns', when she took herself off to bed and refused to come out. Sometimes this would last a couple of days and at other times as long as three weeks. She would emerge only to go to the toilet or poke around in the cupboard in the kitchen in a desperate search for something she actually wanted to eat. Dunk's railwayman father had accepted these trips to a parallel universe without fuss, and his relaxed approach to the strangeness of their family life had engendered in Dunk and his sister Joy an altruistic and easy-going temperament.

In his tiny, shambolic home, Dunk surveyed Gina as she stared at the loud television which was his constant companion.

'Tell me something about yourself, love,' he said to her. 'Where do you come from? Have you got family? What am I going to do with you?'

Gina never liked these verbal excursions other people tried to take into her life. She grunted something unintelligible in reply but Dunk was not to be put off.

'Come on, Gina,' he said. 'You've got to give me something. I've got to know a bit of who you are. You can't just stay here if I don't know nothing about you.'

'I don't want to talk about Gina,' said Gina. 'She's a person who's fucked. Let me stay here, please. I like it.'

She genuinely did like it. For the first time, she felt she could truly be at ease. In this grubby little place, with this big lump of an old man, she felt protected and relaxed. Sexual favours seemed a small price to pay for using him as a stepping stone to greater glory with Morrissey. Although she could not really articulate it in her muddled brain, somewhere down deep she was well aware that she could be lying in a dark wood with a ligature round her throat or floating face down in some dank canal.

'Please, Dunk, I like it here,' she said again.

Dunk grinned. It was a compliment and one he couldn't really understand. Why did this much younger, albeit weird woman want to be here in this neglected hovel? Perhaps she really liked him.

'Well, let's play it by ear then, you funny girl,' he said fondly. He looked her up and down and took in the shabby, stained skirt, the over-large, nylon cardigan and the dirty slippers.

'Listen,' he said. 'We'll take you to the shops and get you some new clothes tomorrow and see how things go, shall we?'

Gina got as near to a smile as she could.

'Yeah,' she said and turned back to the telly.

Later that night, Dunk bathed Gina as if she was a child. Gina sat in the scummy bath quite contentedly as Dunk lathered up an old flannel and ran it over her back. He put shampoo on her hair and massaged it into her scalp, rinsing it with water poured from an old plastic jug his wife had used for cooking.

It was Dunk's complete acceptance of her as she was now that Gina found comforting. Even through the fug of her illness and the deadened edges of her emotional responses she could sense the disappointment Keith carried behind his resigned smile and his regret that he seemed to have lost her forever. Gina was aware she would never really get better and something told her that she would be better off with Dunk than with those people who mourned the loss of her old self and moved round her like wounded ghosts.

That night as they lay in bed together, Dunk with his arm round Gina, exhausted after brief yet energetic sex cut short by premature ejaculation, Gina closed her eyes and smiled. The voices had quietened a bit. She believed that the nearer to Morrissey she got, the less they harangued her. She was sure that a meeting with him would transform her into what and who she wanted to be.

The following day the pair set off into town to buy Gina some clothes. Dunk, as ever thinking of saving a few pence, even though he could afford to pay more, jumped off the bus with Gina near a factory outlet shop which seemed to be selling a selection of clothes for depressives. Gina looked doubtful until a record shop next door to the factory shop caught her eye because there was a picture of Morrissey in the window. Clasping Dunk by the hand, she dragged him towards the shop.

'Come on,' she said excitedly. 'Let's go in here instead.'

A young man stood at the counter with an image of Morrissey on his T-shirt. Gina felt she was getting closer to her love all the time. It didn't occur to her to feel guilty about Dunk. Dunk was safely installed on a different planet from Morrissey; he didn't really figure in her calculations.

Gina approached the young man who was surprised to see what he considered to be two inapproprate old people cluttering up his shop.

'Can I have your T-shirt?' said Gina. 'Please, I'll give you anything.'

'I'm sorry, love,' said the shop assistant disdainfully. 'I need it.'

'No, I need it,' said Gina. 'It's a matter of life and death.'

'You trying for the Wolverhampton gig?' said the assistant, somewhat incredulous that this tramp of a woman could have any idea about Morrissey and his tour schedule.

Something made Gina say yes.

'I can't, love,' he said. 'I'm sorry.'

'Please,' came back a small but determined voice.

Something about the desperation in Gina's voice caused Dunk to step forward.

'Come on, mate,' he said. 'I'll give you a tenner for it.'

'You're joking, aren't you?' said the boy. 'I paid twenty for it.'

The tense auction that ensued was something to behold. A small audience built up around them consisting of an ertswhile Hell's Angel from Chester and a couple of punks, all of whom felt moved to ally themselves with the underdog.

'A hundred and twenty,' said Dunk, eventually, 'and that's my final offer.'

'Come on, mate,' said the Hell's Angel. 'For fuck's sake let them have the bloody thing.'

There was a mild threat in his voice which the assistant could not ignore. Eventually he caved in and said, 'Oh, all right then, hang on.'

He disappeared into the back of the shop and came out with a carrier bag which he handed to Gina. Her face crumpled and she began to cry.

The little group clapped and whooped and Dunk handed over twelve ten-pound notes, double his budget for Gina's new wardrobe.

'Oh, thank you,' said Gina and kissed a surprised Dunk full on the lips. The audience felt a very slight ripple of disgust run through them but continued to whoop and cheer.

'Let's go home,' said Dunk.

They passed a newsagent's on the way home and Dunk bought a *Daily Mirror* and some tobacco while Gina chose a KitKat and an *NME* with Morrissey on the front. Normally Dunk would have added something from the top shelf to his purchases because his sexual energy demanded that he have some focus for his lone nocturnal activities. But in deference to his new 'friend' (he didn't really know what to call her) he forwent this pleasure. After all, he said to himself wryly, I've got the real thing now.

At home, he lovingly hand-washed the T-shirt for Gina, which even Dunk with his minimal attention to personal hygiene surmised had been worn for at least a week. It hung, dripping, in the bathroom and every ten minutes or so Gina fluttered towards it to check whether it was dry or not. Eventually, after many hours, she plucked it from the mouldy shower head on which it was hanging, despite the fact that it was still slightly damp, and a beatific smile spread across her face as it appeared from inside the T-shirt.

'Blimey,' said Dunk. 'You don't half like this geezer, don't you?'

'Love,' said Gina, correcting him. 'Love.' And seeing a shadow flit across his face, she for the first time in years considered someone else's feelings and said, 'And you're fucking brilliant too, Dunk.'

Dunk smiled.

Chapter 26

The five days before Morrissey's gig dragged interminably for Alice, with an attendant anxiety that somehow everything would go wrong. The Smiths split, which had occurred the year before, had been a terrible blow and had made her depressed for days, but the news that Morrissey would carry on alone had lifted her spirits and given her hope for the future. In truth, Alice didn't really care about the members of the band or Johnny Marr, she was only interested in Morrissey. He was the only one she considered really held her life in his hands. He was the one who knew her inside out, who understood her lonely weird life and had the answer to where her damaged soul could proceed in a world full of dark dreams and sadness.

As the days passed, there was no news of Gina and Keith and Alice persuaded themselves that she was probably all right and that at some point she would reveal herself somewhere in the country in a disturbed state and be arrested by the police and brought home. This transition from constant worry to uneasy acceptance had been tackled by each of them in their own way. Although Keith knew Gina was chaotic and vulnerable, he had faith in the nature of other human beings and convinced himself that she was safe. Alice had managed to transfer her worry into a parallel universe and to her it was almost as if Gina had gone on a long holiday and at some point would turn up with some tasteless souvenirs and a dirty tan.

Keith found that he missed Gina in a strange way. He didn't miss the chain-smoking, unrecognisable person that she had become, but he thought more about their initial meeting and their courtship than he had for years. Most days he would drive out in the evening in his little van, scouring the roads and streets in nearby small towns where he thought she might be. Wobbly and Bighead were doing the same and coming home frustrated and tired most evenings. Bert, too, spent his days running through his memories of how Gina had been as a girl, a wild teenager and a hot-headed woman, with a degree of affection he had not felt at the time.

He missed his wife, too, and was surprised by the strength of his feelings, given that after five or six years of marriage they had merely rubbed along in a rather grumpy fashion. But behind that there had always been the unspoken understanding that they were two halves of a whole, Bert dealing with the outside practicalities of life and Violet keeping the home and fostering what emotional stability she could in her wayward children.

Marie Henty, meanwhile, played a waiting game. She observed the depleted little family consisting of Keith and Alice with a great deal of fondness as they coped with the trauma of their missing member. Marie was desperate to offer them more help and support but she was wary of being seen to try and muscle in on their vulnerability. So she sat at home in the evenings, trying not to think about Keith, and staying her hand as it wandered towards the telephone.

Keith did call Marie a number of times, but he was reluctant to introduce her into the household while Alice was there, because he could not fathom Alice's feelings about himself and Marie and he felt too weary to plumb those depths until the situation with Gina was resolved. He spoke to the hospital at regular intervals, although each call was pretty much a carbon copy of the last, as no new information about Gina's whereabouts relieved the pattern of their conversations.

Finally the big day dawned and Alice woke excitedly from a shallow sleep. She had decided to get the bus into Wolverhampton and then, after the show, make her way across to Norman and Jennifer's, hoping that by the time she arrived they would be soundly asleep in their twin beds in the cream-coloured room with its nylon floral curtains.

Keith could see the excitement in every aspect of Alice's demeanour. It was as if she was preparing for the most important rendezvous of her life. She spent four times as long as usual in the bathroom, slapping things on and pulling things out and generally trying to create a sophisticated, educated townie out of a rather natural, artless country girl.

Alice had packed and repacked her rucksack, undecided about whether to wear her Morrissey T-shirt all day or lovingly fold it and try to find a women's toilet to change into it. Eventually she decided she would wear it under a jumper; as she approached the venue, the jumper would be discarded and she would walk into the place, free and deserved, a reward for all her commitment over the years.

She was so excited that she decided she could not possibly wait until the afternoon to travel; she would break her journey at Ludlow and meet Mark for a midday meal before she journeyed on to Birmingham and from there to Wolverhampton.

She and Mark sat in De Greys in Broad Street, he staring at a huge steaming bowl of soup and she picking bits off a cheese and pickle sandwich.

'I'm rather jealous,' said Mark, 'about your adventure today. I wish I was coming too.'

'But you can't stand Morrissey,' said Alice, wishing she was going to the gig with him. Part of the churning she felt inside her was due to the fact that she was making this trip alone.

'It's not him particularly,' said Mark, 'it's your loyalty and your complete absorption in him that I envy. I don't think I ever managed it with anyone. Maybe I'm just not that sort of person.'

'You're lucky,' said Alice. 'I've used him as a crutch over the years to keep me going and to put me somewhere other than in my own life. He's there in my head all the time and I feel him watching me in some way, knowing what my life is about and wanting it to be better.'

'Well, if it's helped, that's a good thing, isn't it?' said Mark.

'Yeah, I suppose so,' said Alice. 'God, there have been so many times I needed not to be in my own life, to have someone I could talk to, when I was alone in bed at night and I could hear my dad crying.'

Mark didn't know what to say.

Alice looked at her watch. 'Will you come and wave me off?'

'Of course,' said Mark.

They walked to the bus stop and stood chatting neutrally about Mark's boring job and the gradual thawing of his relationship with his dad.

'He hasn't got another son,' said Mark. 'He's got to come to terms with what he's got and I think my mum has managed to chip away at him and make him think a bit.'

The bus pulled up and Mark grabbed Alice, gave her a hug and kissed her on the mouth.

'I wish I was Morrissey,' he said, 'and in some ways to you . . .'

'Why?' asked Alice.

'Because you seem . . .' Mark's sentence tailed off. 'Oh nothing,' he said. 'Have a brilliant time, call me when you get back.'

'Will do,' said Alice.

She got on the bus and moved to sit at the back so she could wave. As her smiling face got smaller, Mark was aware of a strange thought he could not shift from his mind: that he would never see her again.

Alice settled down in her seat and enjoyed the silent progress of the bus through the Shropshire countryside. Two chattering women in their seventies who were going to visit a friend in Birmingham spoke barely at whispering level and seemed afraid that this young woman two seats back would somehow take the content of their conversation and use it against them.

Alice arrived in Birmingham some hours later and changed buses at the grimy bus station, feeling a little bit apprehensive as she drew nearer to her destination.

She arrived at about six o'clock, with an hour or so to go until the event began.

To come from her silent and solo adoration of Morrissey to a huge crowd who absorbed and analysed his every word and felt that he spoke only to them was traumatic and inspiring all at the same time. The streets were teeming with an army of people under the age of twenty, all of whom seemed to be dressed in a uniform specified by Morrissey himself. Quiffs, cardigans and NHS glasses were everywhere, scuffles were breaking out between groups of excited people and Alice felt frightened by it all rather than borne aloft on the sheer uncontrolled exuberance that filled the air like drugged oxygen.

There were obviously far too many people to fit into the civic hall and Alice wondered what would happen. It was clear from the atmosphere that things could turn nasty at any time and Alice wondered how best to deal with it.

As she was tossed about in the sea of people, catching odd snippets of conversation from what were mainly young men, she decided to find somewhere to get herself together, remove her jumper and head on into the show. She wandered around looking for a toilet where she could stow her jumper in her bag, have a pee and check her appearance, but the only one she could find had a long, snaking queue of young girls chattering excitedly.

Alice decided to find a quieter place off the beaten track. In a quietish street and despite the cold, she lifted her jumper over her head, opened her rucksack and started to stuff her jumper into it.

As she was doing this, she failed to notice a group of young men, two of them skinheads, heading towards her down the narrow street. They stared at her.

'Look, Mac,' said one. 'She's got a fucking Moz T-shirt. That's what you need, mate, or you won't get in,'

The Mac in question looked her up and down.

'Give us your T-shirt, love,' he said in an emotionless voice.

Alice's heart thudded.

'No,' she said. 'I need it to get in.'

He continued to stare at her while the others looked at the ground and laughed nervously.

'Look, I've asked nicely,' he said, 'and now I'm getting angry.'

How on earth, thought Alice, do I get this monster to leave me alone?

She barely had long enough to articulate this thought before she heard Mac say, 'Hold her, lads,' and he pounced on her like an animal, pulling, grabbing, grunting until she felt the T-shirt tear and lift over her head. She could hear her own voice, weak and pleading, saying to him, 'Oh please don't, please don't.'

Two men let go of her arms, someone giggled and one of them at the back caught her eye and looked ashamed to be part of this assault.

Alice fixed her eyes on him but there was nothing he could do. Mac held her T-shirt triumphantly aloft for a second and then began to pull it over his own head.

The one she'd been staring at spoke.

'Mac, for fuck's sake, she's only a girl, give it back, mate.'

Mac turned to him. 'What did you say?'

The boy looked back at him for a brief second, then his gaze dropped to the ground.

'You fucking tosser,' said Mac. He grabbed the boy's ears and headbutted him with huge force on the bridge of his nose. The boy fell to the ground and Mac kicked him in the back, laughing, before the group turned and headed away, joke-punching each other and singing, 'Morrissey, Morrissey, Morrissey,' like a football chant.

Alice looked up from her foetal position on the wet ground

and began to cover herself up with her jumper. Then she noticed the bleeding boy leaning against the wall.

'Are you all right?' she said and, without thinking, put her hand out to touch him.

He propelled himself away from her and scrambled to his feet.

'Fuck off,' he cried over his shoulder as he ran. 'Fuck off, you stupid cow.'

Alice sat on the pavement for about five minutes. She felt she should cry but couldn't because she was so angry. Angry that she could be bullied like that, angry that she was too weak to fight back, angry that the so-called genius, vegetarian, fucking Morrissey allowed his fans to behave like that.

She decided to do her best to get into the civic hall. She would not be cheated again, especially by scumbags who were no more fans of Morrissey than Wobbly and Bighead. Oh, how she wished they were here, with their huge fists and their pit-bull temperaments. She could almost have enjoyed watching those boys get beaten to a bloody pulp.

Alice followed the crowds and the noise until she stood outside the entrance to the civic hall. It was ten minutes from the start of the show and she could see that hundreds of people outside were not going to get in. She manoeuvred herself through the throng until she stood staring up at the face of a security guard.

'Someone mugged me and nicked my Morrissey T-shirt,' she shouted above the noise.

'Good one, love,' said the guard. 'You're only about the four hundredth person to try that on me tonight.'

'But it's true,' shouted Alice.

'Out the way or you're going to get hurt,' said the guard. 'You're not getting in, all right?'

Alice could not believe her night had turned to dust. Tears began to sneak out of the corners of her eyes and blurred the angry and ridiculous scene in front of her. She tried to see if there was a path through the madness when a face appeared in the crowd that made her whole body react as if a wave of electricity had run through it.

'Mum!' she shouted. 'Bloody hell! Jesus Christ! Fuck! Mum.'

It was Gina, cutting a swathe through the crowd with a look of determination on her face. Alice stepped towards her and above the noise shouted, 'Mum! It's me, Alice. What are you doing here?'

Gina looked at Alice as if she didn't really know her and then an expression of recognition flitted across her face.

'Alice,' she said. 'Have you come to see Morrissey?'

'Yes,' said Alice, 'but some boys took my T-shirt and they won't let me in.'

'Never mind,' said Gina. 'I'll see you later.'

She headed towards the same security guard who had just turned Alice away and pointed at her chest. Until that point, Alice hadn't even realised she was wearing a Morrissey T-shirt.

The security man nodded curtly and ushered her through.

'Mum!' shouted Alice. 'Come back, I need to talk to you.'

Gina shot her a look then turned round and entered the hall with all the other fortunate people who had a passport to their hero.

Alice was at a loss. Should she call the police? Her dad? Mark?

She moved away from the crowd and tried to find a phone box. After walking around for a few minutes, she eventually spotted one of the familiar red boxes and found some change in her pocket. She opened the door. There was an overwhelming stench of urine, not something she was familiar with in the local call boxes at home. She lifted the receiver to listen for a dialling tone. There was nothing. Alice banged the receiver on the side of the box. Still nothing.

'Shit,' she said aloud to herself. 'I'll have to sort it out on my own.'

She wandered back to the front of the civic hall. There were still crowds of rowdy, angry people who hadn't been able to get in, although some realised there was no point in hanging about and started to drift away.

Mercifully Morrissey did a rather short set and it didn't seem very long before the people inside started to pour out.

Alice had positioned herself in the middle of the doors so that she had a reasonable view of every single person exiting the building. Eventually, carried along by the crowd, she saw Gina coming towards her.

'Mum.' Alice grabbed her mother's arm. She could tell

immediately that her mother was somewhere between seda-
tion and wild-eyed madness.

'Mum, you've got to come home. We'll help you sort things
out.'

Gina looked at her daughter. 'I don't want to come home.
I'm happy where I am.'

'Where is that?' said Alice desperately. 'And who with?'

'Got to go,' said Gina breezily and headed up the road
more jauntily than Alice had ever seen her.

'Mum.' Alice tried to hold her by the arm.

Gina shook her off. 'Leave me alone,' she said dangerously.

'Please, Mum,' said Alice. 'Please.'

They reached a huge lorry. Gina banged on the door and the
driver leaned across and opened it. Gina began to climb up.

Alice craned her neck to see who the driver was.

Inside the lorry, Gina turned to Dunk and said, 'Let's go,
I'm starving.'

'Righto,' said Dunk. He could see a young woman trying
to peer in. 'Who's that?' he asked.

'My daughter,' said Gina. 'Come on, Dunk, I want to go.
Bye,' she said to Alice, motioning her to move away from
the door.

Alice stepped back, Gina slammed the door and the huge
lorry wheezed away.

Keith was pottering around in the kitchen, putting the kettle
on and making toast. The phone jingled in the corner.

'Dad, I just saw Mum at the Morrissey gig,' Alice had said

in a voice thick with distress. 'She's gone, she went off in a big lorry with someone. I didn't see who. Dad, I . . .' Her words stopped and after a short pause, a man's voice came on the line.

'Keith, it's your dad. I was worried about your Alice getting to our house so late at night, so I came over to Wolverhampton to look for her and I found the poor girl in a right state.'

'Is she all right?' said Keith. 'What's happened?'

'Well,' said Norman, 'from what I can tell, she didn't get into the show because some thugs nicked her T-shirt off her and they wouldn't let her in, but she saw Gina getting in there and waited for her to come out. I think they spoke briefly but then Gina ran off and jumped in a lorry and that was it, gone like a puff of smoke, who knows where.'

'Oh God,' said Keith. 'Shall I come and get Alice?'

'No, you're all right,' said Norman. 'I'll take her home to me and your mum's and drop her over tomorrow. Is that OK?'

'OK,' said Keith. 'Thanks, Dad. I'll see you in the morning.'

An exhausted Alice arrived the next morning, looking like a tearful ghost. Keith managed to glean a few more details of the previous night's events and then sent her up to bed for the day.

He called Marie Henty.

'I'll come over straight away,' she said, 'and we'll discuss what to do.'

They sat in the little front room with a cup of instant coffee and talked.

'She must be OK,' said Marie. 'She can't be being held against her will by someone or why on earth would she be running around Wolverhampton with a Morrissey T-shirt on to get her into the concert?'

'I can't imagine,' said Keith, thinking how sweet the word 'concert' was coming from Marie's lips. 'What shall we do? Should we call the police? What?'

Marie put her hand on his. 'We could try the police. And I could ring the hospital, see if there were any patients on the ward that might be the man in the lorry, or anyone who knew him.'

Keith nodded. He would speak to the police and Marie to the hospital. Neither held out much hope, but it was all they could do.

The hospital threw up no clues and Keith felt even more hopeless after he had visited the police station and given some details to a bored young female constable. He felt there was no point going to Wolverhampton, Gina could be anywhere by now. But in a little corner of his mind he was slightly reassured by the circumstances of Alice's meeting with her chaotic mother, although he worried that this feeling was mainly due to his strong wish for Gina to be safe.

Wobbly and Bighead didn't seem surprised by what was going on and Keith's news was met with a curt yet strangely friendly nod when he drove up to their cottage to tell them. Keith refused their offer of a cup of tea and managed to escape back home, thinking to himself that this was the most solicitous exchange they'd had for ages.

Mark listened with a serious expression to Alice's description of the events of 22 December. He felt so sorry for her; it seemed so unfair that her difficult life had not been somehow briefly put on hold by her trip to see Morrissey. He suspected Gina would never come home and that this would leave Alice suspended in her guilt-filled universe, where only her dependency on and obligation to her lovely father were important.

Marie hoped Gina would never come home but she knew this was a rather adolescent hope and that there could be no conclusion to Keith and Gina's marriage if she did not. And marriage was Marie Henty's aim. She had tried to deny this fact to herself but couldn't banish the feelings of longing from her mind any more. She sat agitated and despondent in her home and wondered if anything would ever change.

Chapter 27

Alice tried to make herself believe that Morrissey and she were destined never to be close and this thought made her feel very sad. Despite the traumatic events that had occurred in Wolverhampton, she had been enveloped in the magical anticipation of being close to him and that feeling had been so strong and so exciting that she couldn't help wanting to feel it again. She asked herself if actually seeing Morrissey would be an anti-climax but she had no way of telling. She thought it was like trying to give up a lover who was denied to her. Although his presence in her life both delighted and tortured her, she wondered if she would ever lead a normal existence with a normal job, a normal partner and a normal family. For some time she had wondered if she was a lesbian. So many of the men and boys she had contact with seemed brutish and utterly insensitive. She looked at her peer group and could almost physically experience them fading into the middle distance, because compared to Morrissey they seemed grey, dull and had nothing to teach her. She and Karen still saw each other from time to time but they were no longer close. Alice could not tolerate the group of young farmers Karen aspired to connect herself to and she was beginning to resign herself to the fact that she would live a life as strange and isolated as her mother's.

She and Mark met often and spent a lot of time together talking about their lives and where they might be going. Mark's relationship with his family had begun to get better, thanks to his mother's efforts. Mark still did not want to move back home from his mean bedsit, because at least there he had some independence, choice and freedom. He had very little but what he had was his and this was important to him. It also meant there was very little to tidy up and the challenge this presented was minimal. Whenever he saw his mother, she always asked him two things: was he getting enough to eat? Was he wearing a vest? Even in the height of summer he expected her to ask about the vest. It seemed to reassure his mum that he had not allowed his life to descend into the anarchy that she constantly visualised when she was on her own at home in front of the television.

Mark responded to Alice's disastrous night as if it was his own experience and could almost physically feel her pain. Karen, however, caught in a world of make-up, evil-smelling hair spray, short skirts and longing, could not understand the finer feelings this strange person had aroused in her friend. One night at a party in the home of an old school friend called Sally, they all sat together talking as Duran Duran blasted out in the background. Karen surveyed the scene for likely partnerings later on. It was a typical mix, a few posh boys, the sons of local farmers whose life at private school had been interrupted by a downturn in their fathers' fortunes and who had returned to the local state school, and some 'useless yobs', as Mark's father called them, feral, unfeeling troublemakers in the mould of Wobbly and Bighead. Most were average young men and women, some still at home, many living a slightly desperate existence in tatty rented accommodation.

Stephen Matthews was there too with a couple of what could be loosely termed 'his friends', although in reality they were two boys whose suggestibility and complete lack of social skills meant they were destined to play second fiddle to a bully.

Karen had pretty much exhausted the supply of available males in the vicinity, either by sleeping with them or frightening them so much they avoided her at all costs. Her well-defined hips and huge chest had ensured that one or two of the boys she had attempted to engage in private fumbling wondered whether they were heterosexual at all, such fear struck at the core of them when they saw her approaching.

Alice and Mark knew the real Karen, slightly desperate and rather lonely, having been brought up in an emotionally cold home where hugs and jokes were in short supply and more attention was paid to good manners and acceptable behaviour than it was to having fun and being close.

Stephen Matthews, despite his black heart and malevolent intent, had grown up into a handsome man. Quite a few girls threw themselves into his path, willing victims, who were then discarded after one night of very bad sex. This furthered the myth within Stephen's head that he was a desirable member of the male sex and, as he said to himself, 'I could have any fucking bird I want.'

This wasn't quite true. There were a few girls in the neighbourhood who didn't want to have anything to do with him because they remembered his behaviour at school towards them or one of their siblings. Stephen Matthews had set himself the task of gradually working his way through them until he had satisfied himself that this self-image was accurate. So over the past couple of years he had got Debbie Sibson so drunk at a party that she could hardly have even known what was happening to her as he dragged her into the garden as if she were a large sack of vegetables and pushed himself upon her. He had ignored the weak protests of Elaine Spry in a friend's bedroom and carried on, convincing himself that because she had gone quiet she was enjoying herself. And he had given Joy Weston ten pounds, calculating that because her family were poor, this would secure him what he wanted. And it did.

The only two girls in his immediate social sphere whom he had not managed to perforate were Karen and Alice.

He hated the tight little trio of these two girls and Mark. He had been glad of the opportunity to hit Mark a few times in the market square recently and abhorred the way 'that fucking nutter' idolised 'that stupid poof from Manchester'. And now here he was at a party with them, boasting to his friends that he would have both girls tonight. His two sidekicks sniggered and swigged cider.

The party progressed pretty much as parties do with no parents present, loud music and plenty of cheap drink. At first the level of excited chatter and laughter was reasonably low, then it began to rise as more cider and cheap lager was poured down throats. The alcohol allowed confidence to grow and soon groups got up and began to dance in the small space that had been cleared by chairs being pushed back, tables folded and paraphernalia thrown into cupboards. The usual people hung around in the kitchen, picking at crisps and mini sausages and listening to gossip about the progress of various couplings.

People wandered out into the garden despite the cold weather and little groups passed round cigarettes from packets of ten. It was hot inside and getting hotter. Mark, Karen and Alice sat lined up on an old settee discussing Alice's disastrous night in Wolverhampton. Karen thought the account of Alice being relieved of her Morrissey T-shirt and bumping into her mad mother who seemed to have hitched up with an ageing lorry driver was a bloody good story.

'I bet Morrissey was crap anyway, Alice,' she said, trying

to find something positive about the night. 'You were better off outside with all the others I would have had a right laugh.'

Alice shook her head. 'Karen, you've got no bloody idea. I'd been waiting for this night all my life. Remember what happened the time before with my nan? I feel like it's never going to happen.' A tear ran down her face and Karen felt absolutely helpless. She couldn't envisage a situation which could cause her such silent grief. Maybe one of her parents dying? Mentally she shook her head. No, not even that.

She put her arm round Alice. 'I'm sure you'll get another chance.'

'I just feel like I won't,' said Alice, 'as if somehow it's destined not to happen.'

Karen had very little ability to view life in the abstract and decided not to explore this statement.

'Come on,' she said. 'Let's have a dance.' She threw off a cardigan which had been concealing the glory of her magnificent chest tightly contained within a gold low-cut top and hauled herself up, grasping Mark by the hand as she did so.

The expression on his face told her all she needed to know about his enthusiasm for dancing.

He turned to Alice.

'Coming?' he said.

To his surprise, she rose; he knew she hated nothing more than to be forced into the swaying awkwardness that was party dancing.

'You go and dance,' said Alice. 'I'm just going outside for some fresh air.'

Karen entered the throng with Mark awkwardly behind her, bouncing a little on his toes in an approximation of dancing. Alice picked her way gingerly through to the kitchen, nodding at familiar faces as she passed them. She opened the back door and the cold air hit her like a wonderful relief. It was a big garden, illuminated near the house by the light from the windows. She chose not to stay there but wandered further down, gradually disappearing out of the light towards a dark clump of trees.

As she sat down on a rickety chair near the trees, she heard a low giggling and her natural urge to flee whatever humanity had emitted the giggling stalled as Stephen Matthews loomed out of the darkness, his face wearing the vacuous expression she had come to know so well over the years.

'Well, fuck me, if it isn't nutty trousers' daughter come out to take the air,' he said, waiting for a reaction from his two lieutenants.

He was rewarded by a snort from the two of them.

The sickly smell of cider was on his breath, combined with a waft of cannabis.

Alice turned to go. Stephen Matthews grasped her arm.

'Stay and have a smoke with us,' he said. 'We all know your old man, the skinny hippy, does it so it won't be a new experience for you.'

'No thanks,' said Alice, her voice sounding thick in the cold air, a combination of fear and anger.

'Oh, don't be like that,' said Stephen. 'We've been waiting for you.'

Alice felt her heart beat a tiny bit faster. She looked towards the house which seemed to have moved back several miles.

Stephen put his arm round her and held tight to her shoulder, adding the smell of sweat and cheap aftershave to her overloaded senses.

'Get off,' said Alice. 'I want to go back inside.'

'No you don't,' said Stephen. 'Let's all have a bit of fun out here, shall we?'

Alice attempted to squirm out of his grasp but before she could, his two friends were on her, Half laughing, half growling, they pushed her to the ground and three pairs of hands began clawing at her clothes and slipping under the outside layers.

Alice opened her mouth to scream and a hand was clamped over it.

'Come on,' said Stephen. 'You know you want it.'

In the parallel universe where Alice was able to coldly observe the incident, she caught herself thinking, Jesus, what a fucking cliché.

She bit the hand that was over her mouth, eliciting a loud cry of pain and then a punch. She screamed as loudly as she could.

'You fucking bitch,' said Stephen. 'Now you're going to get it.'

Alice continued to scream and as dirty hands with bitten

nails attempted to drag off her jeans, she became aware of two extra voices shouting and then two bodies joining the squirming heap on the ground.

She was pulled up by a strong hand. Mark and Karen were beside her.

'For fuck's sake, Stephen,' yelled Karen.

For a second shame flitted across Stephen's face and then he regained his composure.

'She came out here for it,' he said, staring at the ground.

Mark and Karen took hold of Alice and steered her towards the house. Alice felt almost too shocked to breathe and when she did, big sobs catapulted out of her.

'It's all right,' said Mark. 'You're OK.'

'I'm sure they didn't mean it,' said Karen. 'Got carried away, I expect.'

'Shall I take you home?' said Mark.

It was only ten thirty. Her dad would still be up. Alice couldn't face either pretending she'd had a good time or telling him what had happened.

'No,' she said. 'I don't want to go home.'

'We'll walk for a bit,' said Mark.

Everyone inside seemed oblivious of the sordid incident that had just occurred in the garden and the music played on loudly and unrelentingly.

Mark found his scruffy jacket and Alice's donkey jacket and they walked out into the dark, each step taking them towards a more peaceful and forgiving night.

It was a long, cold walk back to Ludlow. They held hands

and occasionally the moon came out and silvered the road ahead as they walked through Wigmore, the little hamlet of Elton and began to climb up towards the forested area of the High Vinnalls. Most of the time they walked in silence, the occasional hoot of an owl and the familiar rustling of woodland creatures accompanying them on their journey.

Just outside Ludlow they paused to look at the imposing dark shadow of the castle and then they descended past the little church and over the weir.

Mark's room looked delightful, a sparse sanctuary of warmth and carelessness. Alice sat on the bed. As he started to remove his coat, Mark grinned and produced a bottle of vodka.

'Found it on the table,' he said. 'Obviously nicked from some mum and dad's drinks cabinet.'

He got some orange juice from the little fridge and poured them two big glasses.

They talked most of the night, sitting at opposite ends of the bed, neither realising that as the night travelled towards the dawn, they inched nearer to each other.

Had Alice been quizzed on the subject of their conversation the following morning, she would not have been able to remember a single thing, but they covered their families, school, Mark's work, Morrissey, world politics, hunting, and Karen, who at this point was on her back in the garden, laughing delightedly, her legs clamped tightly round Stephen Matthews.

Eventually the conversation came round to the pair of

them and their friendship over the years. Fuelled by the cumulative heat of each glass, Mark looked solemnly into Alice's face and said very quietly, 'Did you know I . . . ?'

He stopped but Alice knew what the end of the sentence was.

Chapter 28

Some weeks after the Second Morrissey Night, as it came to be known, the phone rang very late at night. Keith, dozing in his chair, sat forward in the armchair and lifted the receiver to his ear.

'Hello,' he said, half asleep.

'I want a divorce,' said Gina.

'Gina?' said Keith.

'Yes,' said Gina. 'Did you hear me, Keith?'

'Yes,' said Keith. 'I did. Where are you? What are you doing? Who are you with?'

He heard Gina say, 'Oh for fuck's sake, Dunk, you talk to him.'

A friendly male voice said, 'Hello, you must be Keith.'

'Yes,' said Keith. 'And who am I speaking to?'

'Look,' said Dunk, 'I'm Dunk. I don't expect you to

understand any of this or like it, but it's true, me and your missus want to get hitched.'

Keith found himself sounding pinched and outraged.

'My wife is a very disturbed woman who needs treatment and must come home,' he said.

'Aw, come on, mate,' said Dunk, 'she ain't that bad, are you, Gina? I've been looking after her since she ran away from that mental place – yes, I know all about it – and since she's been with me, she's been fine.'

Keith said helplessly, 'Look, we need to talk face to face. Can you come here?'

'Hang on,' said Dunk, and Keith heard him place his hand over the receiver and then a muffled argument.

'All right,' said Dunk eventually. 'We'll come over at the weekend, but don't you go calling them mental doctors or Gina and me will never forgive you.'

Keith woke Alice and phoned Marie, who drove over in her dressing gown.

'What did he sound like?' said Alice. 'A bit pervy?'

'Evil?' said Marie.

Keith shook his head. 'I know it seems weird but he sounded nice.'

The two women looked at him as if he was the one with a chronic mental illness.

'I think we should have the police standing by when they come,' said Marie.

'Yes,' said Alice, 'me too.'

Keith looked at them both. 'We are not going to do that.

We are going to meet this man, assess the situation and then call the police if necessary.' The normally gentle, humorous timbre of his voice was shot through with a hitherto unheard steeliness.

Marie and Alice nodded.

And so Dunk and Gina arrived at the cottage on Saturday morning in Dunk's enormous juggernaut of a lorry which completely blocked the lane for the duration of their visit.

Keith observed the almost gentlemanly way in which Dunk helped Gina down from the cab, their closeness, and Dunk's very obvious fondness for her. He felt no jealousy or anger but was slightly ashamed of himself when he realised that he had not seen his wife as anything other than a problem for so many years now, she had ceased to be a person and a woman to him.

It wasn't a long visit. Tea was made, Gina slurped a bit and let biscuit crumbs fall down her front, but Dunk didn't seem the least bit embarrassed or censorious. He simply dabbed her chin with his hanky, brushed the crumbs from her face and went back to holding her hand.

By the end of half an hour, Keith had agreed to everything Gina and Dunk wanted. Alice had also warmed to Dunk and as much as she wanted her mum and dad to stay together, she could see that this big lump of an ageing lorry driver was a far more loving and caring partner than Keith could ever be now.

At the door, Keith and Dunk shook hands.

'Thanks,' said Keith simply.

'No problem,' said Dunk.

Once Gina had freed everyone of their obligation to live a life tied to her illness, Keith and Alice became aware of an enormous number of possibilities in both their lives.

But nine months later their thoughts of travel, new houses and different people had all melted away.

Finale

A beautiful September day burst open with the rising of the sun, the best type of day to stand back and take in the unparalleled, uniquely English beauty of the Herefordshire countryside. It was more than they, as a family, could have hoped for.

Gina and Alice got up at six, to give themselves plenty of time to prepare for what was going to be the strangest day the village had seen for many years, a day in which all its members could play a part.

They joined Marie outside the village church and waited for their respective future spouses to walk them through the lych gate to be married by a new, fresh-faced vicar, Tom Akins, who was blissfully unaware of the mayhem the Wildgoose family were capable of.

The ceremony itself was a strange hotchpotch of favourite hymns and a Morrissey anthem, chosen by Gina and Alice to accompany their process up the aisle. Tom Akins had been a little reluctant when he heard the content of 'There Is A Light That Never Goes Out'; he considered the words, 'If a double-decker bus kills the both of us', slightly morbid for a wedding ceremony, but both Gina and Alice were so determined, he was unable to refuse them.

Wobbly and Bighead had managed suits of sorts and Bert had been primped and scrubbed so thoroughly that he looked every inch the proud father and grandad as he shuffled up the aisle with Alice on one side and Gina on the other. Alice was wearing a plain but beautiful lavender dress, and Gina wore what seemed to be a female clown's outfit.

Marie Henty came behind dressed in a fussy cream frock, escorted by her confused father, a retired surgeon who had come down from the Lake District for the weekend with Marie's mother. Joan Henty was relieved to see her only daughter at last hitched, even if it was to this hippy with the odd family. Norman and Jennifer were ecstatic that finally they had a daughter-in-law to boast about.

The villagers had all piled into the church too, including Doug, red-faced and grinning at this marvellous outcome to many years of chaos, strain and heartache.

Then came Dunk, Keith and Mark, the prospective husbands, all smiling broadly and hardly able to believe that things had turned out so well for all of them.

Dunk was resplendent in a badly cut, cheap suit adorned with several incongruous gladioli, an intervention of Gina's to remind her of her hero Morrissey, who seemed to all of them to be present at a ceremony that to some extent he had been responsible for.

After a short service the three couples were pronounced men and wives and they all returned back up the aisle to stand smiling and blinking in the late summer sunshine.

Bouquets were thrown, two of which were caught by May Budd and Annie Wilsher who, looking up at the Wildgoose family in her triumph, secured a wink from a very frolicsome Bert. The third bouquet fell on Doug's head, causing a ripple of laughter round the group and some very rude jokes from Bighead and Wobbly.

Due to financial constraints, everyone had decided that the best place to hold the reception was back at the cottage. Keith and Alice had scrubbed, hoovered and washed the place until it looked as good as it possibly could, which was faded and worn out. Beer, wine, sausage rolls, cheese and cake had been purchased from Hereford and was all laid out on trestle tables in the front garden.

The phalanx of newlyweds moved up the hill with family and villagers and tucked themselves into the little garden to begin the festivities.

As the sun began to go down, Wobbly and Bighead announced to the assembled party that they had a surprise for the newlyweds and Wobbly went to the van and returned with the biggest rocket anyone had ever seen.

'Right, you fuckers, stand back!' he shouted.

Jennifer shuddered at the language and Norman looked embarrassed.

Bighead cleared a space and moved everyone back behind the rocket which he had got cheap off a bloke in Cleobury Mortimer. He stabbed the rocket into the ground. Bighead produced a box of matches and lit the fuse.

Everybody held their breath. As the fuse neared blast-off, the rocket slipped from its position pointing directly at the stars and started to sink towards the earth. Without warning and with a huge whooshing noise, it took off straight towards Gina and Keith's cottage. It hit the window in the front and went clean through it, landing with a massive bang in the tiny front room.

Everyone hooted with laughter and then looked at each other as if trying to isolate a responsible person to deal with the problem.

Within seconds the front room was alight and smoke began to pour out of the window.

'Bollocks,' said Wobbly. 'Shall I get round the back and get some water?'

'Wouldn't it be a good idea to call the fire brigade?' said Jennifer.

'Yes,' said Keith to both questions, but before anyone could move, Gina laid a hand on Keith's arm.

'It's a shithole,' she said. 'We were never that happy there. Shall we just leave it?'

'Do you know what?' said Keith, very tipsy and very happy. 'It's not even ours and we've paid too much rent for the place over the years. It's probably insured, so yes, why not?'

So the assembled party stood there and watched the enormous bonfire, all of them overtaken by a kind of celebratory madness. Bighead and Wobbly, fuelled by beer and wine, whooped round it like children. The orange glow could be seen for miles around and some elderly people wondered if a war had started and the beacons had been lit.

Alice stood with her arms round Mark, wondering whether the physical destruction of her home could wipe out all the bad times in her head. There was nothing there that she really cherished. The Morrissey letter was inside her mother, the only thing of real value that couldn't be replaced.

Mark stood next to her wondering when, if ever, he would tell her that the letter had been from him.